CONQUERED CITY

CONQUERED CITY

A Novel by *VICTOR SERGE*

*Translated from the French and with
a Foreword and Biographical Note by
Richard Greeman*

*Doubleday & Company, Inc., Garden City, New York
1975*

With the exception of actual historical personages, the characters are entirely the product of the author's imagination and have no relationship to any person in real life.

VILLE CONQUISE was published in Paris by Les Éditions Rieder in 1932, and republished by Les Éditions du Seuil in 1967.

Library of Congress Cataloging in Publication Data

Serge, Victor, 1890–1947.
 Conquered city.

 Translation of Ville conquise.
 1. Russia—History—Revolution, 1917–1921—
Fiction. I. Title.
PZ3.S4838Co [PQ2637.E49] 843'.9'12
ISBN 0-385-05748-2
Library of Congress Catalog Card Number 75–25099

FOREWORD

by Richard Greeman

How short our historical memories are!

When Alexander Solzhenitzyn was expelled from the U.S.S.R. last year—having established himself, mainly through works published abroad, as the literary conscience of his homeland—the event was hailed as unique. Yet forty years ago the author of the present work, Victor Serge, was similarly expelled, similarly deprived of his Soviet citizenship—heaped with abuse as a renegade but nonetheless allowed to live and to continue writing, in exile, the truth about the momentous events he had witnessed.[1]

The attending circumstances were also in many ways similar. In 1935, when Serge was expelled, Stalin's government was seeking *détente* with the capitalist democracies in the hope of forming a defensive alliance against a new and rising world power: Nazi Germany. Then, as now, liberal concessions were the order of the day. Like Solzhenitzyn, Serge had a literary reputation in the West, particularly in France. His pamphlets in defense of the Soviets, his journalistic accounts of the great days of the Civil War, his translations and portraits of Lenin and other revolutionary leaders had stirred the sympathies of French readers for over a decade; his first novels (including the present work), written in internal exile under the surveillance of the secret police and published abroad, had stirred the imagination of the West by their utter *truthfulness*, as did Solzhenitzyn's two generations later.

There had been inquiries and protests about the constant harassments to which the writer and his family had been subjected by police and government officials: expulsion from the Writers' Union, denial of permission to work, forced changes of residence, searches,

[1] For further details about Serge's life and works, see my biographical note at the end of this volume.

arrests, interference with correspondence—ultimately administrative exile to Central Asia. Among those who had expressed interest in Serge's welfare were men like André Gide, André Malraux, and Romain Rolland, whose good will was valuable to the Russian propaganda machine. Serge's existence, on the other hand, was a thorn in its side. He was too well known abroad to simply "liquidate" (in any case, the great purges were still on the horizon), and too unbending in his principles to tame through official favor. So Stalin expelled him, just as Brezhnev expelled Solzhenitzyn forty years later, all the while denouncing him as an enemy of the people in the hope of neutralizing him as a voice for the revolutionary movement *within* Russia.

There are other, deeper similarities between the two cases. Both men had fought to defend their Soviet homeland: Serge in the 1919–21 Civil War, Solzhenitzyn during the Great Patriotic War of 1941–45. Both had endured years of confinement and non-person status in that absurd and cruel world of political prisoners and political policemen which Solzhenitzyn has called "the Gulag Archipelago." Both had found the courage to think and to write for themselves, with little hope that any line then penned would ever see print; for writing the truth had become a consuming passion for both of them. Both were Russians to the core, with a deep love of their land and a strong sense of Russia's unique destiny, her vastness, and her deep-rooted contradictions that harks back to Tolstoy and even earlier, to Gogol himself.

But here the similarities end. In 1935 there were no Swiss bank accounts waiting for Serge and his family when, stripped of most of their belongings (including several manuscripts never recovered), they were escorted across the border. No Nobel Committee awaited Serge, nor did publishers press him with lucrative offers or journalists flock to hang on his every word. Ill and penniless, supported by a few friends on the independent left who were scarcely better off than himself, Serge was forced to fall back on his old trade as a typesetter to earn a precarious living in Brussels and Paris. Still he continued to pour his passion into a stream of novels, pamphlets, and exposés which even the vicissitudes of the Nazi occupation and further exile (to Mexico in 1941) could not cut off.

Nor was Serge a stranger to the ways of our Western democracies, to their slums, their prisons, their factories, their detention camps, their free press which is only free to those who own one.

Unlike Solzhenitzyn, whose view of the capitalist West seems to have been formed by a simple process of inversion—a cynically naïve reversal of Russian "anti-capitalist" propaganda—Serge had grown up in the slums of London and Brussels and seen a brother die of starvation and neglect. Serge knew both worlds intimately. As early as the 1930s, he saw through the bogus dichotomy of "Communism" vs. "Freedom" and recognized the outlines of a new world order of bureaucratic state-capitalist powers taking shape in Stalinist Russia, Fascist Germany, and, in a milder form, in the West of the Pop Front and the New Deal.

Further, Serge foresaw that the monster corporate states, whatever their ideological banner, were in reality controlled by power-hungry cliques and hell-bent on a collision course of world war, despite the constant talk of "peace" and *détente* and the constant shift in alliances among the power blocks (e.g., the Stalin-Hitler Pact of 1939, forerunner of the Nixon-Mao *entente* of 1972). Small wonder that George Orwell was among the first in the English-speaking world to recognize Serge's remarkable talent as a writer and stature as a prophet.

By contrast, Solzhenitzyn arrived in Switzerland in 1974 like a man arriving from Mars, and even his most respectful readers were shocked and disappointed by his naïve statements to the assembled press. For example, he saw only "selfishness" in the general strike of the British coal miners, then parading their wasted, consumptive bodies and courageous, indignant hearts on the picket line in defiance of the Tory government's ban on strikes. A past victim of forced labor himself, Solzhenitzyn could not recognize it in the form of wage-labor. Serge, on the other hand, had worked in a mine in northern France as an adolescent. Like Orwell (*cf. The Road to Wigan Pier*), he knew that the only freedom the miners enjoyed was the freedom to starve or to die a slow death from disease, overwork, and poverty in the pits. He knew that the true "selfishness" was that of the mineowner, officials, inspectors, and their servile representatives in press and Parliament: the selfishness of those who put a higher value on profit, productivity, and power than on the lives of those whose sweat produces all wealth.

The press listened breathlessly while this man from Mars pondered the "plumbers" affair and wondered aloud how the United States Government could allow a man like Daniel Ellsberg to remain at large. Yet Solzhenitzyn himself—having published the suppressed truth about forced labor in the Soviet Union—can only be understood as a Russian "Ellsberg," illegally releasing state secrets and "disgracing" his government in the name of a higher patriotism.

Here again, Victor Serge had no such patriotic illusions. Alas, there were no reporters flown in from around the world to record his truly profound understanding of the Russian purges, the Communist betrayals in Spain, the Russo-German alliance, and the coming war. His carefully documented exposés and brilliantly formulated prophecies appeared in the form of penny pamphlets on cheap paper printed in obscure left-wing publishing houses. His tragic (yet somehow optimistic) vision of the world came across in his novels of men and women caught up in the forces of revolution and counterrevolution. (These, at least, were read fairly widely until the Nazis invaded France, destroyed the press, and burned Serge's works. The present translation—the first in English—was made from a copy preserved by the underground.)

To me, however, the difference between Serge's outlook and that of Solzhenitzyn lies deeper than any accidents attributable to the latter's naïveté about the West. The roots of this difference lie buried in the various strata of the Russian soil.

Serge's vision is one of revolution in action. Like his American contemporary and friend, John Reed, Serge actually witnessed the Russian Revolution in its birth throes, when "Soviet" power still meant the actual power exercised by councils of workers, peasants, and soldiers, freely associated and struggling voluntarily for Bread, Peace, and Land. This movement was perhaps the greatest outpouring of popular creativity, of masses taking their destiny into their own hands—in other words, of freedom—our epoch has seen. In any case, it was the first of its kind, and its impulses marked Serge for life.

For Solzhenitzyn, born a generation later, the "Revolution," portrayed in Stalinist schoolbooks and statuary, could never be dissociated from the reality of the existing Communist regime that had usurped its banner while repressing its essence. He could see its heroism during the great struggle against the Nazi invaders, its baseness in the treatment of its own returning veterans, its ugliness in its utter contempt for the dignity of human beings. With his passion for truth, Solzhenitzyn has labored ceaselessly to pull back the veil of official lies and get at the reality of life as it was, and is, lived in Red Russia. He has accomplished much in the cause of freedom. But the truth about the initial spark, the essence of that Revolution —buried under fifty years of official lies and tons of mendacious historiography—has remained inaccessible to him; above all, perhaps, because it lies beyond his immediate experience. As long as he has his personal experience (essentially the war and the Stalinist terror) to guide him in his search for the truth, he stands on firm ground and speaks with resounding and incomparable authority. Beyond this (and the *artistic* failure of his novel, *1914*, is sufficient evidence) he flounders.

Serge speaks with the authority of one who was there from the beginning, who knows the *reason* behind the mountain of lies, the *logic* of the terror, the concentration camps, and the brutality, which both he and Solzhenitzyn risked so much to expose. Serge understood the secret locked away in Stalin's heart, the secret that drove him from one atrocity to another, from forced collectivization and Stakhanovite speed-up to the paranoid creation of the greatest police-state bureaucracy the world has ever known. It is the secret that haunts his successors in the Kremlin to this day.

That secret is fear. Fear of revolution. Fear of a revival of 1917–18, when the masses overthrew the Czar, drove out the generals, expropriated the aristocrats and the bourgeois alike, and went on to create their own democratic power in the Soviets. What happened once can happen again. (Our own leaders may well experience such fears as we approach the Bicentennial of the American Revolution on the eve of our greatest national crisis since the Civil War).

This vision of living revolution is at the heart of Serge's understanding of the world, and it is a dynamic one. Having witnessed it, experienced it thoroughly, he remains, despite all setbacks, tragedies, and contradictions, essentially a libertarian and an optimist. Solzhenitzyn, equally passionate about truth but lacking any concrete historical experience on which to base a realistic faith in humanity's power of self-regeneration, falls back on the principle of authority. Like Dostoyevsky after the experience of *The House of the Dead*, he internalizes and spiritualizes the problem of evil and acquiesces in the proposition that the powers that be, however blundering, cruel, and unworthy, are ordained by God. Hence his spiritual authoritarianism, so strangely out of keeping (to our Western eyes) with his role as critic and dissident.

*

Yet Serge, for all his revolutionary optimism, was no less anguished by the problem of evil, and nowhere is this anguish more evident than in *Conquered City,* his bleakest, most tragic novel.

The title itself is a many-layered irony. Petersburg, the conquered city in question, is first of all Czar Peter's city, the window on Europe conquered from the wilderness through the despotic will of a Westernizing tyrant. Twin capital of the Empire, it has perennially symbolized the conquest of the old Russia by the new, of the Slavic by the European, of the mystical by the rational—and of the people by the imperial bureaucracy. Now, by a twist of fate, it has fallen to the revolutionists. Its elegant palaces, busy offices, and gigantic factories have been conquered by ragged soldiers and exasperated workingmen. Conquered from within, as it were. Yet it is also under immediate peril of conquest from without. White armies, backed by the Western democracies, are at the very gates of the besieged revolutionary city. Meanwhile, within its walls the revolutionists find themselves everywhere surrounded by enemies—spies, traitors, speculators, ex-bourgeois and ex-aristocrats, as well as exhausted, discouraged citizens of all classes—more or less consciously in league with the Whites outside the city gates.

Far from having "conquered" this city, the revolutionists are painfully conscious that they are only camping out in it, precariously perched on a pinnacle from which any fall is deadly—their shabbiness and poverty incongruous against the background of august imperial splendor.

But the ironies do not end here. The revolutionists have conquered the city, conquered power, only to find themselves conquered *by* power and the problems attendant on its use. In his earlier novels, *Men in Prison* and *Birth of Our Power,* Serge had explored the ironic theme of victory in defeat: the revolutionist who, from the depths of prison or exile, sees the inevitable crumbling of the system that oppresses him and recognizes its terrified weakness in the very ferocity it unleashes against him. Here the situation is reversed. The revolutionists have taken power and the theme is the tragic one of defeat in victory.

Having wrested the weapons of repression from the hand of

the slavemaster, the free bondsman is faced with an awful dilemma. To lay these terrible weapons down is to court martyrdom—the fate of the Communards of 1871 and countless rebels before them—in other words, to invite their own massacre and the death of hope. (Danton expressed the dilemma in its classical form in the eighteenth century: "Those who make revolution halfway are only digging their own graves.") On the other hand, to wield these weapons is to be trapped in the awful dialectic of terror, and the problem is how and where to stop.

Conquered City is about the Terror: the Red Terror and the White Terror. But mainly about the Red, about the Communists who have dared to pick up the weapons of power—police, guns, jails, spies, treachery—on the gamble that by wielding them with purity, in a righteous cause, they can save the city and put an end to the need for terror, perhaps forever. Those who wield these weapons know they are doomed, one way or another. *Conquered City* is their tragedy and testament.

Like Sophocles' *Oedipus the Tyrant,* Serge's tragedy follows the outer forms of a "detective story," in which the hero, who is both the savior of the city and its *tyrannus,* attempts to track down evildoers and rid the city of corruption. By a twist of fate, the purge of the city leads to the hero's self-discovery and self-punishment. Oedipus won power in Thebes by his heroism against an external threat, symbolized by the Sphinx and its riddle. Later, faced with an internal peril, the same weapons that brought him victory—unflinching intellectual clarity combined with boldness of action—bring about his doom. . . . Serge's protagonist, unlike Sophocles', is a collective, as opposed to individual, tyrant-hero and is portrayed through a chorus of characters welded together in a collective entity—the Party. But the broad outlines of the action—the threatened city, the heroic effort to purge it, the hero's inner struggle with growing self-awareness, and his ultimate self-destruction—are consistent with Sophocles'.

Serge's drama unfolds at the very heart of the Red Terror, within the organization that became its cutting edge during the Civil War: the Special Commission for the Suppression of Counterrevolution and Sabotage, best known by its Russian acronym, the Cheka.[2] The novel opens on a frosty night in 1919 in the guardroom

---

[2] I have chosen to retain the rather awkward phrase, "Special Commission," rather than the shorter and more familiar "Cheka" in my translation for two

of the Petrograd Special Commission and closes in the same locale roughly a year later. In the interim, two things have happened. (1) The city has come close to falling under the double impact of starvation, disease, poverty, discontent, and treason within and the powerful enemy without; yet at the last minute it has roused itself to one final heroic effort at survival in order to keep open the possibility of a less brutal future. (2) In the process, the collective protagonist has been all but destroyed—devoured by the task, overwhelmed by its contradictions, betrayed by its own scruples. That is the whole story.

This is tragedy at its highest, conceived as only a modern could conceive it; and Serge is able fully to realize its essence in the form of the novel. Here we have the sweep of vast armies, the fate of cities and empires, an action of great moral seriousness entwined with the fate of heroic and essentially good, if flawed, individuals. Running throughout are the tragic themes of fate, here incarnated in its modern form as historical necessity, and of man's freedom, incarnated in the will of the revolutionists to *change life*. The protagonists, in their agony, all attain high levels of self-consciousness and moral awareness. (This is true even of the White Guards, Danil and Nikita, whom Serge portrays with stunning insight.) Their fate, underscored by the tragic ironies of victory in defeat and defeat in victory, remains problematical.

The author was a participant in the events he describes, and at one point in the narrative he takes the stage in his own persona. He wrote the book ten years after the event under circumstances in themselves tragic and ironic. By 1930, Serge had been expelled from the Communist Party and the Writers' Union, deprived of a means of livelihood, tracked and arrested by the G.P.U. (successor to the Special Commission of 1919–21). He had seen the best of his comrades of the Revolution decimated through their reckless heroism during the Civil War or purged by the new bureaucracy of Stalinist opportunists and office seekers who were making his own existence a living hell. His wife had been driven mad by the persecutions, which had also affected his son and other innocents.

---

reasons: (1) because Serge, faced with the same choice in the original French text, did likewise and (2) because the actual name restores the historical reality of a "special" (i.e., supposedly temporary) commission of delegates elected to deal with an emergency. To me, "Cheka" evokes only the idea of a secret political police, into which the Special Commission, alas, all too rapidly evolved.

Serge wrote the novel under strict surveillance and sent it abroad in sections, never knowing whether they would successfully pass through the censorship or see the light of day. These material circumstances in part explain the relative obscurity of portions of the text. For example, public figures like Lenin, Trotsky, Zinoviev, and Dzerzhinsky are not mentioned by name. Yet they all appear on the stage, particularized by their function and described through their unmistakable physical appearance and characteristic gestures.

It is impossible to say whether these obscurities were merely circumstantial ruses against the threat of censorship. In any case, they are characteristic of Serge's style which, especially in this novel, attains a density and tension that are extremely challenging to the reader and translator, even when one is "in on the secret" as it were. This density flows from the author's own deeply felt ambivalence toward the material itself. The bleak grandeur and ironic tension of *Conquered City* reflect the author's inner struggle with the most serious and passionately debated question of our epoch: Can humanity free itself from oppression and barbarism, given the necessity to employ violent means—the only ones available—to this end?

Serge cast his answer to this stern yet unavoidable question in the form of a tragic novel. It is for the reader to absorb and judge for him or herself. Ultimately, the question will be decided in a practical manner, in the streets. As recently as 1968—yes, our historical memories are short!—it was posed anew in the revolutionary streets of Paris, of Peking, of Prague, of Hue, of Memphis, of Chicago. And 1968 was but a dress rehearsal of momentous events yet on the horizon. . . .

History only repeats itself for those who are unable to learn from it. We might add that this is not always their fault. Tyrants invariably do their best to see that it is falsified to the point of being unrecognizable, while pedants add the finishing touches by making it seem obscure and irrelevant. Yet historical understanding is essential. It is the basis of the tragic optimism of Victor Serge. With every line, Serge seems to be telling us that things need *not* always work out the same way; that, given different circumstances and the understanding of past errors, the tragedies of yesterday may be transmuted into tomorrow's victories. That this is his purpose in writing is evident in the dedicatory lines with which he prefaced *Conquered City*.

Tragedy invariably raises universal questions, but it always raises them in a concrete, particular form. This is especially true of historical tragedy. The problem of power, of violence and counterviolence, is universal; but the *particular* form it took in revolutionary Russia in 1918–21 was the Cheka or Special Commission. Since the drama of *Conquered City* revolves around this *particular form* of revolutionary terror in a specific context, it is fitting to conclude this introduction to the novel by quoting Serge's own final political judgment on this question.

The following paragraphs were written during Serge's Mexican exile in the darkest days of World War II. They are taken from the concluding chapter of his *Memoirs of a Revolutionary,* a chapter significantly entitled "Looking Forward":

The participant and witness of our epoch's events must be driven to pronounce against historical fatality. It is evident that the broadest outlines of the historical process are the product of factors outside our grasp and control, which we can come to know only in an imperfect, fragmentary fashion. But it is no less evident that the character, and even in certain cases the direction, of historical events depends to a very large extent on the caliber of individual human beings. When the Central Committee of the Bolshevik Party met in December 1918 to study methods of attacking domestic counterrevolution, it had a conscious choice to make among the weapons it could present to the new regime. It *could have* instituted public revolutionary tribunals (allowing secret trial in certain specified cases) and, within these tribunals, permitted the right of defense and ensured judicial strictness. It *preferred* to set up the Cheka, that is to say, an Inquisition with secret proceedings, and to exclude from this body any right of defense and any control by public opinion. In doing this, the Central Committee probably followed the line of least resistance; it also followed psychological impulses which are comprehensible to any student of Russian history, but which have nothing in common with Socialist principles.

Durham, Connecticut[3]
February 1975

[3] The translator wishes to thank Marc Slobin and Duffy White for help with the Russian spellings and Adam Dibbell for his editorial assistance.

CONQUERED CITY

THE CONQUERED CITY

1

The long nights seemed reluctant to abandon the city. For a few hours each day a gray light of dawn or dusk filtered through the dirty white cloud ceiling and spread over things like the dim reflection of a distant glacier. Even the snow, which continued to fall, lacked brightness. This white, silent, weightless shroud stretched out to infinity in time and space. By three o'clock it was already necessary to light the lamps. Evening deepened the hues of ash, deep blue, and the stubborn gray of old stones on the snow. Night took over, inexorable and calm: unreal. In the darkness the delta resumed its geographical form. Dark cliffs of stone broken off at right angles lined the frozen canals. A sort of somber phosphorescence emanated from the broad river of ice.

Sometimes the north winds blowing in from Spitsbergen and farther still—from Greenland perhaps, perhaps from the pole across the Arctic Ocean, Norway, and the White Sea—gusted across the bleak estuary of the Neva. All at once the cold bit into the granite; the heavy fogs which had come up from the south across the Baltic vanished and the denuded stones, earth, and trees were instantly covered with crystals of frost, each of which was a barely visible marvel composed of numbers, lines of force, and whiteness. The night changed its aspect, shedding its veils of unreality. The north star appeared, the constellations let in the immensity of the world. The next day the bronze horsemen on their stone pedestals, covered with silver powder, seemed to step out of a strange carnival; from the tall granite columns of St. Issac's Cathedral to its pediment peopled with saints and even to its massive gilded cupola—all was covered with frost. The red granite façades and embankments took on a tint of pink and white ash under this magnificent cloak. The

gardens, with their delicate filigree of branches, appeared enchanted. This phantasmagoria delighted the eyes of people emerging from their stuffy dwellings, just as millennia ago men dressed in
pelts emerged fearfully in wintertime from their warm caves full of
good animal stench.

Not a single light in whole quarters. Prehistoric gloom.

People slept in frozen dwellings where each habitable corner
was like a corner in an animal's lair: the ancestral stench clung even
to their fur-lined cloaks which were never taken off or which they
put on to go into the next room, to pry up a few floor boards in
order to keep the fire going—to get a book—or to empty the night's
excretions at the end of the corridor onto piles of excrement likewise covered by the lovely frost whose every crystal was a marvel
of purity. The cold entered freely through broken windowpanes.

The city, crisscrossed by broad, straight arteries and winding
canals, surrounded by islands, cemeteries, and huge empty stations,
sprawled over the tip of a narrow gulf on the edge of a white solitude . . .

but the nights, unreal or studded with constellations, reigned
implacable and calm, and during those nights skiers armed with
heavy Mauser pistols, carrying fifty lovely pointed bullets, a flask of
brandy, four pounds of black bread, twenty lumps of sugar, a well-
forged Danish passport, and a hundred dollars sewed into the lining
of their trousers, moved resolutely with long strides into that desert
where nothing was worse than meeting another man;

and women clutching their children by the hand, old men, cow-
ardly men, all of them cringing against the great wind of the ter-
ror, deadlier still than the polar blasts, likewise entered that desert
of ice led by traitors and spies, guided by hate and fear, sometimes
hiding their diamonds, like convicts their money, in the secret and
obscene folds of their flesh.

Seen from high above, from the red-starred airplane circling
overhead every morning, the Neva looked like a thin white snake
darting two thin blue tongues into the desert from its open mouth.

The half-empty slums were hungry. The factory chimneys no
longer smoked, and when by chance one started smoking the
women, huddling in their rags at the door of a communal store,
watched that bizarre smoke climb with bleak curiosity. "They're
repairing cannons. They get extra rations. . . .—How much? How

much?—four hundred grams of bread a day; yeah; but it's not for us, it's only for *them*. We know who works in that factory, the bastards. . . ."

Grimy red flags hung over the doors of old palaces, oxblood in color, built by Master Bartolomeo Rastrelli, who delighted in eighteenth-century Italian elegance with its gracious structures beribboned like shepherdesses. They had been mansions of empresses' favorites, of the conquerors of the Crimea and the Caucasus, of great lords owning millions of souls, ignorant, intriguing, and thieving nobles whom the Secret Chancellery subjected to torture one day before exiling them to the forests of the east. When guides from the Department of Political Education explained to simple folk who had come to the capital to attend government conferences that these palaces were the works of the architect Rastrelli, the visitors quite naturally heard "the works of one who was shot," for in Russian *rastrellanny* means "shot." The palaces and mansions dating from Napoleonic times, more austere, with noble symmetrical pediments placed over mighty colonnades, bore the same red rags over their doors. The different periods of the Empire had thus marked the streets with imposing structures which might make you dream at night of the tombs of the Pharaohs of a Theban dynasty. But the ashes of *this* dynasty were still fresh in a bog in the Urals; and *these* tombs, those of a regime to be sure, bore signs: R.C.P. (b). SECOND DISTRICT COMMITTEE; R.F.S.S.R. PEOPLE'S COMMISSARIAT FOR PUBLIC EDUCATION, ADMINISTRATION OF EDUCATIONAL SERVICES FOR BACKWARD CHILDREN; R.F.S.S.R. SCHOOL FOR RED COMMANDERS OF THE WORKERS' AND PEASANTS' ARMY. People were working in these dead palaces—dead because they had been conquered, uncrowned because they were no longer palaces. The machine guns squatting in the vestibules, often in the shadow of huge stuffed bears who used to hold out trays for visiting cards, seemed like beasts of steel, silent but ready to bite. The noisy clatter of typewriters filled rooms designed for princely comfort; a coarse conqueror, Comrade Ryjik, was sleeping with his boots on in an elegant Louis XV room on the same divan where, eighteen months earlier, an old epicurean of the august race of the Ruriks amused himself by staring full of enchantment and despair at naked girls. Now this epicurean was stretched out someplace else, no one knew where, in an artillery range, naked, with a bristly beard, and a hole clean through his head, under two feet of trampled earth, four feet of snow, and the nameless weight of eternity.

One flight up dossiers were filed in boudoirs which had been divided into offices by unpainted wood partitions; an odd collection of requisitioned mattresses was laid out on the floors of the great reception rooms, transforming them into dormitories. Huge crystal chandeliers still tinkled weakly when trucks passed. Humbled captives, who in the old days might well have climbed the marble staircases of this very mansion with dignified steps under the impassive gaze of liveried footmen, now waited in the cellar to be transferred to the Special Commission.[1] Every once in a while the bored sentry sitting, elbows propped on a dirty table, at the door to the cellar stairs would get up, wearily shoulder the strap of his rifle, carried muzzle down, and go to open the padlock of this prison.

"All right!" he would say, not unkindly. "Financiers to the crapper, three at a time!"

With familiar shoves, he herded the heavy stumbling forms down the narrow corridor; they paused a moment at the sight of the dazzling snow in the courtyard. . . . Snoring came from the former kitchens, where the guardroom had been established.

Ryjik could no longer keep track of the time. His days had neither beginning nor end. He slept whenever he could, by day, by night, sometimes at the beginnings of departmental committee meetings when the speaker was long-winded. At such times he would doze off in his chair, head thrown back, red-mustached mouth open; and his limp hands, draped across his knees, expressed in their sudden stillness an enormous weariness. For a long while the telephone—that bizarre little voice designed to capture the ear, that voice that made you think of insects scratching underground— had made him nervous and anxious. Now he dictated and received orders over the phone, and he copied down telephone messages in his large schoolboy hand on the backs of cigarette boxes: "Transmit to Committees of Three: Complete requisition of warm clothing within twenty-four hours." "Remove a barrel of herring from ware-

---

[1] All-Russian Special Commission for the Suppression of Counterrevolution and Sabotage, established December 1917 and best known by its Russian acronym, *"Che-Ka"* or Cheka. Replaced in February 1921 by the G.P.U. or political police.—Trans.

house 12, cut back the men's rations." "Arrest the first ten hostages on the list transmitted by the Committee of Five . . ."

He listened, his eyes wandering, dazed from the day's fatigue, in front of the telephone table, dotted with the crumbs of black bread. "Hello, Gorbunov? Get me Gorbunov. Is the raid over?" The shapeless insect scratched away at the earth in its hole and somewhere far off an unknown voice answered brutally: "Gorbunov has a bullet in the groin; buzz off." And the line went dead. Ryjik cursed. The bell rang again with joyful urgency: "Hello! Is that you, Ryjik? The Saburov Theater is giving away twenty tickets to *The Little Chocolate Girl* . . ." The door had creaked behind him, he sensed a comforting but vaguely irritating presence: "Xenia?" "It's me. Go to bed, Ryjik." Xenia wore a grass-green soldier's tunic and steel-rimmed glasses; the holster of an automatic hung from her belt. She was carrying a book. Ryjik, in his great weariness, dreamed of two soft firm globes of flesh and a warm mouth. Xenia looked at him sedately: "Tomorrow at six. Department meeting." He blushed. "Okay. Good night." He went down the marble staircase. A kind of senseless anger was brewing within him against this young woman who was so simple and frank around him that her very presence banished the idea that they could ever be, even for an instant, face to face as man to woman, disarmed by each other and abandoned to one another.

In the deserted library, next to the great Dutch earthenware stove, two soldiers were playing chess in the glow of a candle. The chess board was a mosaic of rare stones incrusted in an elegant little stand; the ivory men of Chinese design, fine-chiseled, detailed, and grotesque. Ryjik leaned against the stove to let the heat penetrate him and closed his eyes. What a job! And what if I'm tired of being strong, after all? What if . . . ? In these moments of extreme weariness he repeated three unanswerable words to himself: "It is necessary." His battery magically recharged itself. This weariness was only the day's fatigue: sleep could dissipate it. The night reigned, magnificently silent over the snows, the square, the city, the Revolution.

"Bushed, Ryjik?" asked one of the players, advancing a pawn. (He was a dark little man with wisps of straw glistening in his unkempt, overgrown hair.) "Me too. Milk was up to twenty rubles in the market today. Sugar was forty. I just got back from Gdov. It's pretty, the country! At Matveevka, get this, a commissar had gone through requisitioning cows and watches. The yokels nearly tore me to pieces. Our supply details are pillaging, running away, or getting massacred. But I did run into some decent guys with guts—from the wire factory. . . . They were sleeping in the station to play it safe. They were smart."

The other player coughed into a dirty handkerchief and said, without raising his small, craggy, hard head:

"I've had it. My wife covered sixty versts by rail and eighteen on foot to get forty pounds of flour from the village. They confiscated them all when she got back. Now she's got a fever. It may well be typhus. I can't even put the kid into the children's shelter; they're dying like flies there. . . . Check . . ."

"Gorbunov has a bullet in his groin," said Ryjik.

"He's a hustler," replied the dark man casually. "I saw him inventorying typewriters. He didn't know the difference between inventorying and requisitioning. He was making off with everything, even cameras. I told him: 'You're a slob, we'll never make a class-conscious citizen out of you.' All he knows is how to spout about 'world revolution.'"

Ryjik was warm now and murky second thoughts were stirring under his brow, in those dark corners where we tirelessly, pitilessly repress a strange multitude of desires, dreams, suspicions, violent impulses, stifled joys, and curbed brutalities. He told the men curtly: "You: stand guard at the prison from two o'clock until five; you: at the door," and went out. The icy night refreshed his face, but he didn't feel any better. People were standing watch in dark doorways in accordance with the edict of the Executive. The night had become cloudy, the snow no longer glistened: it was like walking through soft opaque ashes which muffled the sound.

⁂

Around 3 A.M., at the moment when night is so vast, calm, and profound it seems definitive, the telephone finally silent, Xenia, alone in the great, parquet-floored hall of headquarters, was writing a few lines on the back of a pass:

> *Revolution: Fire*
> *Burn out the man of old. Burn yourself.*
> *Man's renewal by fire.*

She held her twenty-year-old head in her hands as she sat pensive over these lines. Regeneration of man through the red-hot iron. Plow up the old earth, tear down the old structure. Recreate life anew. And in all likelihood perish yourself. I will perish. Man will live. Yet still a dull anxiety. Is that too the man of old resisting? Victory, smile into the void: Very well, I'll perish, I'm ready. "Ready." She said it out loud. The word came back to her from the silence and the limitless night with a long inner echo. She didn't sense that there was anyone behind her.

Ryjik approached quietly, treading so lightly that the floor didn't creak under his suede boots; slightly stooped, brow hot, hollow-eyed, carrying a great simple decision within him. He placed his hand heavily on the young woman's shoulder. The warmth of that shoulder passed instantly through all his nerves. To gain a few seconds, the infinity of a few seconds, he asked:

"Writing, Xenia?"

"Oh, it's you!"

Without any surprise, not even turning all the way around, she nodded at the lines she had just scrawled.

"Read it, Ryjik. And tell me if it's all right."

"Burn out the man of old. Burn . . ."

Ryjik straightened up, totally subdued.

"All right? All right? I don't know. I don't like romanticism. Empty phrases. Everything is much simpler: imperialism, class war, dictatorship, proletarian consciousness . . . See you tomorrow."

He turned on his heels, a solid block. The leather thong of his Nagan revolver slapped against his leg. He went through the black corridors with the dogged step of a sleepwalker, threw himself on his bed in the dark, and passed out.

. . . That night only seven cars of food supplies arrived in the city. (One was pillaged.) Forty suspects were arrested. Two men were shot in a cellar.

2

Each day the sun rose slowly, late, at an hour when in other cities of the world, of whose existence people here were abstractly aware, the pulse of life was already beating ardently. London, Paris, Berlin, Vienna. Did they really exist? London Bridge with its river of humanity crossing the Thames furrowed in the fog by dark tugboats with lingering, hoarse whistles? Was it possible? Were there still crowds in Piccadilly as in the old days, crowds on the corner of the Rue du Faubourg Montmartre, armies of ants going about their mysterious business around the Porte St. Denis, on the Alexanderplatz—long since washed clean of the blood of the Spartacists—in the great Gothic shadow of St. Stephen's and the despair of Austria! Phantom capitals belonging to the past and to another world which could only be glimpsed through the new prisms of this city: expected uprisings, outcome always in suspense, dispatches, stunning as blows, from the Rosta wire services proclaiming endless crises, the collapse of old nations, thrilling upheavals. Gaudy posters attacked the counterrevolutionary alliances: Lloyd George and Clemenceau, potbellied, wearing top hats, personally aiming battleship deck guns at the Revolution. Night came, merging bit by bit into the stones, the dwellings, the great empty courtyards, the cellars, leaving imperceptible traces of shadow behind; and on the walls gray sheets of newsprint announcing:

Leaving or entering the city without special permission prohibited.
Cloth coupons to be distributed in the near future: one for every 8 people.
Extra requisition of mattresses for the Red Army.
Nationalization of bathhouses. (Closed, in any case, for lack of fuel)

Mobilization of Latvian Communists.
    NO ONE WILL ESCAPE
    THE INEVITABLE
"... *verdict of history, verdict of the masses* ... *riots in Milan* ...
Today Italy, tomorrow France, the next day the universe ... (A
white flame of unstuck paper flapped against the wall in the cold wind.)
Signed, Kuchin.
    Dance Lessons, from 4 to 8. Modern interpretive and ballroom danc-
ing, waltz in a few days. Moderate prices. Tel. 22.76. Madame Elise,
certified graduate."

The street ran straight, all white. Night stretched out over
damp-stained building façades and lingered in dark windowpanes.
People still stood guard in doorways. They were mostly women,
hands buried inside the sleeves of old cloaks, wizened faces
wrapped in woolen scarves. Some of them emerged from the stones
and moved slowly through the snow like little old ladies in paint-
ings by the elder Breughel, feet laden by rubber boots, toward
Communal Store No. 12. There they gathered like woodlice in a
hole.

Around ten o'clock the street took on a feeble animation. People suddenly rushed by on urgent, necessary, imperious, deadly
tasks. They moved quickly, similar in their diversity—uniforms and
black leather—men and women alike, young or ageless, carrying
overstuffed briefcases under their arms: dossiers, decrees, tran-
scripts, theses, orders, mandates, absurd plans, grandiose plans,
senseless paperwork and the quintessence of will, intelligence, and
passion, the precious first drafts of the future, all this traced in little
Remington or Underwood characters, all this for the task, for the
universe; plus two potato pancakes and a square of black bread for
the man carrying these burdens. This was also the hour when those
who had accomplished the tasks of the previous night returned
homeward, chilly and agitated with oddly wrinkled yellowed faces,
yet feeling a final rush of energy mixed with their fatigue.

✿

This was the hour when Xenia went home. She found an old
woman, in a room filled with bitter smoke, kneeling on a floor covered with scraps of bark, ashes, and wood. A square stove of freshly
laid unfaced bricks, which occupied the whole middle of the room,
proclaimed the intrusion of primitive poverty into this ravaged

household. Unmade bedding had been left lying on the couch. The old woman half rose and turned toward the tall blond girl with a fresh, erect body who came in from the night, from the committee, from the unknown, with revolting words on her lips and criminal theories under her high forehead. (Only yesterday, it seemed, that brow had shown between the twin ornaments of flaxen braids.)

"Well, well, well, look at your mother, look at her, kneeling in ashes and filth, hands all black, eyes watering from smoke. The chimney won't draw, can't you see? And *you* won't be able to make it work with all your ideas about the new life! Lovely, the new life. Filimochka won't take money for his milk any more: 'I've got a trunkful,' he says, 'of those worthless bills. I'm going to have my *isba* wallpapered with 'em,' he says, 'give me some cloth.' . . . Well, answer me, answer, won't you!"

Mother and daughter stared at each other, enemies; the one, her gentle face distorted by desperate anger, the other turned in on herself, feeling the excitement of her walk through the snow suddenly fall away from her and fatigue weigh down her thoughts. (Inside her mind a little voice, clear, yet barely audible, was whispering: "I see you clearly enough. You are my mother and you are nothing, and I am nothing. You are incapable of understanding us, you are blind. You can't see that the Revolution is a flame, and the flame will burn us—you: full of pain and spite in this misery; me: anywhere, happy and consenting.")

She said:

"Let me help you, Mama, I'm not tired. . . ."

Then, sharply:

". . . And you know, if this is new for you, it's because we were privileged. Millions of women have never known any other life."

The mother kept silent, blowing on the fire, in the age-old pose of women before the hearth. Heavy blue curls of smoke floated through the room, as in a nomad's tent when the wind is bad. A breath of frozen air came in from above the window through a vent which opened out on a morning as vast as a steppe.

Undressed and in bed, the girl once more became the smooth-browed child she had always been; her close-cropped hair added a bright touch. The mother brought her a bowl of warm milk and watched her drink, softened, recognizing the greedy pout of lips that used to take her breast.

Xenia listened to the noises of the house dying away inside her. The fire caught at last, the window was pulled shut. Someone knocked. It was the secretary of the Poor People's Committee of the House; he asked for Andrei Vassilievich: another registration of ex-officers had been posted.

With the communicating door open you could just hear Andrei Vassilievich's bass voice arguing, in the next room, with his habitual visitor, Aaron Mironovich, who also wore a beard but was round-shouldered, fat, and smiling. The secretary of the Poor People's Committee was speaking too softly. "Speak louder," said Andrei Vassilievich, "she's asleep. She came home exhausted." "All right. So yesterday we moved out the general's furniture; the clubroom of the house is being set up in his place." "And the comrades stole everything, eh?" Andrei Vassilievich asked gleefully. "No, not everything, for the sailor from the *Vulture* stayed until nightfall. But I can sell the old oak dining-room set: Grichka took the Karelian birchwood bed . . ." The muffled laughter, muffled perhaps by the sleep weighing on these voices, drifted slowly off. These scum should have been arrested a long time ago, and Uncle Andrei with them. . . .

"How much?"

"Six thousand."

They were seated around the samovar, huddled in their furs, sipping tea through tiny pieces of sugar held between their teeth. Happy not to be under arrest, they discussed the news of the day while carrying on business. "Did you read, Aaron Mironovich, that they are nationalizing the news dealers' business, now that there is no more paper, no more newspapers, and no more business?" Andrei Vassilievich's hands were holding a miniature composed entirely of hues of blue, gray, and pink—you might have thought it was painted with colors borrowed from the flowers of the field—depicting a young officer. "Come, four hundred; take it, Aaron Mironovich, and I'll leave you half the butter." Without us, they told each other, the city would die of hunger: and how many art treasures would be lost! What they call speculation is the heroic struggle of energetic and competent men against famine. What they call looting the national wealth, in this great anarchic looting known as expropriation, is in fact the rescue of the treasures of civilization. Whatever is stolen is saved. Whenever Andrei Vassilievich expressed these ideas in front of Xenia, he would draw himself up in his chair, his voice trembling with bitterness:

"When Razumuskoe was sacked, the *mujiks* carried off Chinese vases in their carts because they were handy for salting down cucumbers. . . . I have seen Mordvins sharing out a chandelier, pendant by pendant. I have seen drunken soldiers smash a Gardner porcelain for fun. . . . And you don't even know what a Gardner is!"

"We would smash all the porcelains in the world to transform life. You love things too much and men too little. . . ."

Then he would turn around so thick-necked, so sure of himself, that his power nearly cut into the other truth:

"Men? But look what you're doing to them. . . ."

(It is necessary to burn. Burn. That's what he can't understand.)

"You love men too much, men and things, and Man too little."

*

The previous year, before the Austrian socialist leader had disappointed two revolutions, the old Horse Guards Street had been called Friederick Adler Street. Few people knew its present name, Barricades Street; the habit of a century was too heavy for it. Number 12 was a tall commonplace dwelling with crumbling courtyards, crushed under the desperate grayness of old apartment buildings. There, for sixty years, meticulous lives had followed their inconspicuous courses. They kept the saints' days there. They ate well there. They slept warmly there under feather beds. There money flowed quietly in from the countryside, from factories, from unknown obscure offices through underground rivulets like sewers. On a blue enamel plaque screwed over the main archway was written: *Property of the Insurance Building Corp.* By order of the Soviet of the 2nd District, a sailor from the *Vulture* had come one December evening and tacked a handwritten paper bearing the seal of the Poor People's Committee lower down on the door: ". . . has been proclaimed national property." Sad-faced businessmen in worn overcoats—the type seen prowling around the consulates carrying property deeds as obsolete as sixteenth-century patents of nobility—still sold and resold that building every two weeks in Helsingfors restaurants. It still brought a fairly good price, but in czarist rubles, which were out of circulation everywhere except among smugglers and traitors.

On the ground floor the frosted glass store windows, now covered with dust and frost, half revealed tarnished mirrors. *Céline, modes parisiennes*. These words were written in gilt script flaring to a flourish at the bottom. Piss-stained curtains were hanging above the bright metal stands designed to show off the latest model hats imported from the Rue de la Paix. A Jewish family was living there. Sometimes, through a crack in the curtain, you could see a dark graceful eight-year-old slip of a girl rocking a bizarre rag doll with a beautifully painted face. An old man emerged every morning; you could only make out a long, drooping profile, flaccid cheeks, and rheumy eyes under his winter cap. He went to sell God knows what in a market place.

The other shopwindow, which used to be a bootmaker's, now belonged to a half-deserted grocery: little tubes of saccharine, flower tea wrapped to look more or less like the genuine Kuznetzov tea of old, coffee made of some kind of anonymous evil-tasting beans. A few sprouting potatoes placed on a porcelain plate attracted the eye like rare out-of-season fruits. What kind of phantom commerce was hidden behind this shadowy merchandise? The *Vulture* sailor talked to the Poor People's Committee about turning the whole shop inside out, as it was certainly full of stolen sugar and flour. Then the committee secretary, a busy little loudmouth with a limp, who claimed to have been wounded in Carpathia and was surely lying, calmed him down without appearing to by reassuring him that he was personally keeping an eye on "that highly suspicious place."

Sometimes you could see an extremely old man in a gray greatcoat sweeping the morning snow in the courtyard; and when another old man in an astrakhan hat passed stiffly by with jerky steps, the two old men exchanged a long angry look. The privy councilor couldn't forgive the regular state councilor for having entered the service of "those bandits" in an office that was certainly run by an illiterate brute. They also met at the Communal Store, where they both went to get their bread ration. The privy councilor, classified in the Fourth Category (non-workers), slowly wrapped his fifty grams of black dough in a cloth which resembled a dirty handkerchief; he waited until the other man, that scum placed in the Third Category (intellectual workers), had picked up his ration, the double, in order to show him, with a sneer which he thought full of irony, the scorn he felt for this traitor's reward. But the privy coun- cilor's toothless grin, intended to express sarcasm, hardly changed the habitual grimace on his sagging, swollen face; and the privy councilor's glance, which fell on the regular state councilor's ration, revealed itself to be charged not with severity but with bleak animal greed.

Punctually at nine o'clock the regular state councilor appeared at the office—Ah! what personnel!—of the district council. He found only the old woman who swept the rooms. The employees came late and the director the latest of all. After going through the newspapers with deep sighs, the regular state councilor opened his files: *Municipal Properties: Habitations To Be Razed (fire- wood)*. . . . Around noon the director, a short fellow with a harsh, blond peasant's face, had them bring him some tea made of carrot parings and gave his signatures. Since he could barely decipher handwritten script and often got the meaning mixed up, they had to read the propositions written in red ink in the margins of typewrit- ten reports aloud to him. He rarely said no, probably only when he had been paid for it. He almost always signed, with a dissatisfied expression.

"House in good repair," quietly explained the regular state councilor standing deferentially next to the director's chair. "Lodg- ing for twelve persons. To be razed in accordance with the decree."

"I do my duty," he would sometimes explain to his neighbor Andrei Vassilievich, in the evening. "I am serving my country. A government, even one composed of madmen and bandits, nonethe- less represents the country; and the people who live under it only get what they deserve. We're tearing down the city, my friend. We're creating a pickle of a housing shortage for the future, let me tell you! When all this business is over with, I tell you, the value of real estate will triple."

He was the best expert in the district.

*

The whole house took an interest in the newborn baby in apart- ment 15. He had emerged from a tired womb in a fireless maternity ward because they hadn't been able to get rid of him in time; and he had been clinging tenaciously to life for weeks now, contrary to all expectations. He inhaled the ammonia stench of his urine under a heap of old furs. He sucked implacably at the exhausted breast of a woman whose face had the radiance of the dying and who told her visitors, opening her large, slightly crooked eyes over her boy:

"He's alive, he's alive! Look at that. . . ."

People were amazed by this triumphant obstinacy.

People brought logs, grain, and lamp oil to apartment 15. They knew the husband was at the front; and the wife of an officer who was also at the front (but on the other side, so that if these two men met one would kill the other or, a prisoner, would put him coldly to death) went to get the mother's bread. These two neighbor women read together, with the same anxiety, the names of cities lost or taken.

A little girl in a red beret still went every morning to the ballet school to learn the arts of toe dancing and leaping. The hurricane will pass, no? But the dance will remain; and the child has talent. When the weather permitted, she would read Andersen's fairy tales on the way, wondering why no magic carpet ever appeared over the bleak housetops. She also read, and carefully repeated when she got home, the penciled notices posted at the Communal Store: "The Third Category will receive two herrings for coupon No. 23 on the ration card. . . ." How sad life is without flying carpets!

Some workers, who were ready to move out at the first alert to avoid having their throats cut in this house where they felt like intruders, occupied the apartment of a lawyer who had disappeared. They had quickly bartered the salable furniture for foodstuffs from some marauding peasants, and they used the rest to keep warm. They had gutted the safe with an oxyacetylene torch but all they found were some ripped-open files from which the sheaves of documents had been torn by the handful. The gaping wound of the safe, which had been turned into a larder, was visible behind the great office desk, on which a lathe operator from the shipyard kept his tools; for as soon as he came home from the factory, where he mostly stood on line for his grain ration, the man fabricated pocket knives out of stolen machine parts which he later bartered for flour. The water pipes, which froze early in the winter, had burst. Their wives went down two floors to get their water at Professor Lytaev's; loudly they longed for their warm old wooden cottage in the old neighborhood with its evening streets bathed in the yellow light of tavern windows. "That was the good life," they said bitterly. "We'll all croak, you'll see. Hard times," they added.

○

A poster announced that the Poor People's Committee was opening the house clubroom with a lecture on the Paris Commune. A blue Vendôme column, broken in half, was falling into scarlet flames. DANCING WILL FOLLOW!!! The lecturer sent by the Central Club Service, a thin archivist with a faded goatee, spoke for an hour without raising his voice, which fell like a fine rain.

The poor man dealt with the history of "all that political butchery" pitiably rewritten to suit the mood of the times, only because it fed him, and with him an ugly wife who suffered with rheumatism. It didn't interest him any more than had, formerly, the genealogical research he did for new-rich families. And he sometimes had to restrain himself so as not to suddenly break out of this obstinate bad dream, wake up, interrupt himself, and say in a rejuvenated voice with the weight of twenty years lifted from his brow:

". . . But let us leave all these terrible and futile things. The work of a poet is much more precious to humanity than all these massacres! Let us speak then of Pushkin's youth. . . ."

At these moments he blinked his eyes strangely, like a dazzled man emerging from the dark; he was afraid of himself and searched the audience for some enemy face in order to surrender to it. Suppressed, his voice rose an octave for no apparent reason: ". . . the evacuation of the Fort of Vanves . . ."

The hall was a ravaged former drawing room, ornamented in the corners by fat-cheeked cherubs made of gilded plaster holding candelabra, and furnished with leather armchairs, prettily fluted and embroidered boudoir chairs, and heavy dirty wooden benches from the neighboring barracks. On the walls hung photographs of the leaders, as they did everywhere. One appeared to be squinting: beneath his huge, balding forehead appeared a crafty, vaguely cruel expression, due to the photographer who, unable to comprehend his real greatness, had tried to give this simple man what he imagined to be the face of a statesman. (". . . It wasn't easy, I assure you," this former court photographer repeated long afterward.) Another darted a brilliant glance into the abstract, through his rimless glasses; and this head, despite its gracious smile and the impression of irony created by its strong lips, thick mustache, and comma-like goatee, made you think of Draconian orders, of telegrams announcing victories, of proscriptions, of a conquering, exalting, and implacable discipline. There was also the unruly hair and flabby smile of a clean-shaven dictator who still appeared slightly overweight through these famine times. There were only a dozen people in this room, but a good wood fire gave it a feeling of well-being that evening. When the lecturer had finished, the *Vulture* sailor asked if anyone in the audience had "questions to ask the reporter." As the hour for the dance was near, the hall was filling bit by bit. Heads turned toward the harmonica player who was sitting near the door with his instrument on his knees. But a soldier who looked like a clay figure from a shooting gallery rose heavily from his leather armchair at the back of the hall. His commanding voice could be heard very easily as he murmured:

"Tell the story of Dr. Millière's execution."

Standing massively with his head bowed, so that all you could see of his face were his heavy bearded cheeks, his sullen lips, and his wrinkled bumpy forehead (he resembled certain masks of Beethoven), he listened to this story:

. . . Dr. Millière, in a dark blue frock coat and a top hat, dragged through the streets of Paris under the rain, forced to kneel on the steps of the Pantheon, crying, "Long live humanity!" The remark of the Versailles guard leaning on the grill a few steps away: "We'll give you humanity up the ass. . . ."

In the dark night out in the lightless street the clay figure joined the lecturer. The sounds of the harmonica faded behind them, devoured by the darkness.

"Here, you must be hungry."

The archivist felt a hard package being thrust into his hands.

"They're English biscuits I brought back from Onega. Those bastards eat, it's not like us."

The archivist took the biscuits. "Thank you. . . . So you've come from Onega?" He spoke out of politeness. Onega, Erivan, Kamchatka, what difference did it make? But the man who had come from Onega had a secret on his lips. His momentary silence was charged.

"I was also in the government at Perm, last year, when the Kulaks rebelled. They cut open the stomachs of supply commissars and stuffed them with grain.

"On the road I had read Arnould's pamphlet, *The Dead of the Commune*. I was thinking of Millière. And I avenged Millière, citizen! It was a beautiful day in my life, and I haven't had many. Point by point, I avenged him. I shot the richest landowner in the area, on the steps of the church, just like that—I don't remember his name, and I don't give a damn!"

After a short silence he added:

"But I was the one who shouted, 'Long live humanity.'"

"You know," said the archivist, "basically Millière wasn't a real Communard. He was only a bourgeois republican."

"It's all the same to me," said the man who had come back from Onega.

3

You had to wander for a long time through the corridors of the university before finding, in the end, the room where Professor Vadim Mikhailovich Lytaev still came on certain evenings to teach his class. It was like being in a city of another time, in the middle of a sort of abandoned monastery. The night and the cold penetrated even here. Hard rectangles of night pressed in through the white frost-ferns on the windows. The blackboard seemed a bay window open on the night. The professor kept his fur cloak on; his students urged him not to remove his hat so that his high, gray brow with its strands of white hair should not be too defenseless against the icy darkness waiting to envelop men. The audience listened, frozen, in their coats. From the height of his lectern, which was dimly lighted by a green-shaded lamp (the only one in the room), the professor could make out only a dozen indistinct forms from which a few sketchy faces emerged, as through a fog. He could be seen a little more clearly. He was an old man of about sixty, thin, erect, and sturdy. Sunken cheeks, parchment lips. Wrinkles surrounded his eyes which, when lowered, were those of the statue of an ascetic, but when raised showed themselves to be warm and brown. You noticed at such moments the delicacy of the nose, which was straight despite its high bridge, the regular mouth, the unruly, graying beard, and that this combination of features formed one of those faces, of somber aspect and luminous expression, which the Novgorod icon painters usually gave to their saints, not out of fidelity to a mystical type but much more probably through the sanctification of some ancient Greek portraits.

The professor spoke of the reforms of Peter I with a passion so sure of itself that it was almost subdued. You had to say Peter I now instead of Peter the Great. Most often Lytaev said simply Peter, emphasizing the strength of the man in the mighty Czar. When his class was over, Vadim Mikhailovich Lytaev entered a present night as vast as that of the past. He followed a path of ice on the Neva, crossing the wide river obliquely toward the Winter Palace. Parfenov usually accompanied him, for they both lived in the center of town. Parfenov walked alongside the master with an even tread which was absolutely silent, as if non-existent. With his felt boots, fox fur coat, and fox hat whose long earflaps hung down over his chest and his heavy shapeless face, he appeared to be only a shadow, huge and light. From a few paces off, you would have taken him for a bear.

The moonlight was diluted by a light, icy mist which allowed only an intense, gray, diffuse phosphorescence to shine through. From the middle of the Neva limitless landscapes were visible. The shapes of palaces appeared dimly above the two circular banks as if on the edge of a lunar crater—black but fluid, shimmering in an atmosphere like an ocean floor. Somewhere to the right, beyond the high granite rampart of the embankment, in the middle of a colonnaded square, a giant reared his horse atop a rocky crag, crushing, without seeing it, a serpent bronze like himself. His hand reached out toward the sea, the north, the pole. Peter: a broad face of power with little insignificant mustaches.

Vadim Mikhailovich was carrying home his scholar's rations, which he had received at the university after waiting two sullen hours among academicians: one pound of herrings, one pound of groats, two pounds of millet, two packs of cigarettes (second quality). He shifted the sharp straps of his knapsack on his shoulders and said:

"Look, Parfenov. We are outside of time. The night was the same on this river centuries ago. Centuries will pass, night will be the same. Two hundred twenty years ago, before Peter came, there were five thatched huts made of logs lost somewhere out there on these banks. Seven men scratched for a living here—for they only counted the males—with their females and their young. Seven men identical to their unknown ancestors who had come from the east. That village was called Ienissari."

"But Peter came," said Parfenov. "And now we have come. How happy men will be in a hundred years! Sometimes it makes me dizzy to think of it. In fifty years, in twenty years, maybe in ten years . . . yes! Give us ten years and you'll see! The cold, the night, everything . . ."

(Everything? What did he mean by that vague word, vaster than the cold and the night?)

". . . everything will be conquered."

They walked a moment in silence. The other bank got imperceptibly closer.

. . . This Parfenov, what an enthusiast! Lytaev smiled in the darkness at the myths that drive men through history.

"Parfenov, you are right to believe in the future. It is the new God, the reincarnation of the oldest divinities, which makes the present bearable. I believe in it too, but differently, for the future is an endless spiral. . . . Are you satisfied at the factory, Parfenov?"

"No. In fact I've had about enough. Vadim Mikhailovich, I'm getting ready to leave you. I have requested permission to leave for the front; the branch secretary is supporting me. I'll get it."

He needed to talk. And Lytaev listened with a kind of vague joy to that young male voice filtered through the harsh sounds of the day. The walk through the darkness on the ice in the midst of this solitude made it possible for the two men to understand each other far beyond the precise meaning of words.

"The factory? It takes us a week to produce what we produced in a day last year. I had to reintroduce the practice of searching the workers on the way out: they steal everything. They came and cursed me: 'Policeman! Have you no shame! You yourself protested against searching in '17, an indignity you said it was! Just wait a little, Commissar, your turn will come. . . .' The worst part of it is that searching doesn't help very much. They tie up packages and throw them out the window. The women workers carry out thread between their legs and linings rolled around their stomachs. I can hardly ask the men on the door to pinch their asses! They thumb their noses at me."

Lytaev replied softly. "Parfenov, they've got to make a living."

"Yes, that's the worst of it. So they steal. With the cloth from the tunics they make slippers that sell for forty rubles on the market. The workers have got to live, but the Revolution must not be killed. When I tell them this, some of them answer me: 'Isn't it killing us?' Some of them have no consciousness at all, Vadim Mikhailovich."

". . . And it's with that blind force, Parfenov, that you want to change the world?"

"With them and for them. Otherwise, they will never be men. Despite them, if necessary. 'Policeman?' I told them. 'Okay, I'm not afraid of words. Insult me as much as you like, I'm your comrade and your brother, maybe that's what I'm here for: but I will defend against you what belongs to the Republic. If someone has to get killed, I don't mind getting killed, with you, as long as the Revolution can live. . . .'"

"Do they understand you, Parfenov?"

Parfenov meditated. "It's hard to express. It seems to me they hate me. It seems like I could get killed. They write in the toilets that I'm a Jew, that my real name is Schmoulevich, Yankel. And nothing can be done about the stealing because it is the hands of hunger that steal. But under all their hate I believe they still understand me, they know I'm right; that's why they haven't yet knocked me off, even though I walk home alone every night."

*

The main entrance to the house had been closed for months as a precaution. Lytaev went in through the wicket gate at the carriage entrance. An old lady, on guard duty, stared at him in the dark. Her response to his greeting was a nod of calculated dignity, which he didn't see, for she disapproved of the idea of such a respectable man consenting to teach under a government of bandits. Having crossed the courtyard, Lytaev felt his way carefully up a narrow stairway smelling of damp and of garbage and knocked heavily at the double door of what had once been a kitchen. He had to identify himself before the servant woman inside would raise the iron bar and unhook the safety chain. "It's me, Agrafena, me. . . ."

A gentle warmth reigned in the study where they were now living around a cast-iron stove and an oil lamp. For thirty years the same feminine face had appeared in front of Vadim Mikhailovich at the calm hour of midnight tea, just before rest; he had watched that face climb through the full light of life, then decline, fade, wane, without losing the clarity of its gaze, the only youth that lasts; he knew that face so well that he forgot it, that he saw it without seeing it, that he rediscovered it at times in his memory with helpless astonishment. —Here we are, old people. . . . What, then, what is life? —The same hands, at first tapered with rosy polished nails, hands he compared to flowers and which he sometimes covered with kisses; then little by little faded, wrinkled, slightly thickened, with ivory hues, placing the same silver service before him. The same voice, imperceptibly changed like the hands, talked to him of the day, which was now over. This evening the hands placed thin slices of black bread and marinated herring in the circle of light; they passed the sugar bowl in which the sugar was frugally broken into tiny crumbs. The voice said:

"Vadim, we're going to have butter. They promised me fourteen pounds in exchange for the Scotch plaid."

Perhaps an image passed rapidly, from very far away, through the two minds or between them (so rapidly, from so far, that they didn't notice it): the image of a couple in a blue brougham, the Scotch plaid on their knees; and the white peaks, the pines, the torrents, the green valleys dotted with steeples, the feudal towns of the Tyrol fled as youth and life had fled.

"Vadim, they conducted a search last night at the Stahls' and made off with a gold watch. . . . Vadim, Pelagueya Alexandrovna received a letter saying that her son died at Bugulma. . . . Vadim, milk is up to thirty rubles. . . . Vadim, my backaches have started up again. . . ."

Vadim listened to these remarks, always the same, and let himself sink into a feeling of sad contentment. This warmth was certain and that other life, that other part of his life, tremendously foreign, tremendously close. He answered softly, distractedly, but with an attentive air, giving the right replies. Relieved of the weight of another day, his mind wandered off to grapple with the usual great worry. "Thank you, Marie," he said, as he had said thirty years earlier, and yet very differently. "I'm going to work for a while." After moving the lamp behind the screen that separated off his nook, he sat down over a needlessly opened book, reached for one of those unfolded old envelopes on the backs of which he took his notes, and began to draw patiently with his pencil: geometric designs in the manner of Arab artists, childlike faces, bits of landscape, animal silhouettes. During these moments of meditation he was always bothered by the temptation to sketch the faces of women with huge eyes and long lashes; but he repressed it with some shame, not really knowing if he was ashamed of the temptation or ashamed of himself for not giving in. . . . He remained there for an hour face to face with his thoughts, no longer expressed in words, like blind men locked into an irregularly shaped room, more worries than thoughts.

Another worry raised its voice at last behind him in the semi-darkness.

"Vadim, you ought to go to bed. You tire yourself too much. The stove has gone out."

"Yes, dear."

The cold had begun to penetrate his motionless arms and legs. He got undressed, slowly, dreamily, blew out the lamp, slipped shivering between the sheets, and stretched out as if "for eternity." And now his mind began to give birth to clear sentences forming, all by themselves, into paragraphs which would have made good sections of articles. "The death rate in Petrograd this year was higher than in the Punjab during the great plague of 1907!!!" "Peter I's great reform seemed to some of the best minds of old Russia the beginning of the reign of the Anti-Christ. . . ." "At the time of Peter I's death, the Empire had been depopulated. . . ." But no, that wasn't it. History explained nothing. What if, in order to understand, it was necessary to think less, to know less? What if things were much simpler than they seemed? A title for a work: *The Fall of the Roman Empire.* What could be clearer? No explanation. What's to explain? *The Fall of Christian Civilization.* No, not *Christian, European.* Not right either. *The Fall of Capitalist Civilization.* If the newspapers were telling the truth, if you could believe the posters in the streets, the speeches at the assemblies, if . . . ?

He remembered Parfenov, asleep at this hour on some make-shift cot, not far from here, in an unknown house, sure of the greatness of men in ten years, twenty years, provided this necessary night could be got through. "They don't know history, but they are making it. . . . But what are they making, what are they making?"

4

I, too, sometimes crossed the frozen river on those arctic nights. The pathway was silent underfoot. It was like moving through the void. I reflected that only yesterday we were nothing. Nothing: like the nameless men of the forgotten village which had vanished from these banks. Between that yesterday and the present, centuries seemed to have passed, or between the times of those men and our own. Only yesterday countless lights were burning along these banks inside rooms where the power, the wealth, and the pleasure of others reigned. We put out those lights, brought back primordial night. That night is our work. That night is us. We have entered it in order to destroy it. Each of us has entered it, perhaps never to leave it. So many harsh, terrible tasks must be done; tasks which demand the disappearance of their performers. Let those who come after us forget us. Let them be different from us. Thus what is best in us will be reborn in them.

Yesterday, we only counted as statistics: labor force, emigration, death rate, crime rate, suicide rate. The best of us also counted in the records: file B, wanted lists, political police, reports, prison rolls. This is no metaphysical void! No commodity is more common and more depreciated than man. Is he even worth the weight of his flesh? They wouldn't let a draft animal starve in the gray autumn fields. But a man in a big city? As far back as I search in my memory, I find not theories but images, not ideas but impressions, brutally imprinted in my nerves and soul, reminding me that we were nothing. Childhood moments in London. There are two of us kids: one will later more or less starve to death. We are playing in the lamplight at building an Angkor Temple. Strident whistle blasts explode in the street, like lightning flashing in all directions in the darkness, crisscrossing through the sky. Because a dark shape, more furtive than a shadow, had spun past the window. The street is an abyss, the windows of the poor open onto infinity. Downstairs some bobbies, carefully avoiding getting bloodstains on their trouser cuffs, are bending over a pile of old rags and flesh. "It's nothing, children. Be still now!" But we had overheard whispering, we discovered a dark infinity in the windows, we sensed the profundity of the silence.

. . . And that hunted Jewish couple, in another city, with whom the child died on a happy June evening. There were no more candles, there was no more money, the room was bare. We had gone without eating in order to pay for the doctor's useless final visit. Reflected light from a café across the street projected the backward silhouette of a sign on the ceiling.

We don't need gas explosions burying miners, communiqués from quiet sectors where thirty men spill out all the blood of their bodies (nothing worth reporting), memories of executions, the history of crushed insurrections, memoirs of deportees and prisoners, we need no naturalist novels to understand our nothingness. But each of us has all that behind him.

The snow track faded on the river bordered by dark granite. The dark shape of the Winter Palace stood out vaguely among the shadows. In that corner—I knew without thinking—between two bay windows dominating a wide panorama of river and town, stood the Autocrat's desk, on which his cigarette holder was lying.

A buddy's jibe: "Man. The thinking reed! They taught him to stop thinking years ago. Today they dry him out, soften him up, and weave baskets out of him for every use, my friend, including the least appetizing. Pascal didn't think of that."

Now things will change. Now we are all: dictatorship of the proletariat. Dictatorship of those who were nothing the day before. I break out laughing, alone in the dark, to think that my papers are in order, that I am using my name—that in my pocket I have an order in the name of the Federated Republic enjoining

"all revolutionary authorities to lend aid and assistance to Comrade —— in the performance of his functions."

and that I am a member of the governing party which openly exercises a monopoly of power, unmasks every lie, holds the sword unsheathed, ideas out in the open.

I laugh climbing the hard snowbank up to the embankment. I trip over black potholes which I know to be white—thus black and white can be one and the same.

A harsh voice, piercing the night, hails me:

"Hey, there! Come out in the open!"

Then, more slowly, as I approach the invisible shouter:

"What do you think you're doing here?"

A ruddy glow spills out from behind the sharp corner of a woodpile. I perceive a heap of glowing coals and, near the coals, a soldier freezing in his long overcoat, which skirts the ground. The man is standing guard over this precious wood, which people come to steal, log by log, from the riverside.

"You got a permit to go around at night?"

I have one. He examines it. Either he doesn't care or can't read. It's a typewritten permit. The typist mistakenly put her carbon wrong side up, and the writing on the back is illegible. It suddenly reminds me of those advertising handbills which, folded, look like halves of bank notes. If I closed my eyes, I could see a piece of the sidewalk at the corner of the Place de la République and Boulevard du Temple again. The soldier hands me back my paper. We are cold. We are both dressed in the same rough gray cloth which looks so much like the Russian soil. We are the dictatorship of the proletariat.

He says:

"They steal the wood; it's incredible how they steal. I'm sure that if I walked around the stock, I'd find somebody on the other side handing logs down to the Neva. There's a hole on the ice out there. A while ago the man on guard finally fired a shot, to scare the thief. He was a twelve-year-old kid, whose mother sent him out every night. She waited for him under one of the gates on the embankment, No. 12. The kid got scared. He fell right into the hole with a log on his head. He was never seen again. I pulled the log out when I got there. I found a wood-soled shoe at the edge of the hole. Look."

There, in the snow turned gold by the glow of the coals, was the dark print of a little schoolboy's foot.

"There's always a strong current under the ice," said the soldier.

✦

He had taken me for another wood thief at first. I could have been one. People steal the wood that belongs to everyone, in order to live. Fire is life, like bread. But I belong to the governing party and I am "responsible," to use the accepted term, that is to say, when all is said and done, in command. My ration of warmth and bread is a little more secure, a little larger. And it's unjust. I know it. And I take it. It is necessary to live in order to conquer; and not for me, for the Revolution. A child was drowned today for the equivalent of my ration of warmth and bread. I owe him its full measure in human weight: flesh and consciousness. All of us alike. And he who is dishonest with himself, who takes it easy, holds back, or takes advantage, is the lowest of swine. I know some. They are useful, nonetheless. They also serve. Perhaps they even serve better, with their oblivious way of profiting from the new inequality, than those who feel guilty. They pick out furniture for their offices; they demand automobiles, for their time is precious; they wear Rosa Luxembourg's picture on medallions on their lapels. I console myself by thinking that history naturally turns these people, despite themselves, into martyrs quite as good as the others. When the Whites capture Reds, they hang the phonies from the same limbs as the genuine articles.

I move on through the night: on the left I should soon see, through this crosshatching of spindly branches, the vast horseshoe of Uritski Square with its granite column and its four-horse chariot surging forward atop Headquarters Arch in a motionless gallop. I think about those bronzes in the same way as I would place my hand on them, to refresh my soul. I too need all my lucidity in order to find my own way through another darkness. On the right, pale lights flicker under a row of high windows, glimpsed slantwise between white columns. The Special Commission works day and night. That is us too. The implacable side of our face we turn to the world. We, the destroyers of prisons, the liberators, freedmen, yesterday's convicts, often marked indelibly by our chains, we who investigate, search out, arrest; we, judges, jailers, executioners, we!

We have conquered everything and everything has slipped out of our grasp. We have conquered bread, and there is famine. We have declared peace to a war-weary world, and war has moved into every house. We have proclaimed the liberation of men, and we need prisons, an "iron" discipline—yes, to pour our human weakness into brazen molds in order to accomplish what is perhaps beyond our strength—and we are the bringers of dictatorship. We have proclaimed fraternity, but it is "fraternity and death" in reality. We have founded the Republic of Labor, and the factories are dying, grass is growing in their yards. We wanted each to give according to his strength and each to receive according to his needs; and here we are, privileged in the middle of generalized misery, since we are less hungry than others!

Will we succeed in overthrowing the ancient law which bends us to its will at the very moment when we believe we are escaping it?

The Gospel said "Love one another" and "I have not come to bring peace, but a sword." Nothing but the sword is left under the crucifix. "Whoever would save his soul will lose it. . . ." Well, I'll be glad to lose my soul. Who cares? It would be a strange luxury to worry about it today. Old texts, old, old inner captivity. What haven't they built on the Gospel! Destroy! Destroy! The main thing is to destroy thoroughly.

To be afraid of words, of old ideas, of old feelings, those feelings that are so firmly riveted into our beings, by which the old world still holds us. A poor fighter he who holds back thinking, when it is necessary to reload your rifle and shoot with the greatest concentration—like shooting at dummies on a rifle range—at the men climbing that hill over there. Simple truths, sure, hard as granite, formulated with algebraic clarity; that is what we need. We are millions: the masses. The class which, owning nothing, has nothing to lose but its chains. The world must be made over. For this: conquer, hold on, survive at any cost. The tougher and stronger we are, the less it will cost. Tough and strong toward ourselves first. Revolution is a job that must be done without weakness. We are but the instruments of a necessity which carries us along, drags us forward, lifts us up, and which will doubtless pass over our dead bodies. We are not chasing after some dream of justice—as the young idiots who write in little magazines say—we are doing what must be done, what cannot be left undone. The old world dug its own grave: it is now falling in. Let's give it a little shove. Millions of men who were nothing are rising into life: they are unable not to rise. We are those millions. Our only choice is to understand this and to accomplish our task with our eyes open. Through this consent, through this clear-sightedness, we escape from blind fate. All that was lost will be found again.

The square is lined with dark old palaces. At the bottom, the Maria Palace, that low edifice with an ill-defined shape. The Imperial Council used to meet there. There's a big Repin painting showing that council: busts of bemedaled old men posing around a semicircular table. They appear through a yellow-green aquarium light which makes them all look dead. At the center, the Emperor, the portrait of an obliterated face. Those thick necks resting on embroidered collars have all been smashed by bullets. If any one of these great dignitaries still escapes us, it is probably that old man with the big bony nose drooping over flabby lips who sells his daughters' old shawls in the mornings at the Oats Market. . . . Thick peasant fingers test and fondle the beautiful cashmeres.

On the right, in the indistinct light falling from the windows of the Astoria, the former German Embassy stands behind its massive columns which support no pediment. There used to be some bronze horses on top. During the first days of the war, furious crowds toppled these statues, threw them down to the pavement from their high granite perch, and dragged them to the neighboring canal where they are still under the ice. Behind the embassy's barred windows there remains only the simple desolation of places long since plundered. Bandits get in through the courtyards and live there, careful that no light can be seen from outside to betray their presence. They play cards, drinking old cognac swiped from the cellars of great houses or fiery brandy fabricated in secret stills on the outskirts of town. Girls with lips painted fiery red, with names like Katka-Little-Apple, Dunya-the-Snake, Shura-Slant-Eyes (also known as The Killer), and Pug-Nose-Marfa-Little-Cossack, who wear luxurious dirty underwear and dresses by the great couturiers, taken from empty apartments, sometimes peer out, invisible, from behind the dark windows of the great hall of the embassy, at our lighted windows across the way.

"The commissars live good," says Katka.

"They sure live it up," says Dunya, "with their short-haired whores, partying every night of the week."

"I know one of them," says Shura, "what a pervert."

Her bitter laughter flashes through the darkened hall. A thin ray of light slides across the floor. A triumphantly masculine voice calls out:

"Hey, girls, we're waiting!"

Another voice, a bass, is humming *Stenka Razin's Complaint*.

There is also the huge dark mass of St. Isaac's with its massive columns, its enormous archangels spreading their wings at each corner to the four corners of the earth, its steeples, its gold-plated cupola visible from far out at sea. . . .

The windows of the Astoria burn until dawn. They are the only lighted ones in town, along with those of the Special Commission and the Committees. Nocturnal labor, danger, privilege, power. The powerful façade repels the darkness like a shell of light. People crossing the square in the evening on the way back home to their airless hovels cast hate-filled looks at the hotel of the commissars ("naturally most of them Jewish") where it is warm and light and where there is food to eat, it's certain, where no one fears house searches, where no one's heart leaps into his mouth at the first sound of a doorbell ringing at night, where no one ever hears rifle butts falling on the doorsteps. . . . Passers-by murmur: "A fine trap. You could catch the whole lot of them at once!"

First House of Soviets. I push through the revolving door. From the hotel desk the single eye of a machine gun fixes its infinite black gaze on me. The machine gunner dozes, his sheepskin hat pulled down to his eyes.

This is the threshold of power. All who cross over this doorstep know what they want, what is necessary, and feel themselves under the great shadow of the Revolution; armed, carried forward, disciplined, by the structure of the Party. Droning voices trail out from the guardroom. A gilded plaque fastened to the open door reads (in French): *Coiffeur à l'entresol*. Another sign in black ink: *Present your papers when requesting your pass*. You need a pass, which you return on the way out, to get in to the people who live in this building; these little papers are then sent on to the Special Commission. Somebody collects them. Somebody has to know who comes to see me at what time. We must not be allowed to be killed with impunity; we must not be allowed to destroy, we must not be allowed to know strangers, for we have power, and the power belongs to the Revolution.

"Evening, Ryjik."

He comes out to meet me, carefully carrying his tin teapot from which scalding steam is escaping. Ruddy stubble covers his face up to his eyes. He is in slippers: the broad folds of a magnificent pair of cavalry breeches (raspberry colored) float around his hips. Why do they call these breeches *gallifets?* Ryjik wears a satisfied smile.

"You're looking at my *gallifets?* What material! Take a look, feel it. A real find, eh? And a love letter in the pocket, my friend. . . . Come up to my room, you'll see Arkadi: I have your newspapers."

Red carpets muffle our steps. This is a huge stone ship, appointed like a luxury liner anchored in the polar city. Wide corridors, oak doors marked with discreet gold numbers. The calm is profound, the warmth—after the nocturnal cold—like a hothouse. Isn't one of these doors going to open on a haughty couple? She, shapely in furs crackling with electricity, her mouth a purple-blue line; he, slender, high cheekboned, a flash of light dancing off his monocle . . .

. . . A champagne bucket behind them in the room leaves a silver glow. They pass like phantoms: I wouldn't even turn around. . . . A door has opened quietly, the phantoms vanish.

"Come on in," says Ryjik, appearing in the doorway.

I can already see Arkadi's oriental profile in a mirror. Shapely in his close-fitting black uniform, his waist cinched by narrow Montagnard belt with sculptured silver pendants, a large metal insignia —silver and red—on his right breast, like a commander's star; he is smoking, leaning back on the divan. Without smiling, he shows his handsome white teeth. Ryjik pours us tea.

"Here are your newspapers," Arkadi says to me. "From now on they'll be a hundred and twenty rubles a copy."

(A hundred and twenty czarist rubles, out of circulation.)

"Your smugglers are too much. It was eighty three weeks ago."

The package, tied with heavy twine, smells of printers' ink. *L'Intransigent, Le Matin,* the Manchester *Guardian, Corriere della Sera,* bought in Vyborg . . . Men, eyes peering out of white furs, ears straining to hear the slightest crackle of branches, cross the front lines bent under the weight of these bundles. Sometimes explosions shatter the absurd silence around them; running, they pull long-range Mausers out of their frozen wooden holsters and crouch even closer to the snow; inside their chests, startled-beast terror changes into the will to kill, and an extraordinary lucidity bursts inside their skulls.

"They're still expensive," I say.

"They say two of their men got killed during the past two weeks: that's certainly worth two raises of twenty rubles a copy. And it's true. Jurgensohn knows that two bodies were picked up in the zone. The place is getting hot."

Ryjik says:

"They haven't delivered any bread for the last three days in the Moscow-Narva district. Ataev claims that the trains take twenty days to reach us instead of eight. Nothing to burn. There's gonna be trouble in the factories."

"Rather!" snapped Arkadi between his white teeth.

"I think we should put out emergency calls for special conferences of non-Party people, or the discontent will break out by itself. I suggested it at Smolny."

". . . better lock up the Left Social Revolutionaries first. . . . According to our informers, they're cooking up something. Goldin has arrived, it must be for a *putsch*."

"Indeed," I say, "I'd like to see him."

"He's staying here, Room 120."

The comrade who's preparing a *putsch* against us is right downstairs. Handsome, daring, and sensual, he seems to have been playing with death—his own and other people's—for years.

"I suggested," resumed Arkadi, "arresting him tonight if not sooner: better before than afterward. The Commission wouldn't hear of it. Misplaced scruples."

The conversation breaks off. Three o'clock sounds. Ryjik wipes his lips with the back of his hand and asks:

"Do you know how people in town spell out S.B.N.E. [Supreme Board for National Economy]?"

A great guffaw is already stretching his jolly red cheeks.

"No? Well, it seems it stands for "Slave But Never Eat." Not bad, eh?"

We laugh. Arkadi yawns. He spends his days and part of his nights at the Special Commission. He does everything himself, with precise movements, a clipped voice designed for command, and shining teeth. Difficult raids, arrests of men who must be taken by surprise before they can fire their Brownings, complicated inves-

tigations, and probably also automobile rides through the rising
mist at dawn down lanes lined with dark pines and spindly bushes
fleshed with white, toward that little wood located seven versts out
on the Novgorod road where . . . In the back seat of the Renault,
opposite two silent Latvians, sit two pale handcuffed passengers
chain-smoking—impatiently lighting a fresh cigarette with slightly
trembling hands from the dying one as if it were essential that this
infinite dying fire should be kept going. . . . An aura surrounds
them. Their sprouting beards (depending on which way the shadows fall) give them faces like evil Christs or pure-browed criminals.
They say that it's cold; they converse about indifferent matters in
hoarse cracking voices. . . . Back in his room—a room identical to
this one, except for a portrait hanging above the couch: Liebknecht's head,[1] thrown back with a horrible red carnation blooming
at the temple—Arkadi pours himself a big glass of confiscated
samogon (Russian "moonshine"), a fiery brew that rasps the throat
and numbs the brain. And so he will be able to sleep until it's time
for interrogations. He has the regular features, narrow, fleshy eagle
nose, and green eyes flecked with yellow and white of a falconer of
Adjaristan, his native land. Adjaristan with its hot rains pelting the
red earth with liquid hail. Adjaristan with its mimosas blooming in
the damp shadows, its tea bushes on pyramidal hills, the palm-lined
walks of Batum, its little Greek cafés, rows of scorched mountains,
white minarets towering over flat roofs, brown tobacco leaves dry-
ing on racks; Adjaristan with its veiled women who are submissive,
beautiful, and industrious.

I open the newspapers: *Le Journal,* wire dispatch in *Le Matin:
Tragedy on Rue Mogodor:* "She was cheating on him; he kills her
and then commits suicide." Do they think they're alone in the
world? Rue du Croissant at this hour: presses rolling breathlessly in
the print shops; bicycle delivery men brush past night revelers as
they slip away on their silent machines. Old Fernand, the good,
melancholy hobo, wanders along the sidewalk headed God knows
where. . . . *Terror in Petrograd.* "Bolshevism is at bay; only its

---

[1] Karl Liebknecht (1871–1919), German revolutionary and martyr. He was the
only member of the Reichstag to vote against the war in 1914 and was jailed
for pacifism in 1916. Freed in 1918, he founded the Spartacus League and was
shot in the head during the workers' uprising of 1919, along with his collaborator, Rosa Luxembourg.—Trans.

Chinese praetorians still defend it. . . ." Arkadi! Ryjik! Listen to
what they are saying about us! Apoplectic Socialists, seeing the in-
adequacy of the blockade, whose inhumanity they condemn, pronounce themselves, with words of triple meaning, in favor of military intervention, on the condition (for Woodrow Wilson is a
prophet) that the sovereignty of the Russian people will not be im-
paired. . . . They dream of bayonets which respect the law. We
sense fear, stupidity, hatred sweating through these printed lines.
How they long for our death back there, for the death of this
Republic whose insignia you wear on your chest, Arkadi, for which
we do every sort of job, which we want to see survive because it is
still the greatest hope, the birth of a new kind of justice, honesty in
deeds and words—implacable deeds and truthful words!—the work
of those who have always been vanquished, always duped first and
then massacred, who were nothing yesterday, who are still nothing
in the rest of the world!

5

Other oases of electricity burning from dusk to dawn: the Committees. Committees of Three, of Five, of Seven, of Nine, the Enlarged Committees, the Extraordinary Committees, the Permanent, Temporary, Special Subaltern, Superior, Supreme Committees deliberating on the problem of nails, on the manufacture of coffins, on the education of preschool children, on the slaughter of starving horses, on the struggle against scurvy, on the intrigues of the anarchists, on agitation and propaganda, on road transport, on the stocking of women's hats after the nationalization of small business, on the consequences of the Treaty of Versailles, on the infraction of discipline committed by Comrade N., on the famine . . . So much thought straining and working everywhere in these messy rooms under the same portraits, in the same atmosphere of neglect characteristic of conquered places where people are always rushing in and out! New dangers were appearing at every turn. The thaw was approaching. Piles of filth hardened by the cold filled the courtyards of buildings and the floors of whole rooms which would be transformed into cesspools with the first warm days. The water conduits had broken in many areas: they would soon be infested with disease. Typhus was already present; it was necessary to head off cholera, to clean up a huge enfeebled city within a few weeks. Kirk proposed to the Executive the formation of an extraordinary Committee of Three with unlimited powers. Kirk telephoned the Urban Transportation Committee: "I need four hundred teams . . ." At the other end of the wire Rubin answered: "I'll give you thirty and you'll feed the horses yourself." Kirk requisitioned the old retired tramway cars and posted notices declaring that "persons belonging to the wealthy classes, aged 18–60," were drafted into sanitation duty. Formed into teams supervised by the Poor People's Committees, this work force would clean up the city. Only 300 disinherited ex-rich people were to be found among the 750,000 inhabitants. Kirk, swearing in English into his stained mustache, ordered roundups in the center of the city and had the trams stopped in the streets to pull off well-dressed people who were adjudged ex-bourgeois by their appearance and sent off to sanitation duty with no further discussion.

Frumkin had no workers to unload trains of foodstuffs; as a result there was a shortage of cars, and the cars in the stations were being pillaged. He announced an obligatory registration of former employees and unemployed functionaries, picked up nine hundred naïve fellows at the unemployment office, and sent them off to the stations escorted by a Communist battalion; but one third of them melted away en route and another third on arriving. The flour sacks, unloaded with unheard-of slowness and clumsiness by the remaining three hundred petits bourgeois, were left under the snow along the tracks: a good part of them went rotten. The black markets were inundated with flour for several days. The great writer, Pletnev, and the brilliant tenor, Svechin, having learned that professors, men of letters, and gracious lawyers, who, under the old regime, had brilliantly defended the Revolutionaries, were being drafted for these "public works," protested to the President of the Soviet against these proceedings, which were "unworthy of a civilized people" and would "end up dishonoring the Revolution." The President had just received a stock inventory from the Town Council indicating that in three days there would be no more food; and from the Railway Commissariat a telephone message begging him to take urgent actions aimed at supplying combustible materials for the lines and raising discipline among the railwaymen; otherwise all traffic would probably halt in less than a week. Kondrati had just announced to him that a strike was brewing at the Great Works. He gazed at the great writer and the brilliant tenor with polite indifference.

"I'll look into it, I'll look into it; we're swamped. . . . Do you need anything?"

Naturally, they were in need of many things, despite the fact that the whole city envied their opulence, which was of course exaggerated by gossips.

"I'll have two sacks of flour sent over to you, Simeon Gheorgh-
ievich. . . ."

The brilliant tenor lowered his chin as a sign of thanks; in this
way his thank you was no more than a silent acquiescence masking
both disdain and servility. Pletnev, whose greatest pleasure—all the
while feigning indifference—was to discover the hidden inner man
("the true brute, the vain, hypocritical madman, who nonetheless
has created God in his image . . .") beneath the masks of the social
man, noted this movement, which was worthy of a flunky taking a
huge tip. The President took him affectionately by the arm.

"Vassili Vassilievich, look at these charts: I thought of having
them sent to you."

Green triangles, connected by straight lines to pink circles, blue
rectangles, and violet ovals, each inscribed with figures and % symbols of percentages, dancing around them like air bubbles in clear
water full of aquatic plants, described the progress of public education over the past year.

"What a thirst for learning!" exclaimed the President. "Look:
the number of teaching establishments has grown by 27%, not count-
ing adult courses, preschool, and the Remedial Service for Deprived Children; altogether, it adds up to 64%, 64%!"

Pletnev, tall, stooped, gray-headed, wearing a gray sweater
under an old English jacket with wide gray stripes, shook his low,
wrinkled forehead, sniffed the warm air of the room with his wide
mujik nostrils, brought his hostile glance back from the green triangles to the pale, flabby, sad, self-satisfied face of the dictator and
said evasively:

"Mmm. Yes. Great progress. Hum. Hum." He cleared his
throat. "I really must discuss the school problem with you one of
these days; quite right."

How to make these confounded great men understand that the
audience had gone on long enough! The President's fingers
snatched a piece of paper just handed to him through the half-
opened door. A decoded message: "According to agent K.: Major
Harris back in Helsingfors. Stop. Negotiations resumed. Offensive
nearing Finland. Informed circles think agreement likely." If an
agreement is likely, that means our existence becomes rather un-
likely.

"Harumph," said Pletnev, restraining the hoarse sounds ready
to burst out of his hollow chest, with the strange coyness of an old

consumptive who had been holding on for twenty years, "you know some funny things are going on in the schools. . . ."

He finally vented his spleen with a sort of growl:

"I know of one high school where four students were found pregnant last month. Of course the old directress is in prison, no one could quite tell me why. . . ."

Finally they left, the one after the other, colliding in the narrow opening of the doorway: the tenor, still elegant in his long overcoat lined with monkey fur, the writer extraordinarily erect, his stiffness accentuating his thinness, a sly expression on his face. Fleischman brushed past them without recognizing them. Tenors and writers were the last thing he could be bothered with at that moment anyhow! He burst into the huge presidential office, with its soft atmosphere of carpets and leather furniture, bringing with him the street, the wind, the cold, dry mud clinging to soldiers' boots. Muddy and booted himself, sheathed in black leather, pockets stuffed, chest crisscrossed with rust-colored straps, his face the face of an inexhaustible old Jew, he unceremoniously picked up the thread of a conversation begun the previous night by direct wire from the front.

"We've got to put a stop to these outrages . . ."

These were not the same outrages, but they had just cost the lives of forty soldiers who had frozen to death near Dno while the overcoats being sent to them were held up in a railroad station because the shipping order hadn't been filled out according to regulations.

Varvara Ivanovna Kossich, the heroine of the Trial of the 206 (1877), had sent an indignant letter to the President of the Soviet of People's Commissars of the Federated Republic demanding an end to the same excesses denounced by Pletnev and Svechin. The letter ended with these lines: "I warn you: you will be held responsible by future generations." The President of the Soviet of People's Commissars was more concerned, under the circumstances, about his present responsibilities. He thanked Varvara Ivanovna for having pointed out abuses of which he was well aware and had her letter sent on to the President of the Soviet of People's Commissars of the Northern Commune. The Party Control Commission was informed about it. Meanwhile, the Poor People's Committees and the population had more or less finished the job of cleaning up the city by dumping most of the garbage into the canals. Public Health reported the first cases of poisoned water. Kirk and Frumkin were about to be censured by the Control Commission when the affair was suddenly forgotten. A bunch of sailors, whom some described as drunk and others as anarchists, had just shot down three militiamen during a brawl. The Wahl Factory had stopped work and demanded two weeks of paid leave for all the workers to go to the country and replenish their food supplies individually. The strike, inspired by Menshevik agitators whom no one dared arrest, threatened to become general. That same night the Special Commission incarcerated seventeen Social Democratic intellectuals, most of whom were strangers to the movement. Among them was Professor Onufriev, the author of an authoritative *History of Chartism*. During the search of his house, a manuscript study on *Democratic Freedoms in England at the Beginning of the Nineteenth Century*, which Commissar Babin mistook for a counterrevolutionary satire, was seized and lost. Several days later a few odd pages were found in a public garden. Pletnev, the great writer, and Svechin, the admirable tenor, once again presented themselves at the office of the President of the Soviet. A harsh article by Pletnev on "The Tragedy of the Intellectuals" was turned down by the official newspapers. This created a fresh incident which was greeted with malicious joy by the foreign press. Professor Onufriev had only been freed for a short while when he died of dysentery. The President of the Special Commission, who drank too much, was replaced by Frumkin. The ruble declined disastrously.

The Commission on Workers' Housing, whose seventeen members received the same food rations as members of the Executive, put the finishing touches on its grand plan for rebuilding the slums. It called for an initial delay of three years and a hundred million rubles credit. The painter Kichak showed a full-length portrait of the President, his hair blowing in the wind, his hand extended in a vague but eloquent gesture which looked as if he wanted to see if it were raining, to bless a crowd, or to politely approve a takeover. In the background there was an armored train so beautiful that no one had ever seen any like it. He charged admission.

The newspapers announced the coming visit of the old French revolutionary, Durand-Pépin, author of a *Plan for the Organization of Socialist Society* in 2,220 articles. *Pravda* (*The Truth*) announced that the situation at the front was improving. The next day it was learned that a catastrophe had taken place near Narva, which was overrun by the Whites. The problem of the front was thrust forward before the problem of nails could be resolved, before boots could be found for the workers in the factories. Typewriters crackled ceaselessly:

ORDER. ORDER. ORDER. MANDATE. EDICT. DECREE No. XXX. DECREE No. XXXX. DECREE No. XXXXX. DECREE . . . Canceling DECREE No. XXX . . . From the Kremlin, by direct wire, the Soviet of People's Commissars of the R.F.S.S.R. implored the Soviet of People's Commissars of the Northern Commune to execute the measures decreed by the central government. The Northern Commune replied: "Impossible. Situation getting worse and worse."

From dusk to dawn, the Committees of Three, of Five, of Seven, of Nine, the Enlarged Committees, the Extraordinary, Permanent, Temporary, Special Subaltern, Superior, Supreme Committees deliberated, planned, ordered, decreed. . . .

❖

"The meeting is called to order," said Fanny.

Her wrinkled face bore the imprint of contradictory forces: vanquished diseases, hidden pride (the stubborn forehead, the sounding glance like a plumb line, the inner shock one felt on first contact with her), warmth, suspicion, and somewhere deep inside a secret instability, perhaps a noble madness, perhaps a half-repressed hysteria.

A brass plaque alongside the door: *S. T. Itin, Certified Dentist*. Cardboard, on the door itself: *Labor's Rights Club*. Crumbling corridors smelling of piss and sweepings; old papers under a coat rack, the surprise of a large mirror in one corner, piles of newspapers tied with twine and covered with a layer of dust, stifling heat; the desolation of a young bride's smiling portrait left hanging over a chimney, of this tiny room itself, furnished with a camp bed, a mahogany table covered with ring marks from glasses, and a broken-down couch. Cigarette smoke, steamed-up windows. Seven heads, so close they nearly touch at times, emerging and receding into the shadows; grave, undistinguished, austere heads; one of them charming, like a black flower fallen from a Persian poet's paradise.

"Goldin has the floor," said Fanny.

He had come from the Ukraine by way of the Volga: Czaritsin

under siege, Yaroslov in ruins, starving Moscow, forty-seven days on the road, leaving behind him the shades of two brothers-in-arms, one hanged by the Whites at Kiev, the other shot by the Reds in Poltava. He had slept in the vermin-infested straw of the cattle cars along with typhus-ridden refugees, wounded men miraculously rescued from unknown battlefields, with raped Jewesses escaping from pogroms, and pregnant peasant women who hid foodstuffs over their bellies and paid for their corner at night by giving themselves standing to the men who ruled the roost. He brought back with him a bullet lodged in his flesh, at the back of his chest, against the spinal column, expressly to provoke the admiration of the surgeons ("You're sure hard to kill!"), a pure and delicious love rent by pride—pride is sometimes only the noble side of egotism—some letters of the young Korolenko discovered in a country house during a guerrilla battle, and the secret correspondence of the vanquished party: five cigarette papers covered with ciphers hidden inside his metal tunic buttons.

He emanated power, a bitter power, somewhat drunk with itself, yet capable of sweeping others along. His style of talking was deliberately unadorned, yet vibrant with heat; its seductive power came as much from a veiled lyricism as from its firm dialectic. He was dark and bony with a thick head of hair, burning eyes, a prominent nose, and an ardent mouth. He wiped out all those faces surrounding him—insignificant for him except for the one which was feminine and beautiful—by pronouncing the single word "Comrades" in a warm voice which conveyed the strength of this formidable brother. Fanny was watching him from the side and judging him severely within her soul: too eager for exploits, not devoted enough to the Party to perform mundane tasks and remain in the ranks. Adventuristic. He brought the six heads surrounding him back to a life as strained and imperious as the health of the Revolution.

Balance sheet: hatred and famine in the countryside, ready to march on the cities armed with nailed clubs as in the Middle Ages. A despairing, decimated proletariat. Paper decrees—impotent, annoying—dropping from the Kremlin towers onto the masses paralyzing the last living strength of the Revolution. The Regular Army, built at the hands of old generals, steamrollering over the partisans, the true people's army. Opportunists and bureaucrats eliminating enthusiasts. A monstrous state rising from the ashes of

the Revolution. "This Robespierrism will devour us all and open the
gates to the counterrevolution. We haven't an hour left to lose."

The head which was as beautiful as a black flower murmured
softly:

"Reconstitute the fighting organization."

"You're crazy!" Fanny cut in sharply. "And you don't have the
floor."

Timofei, of the Great Works, rose, filling the tiny room with his
shadow. He had large, sky-blue eyes set in a craggy face like a
clenched fist.

"Department B wants a strike; Department A is hesitant but
will go along. The best of them are with us, the rest are worthless
anyway. Morale among the women is excellent. They'd be ready to
smash up all the cooperatives in a single morning. Liaison with the
Wahl Factory has been established."

Kiril, who had gone through the experience of the 1914 strikes
and of three years in the mining towns of northern France, advised
caution: don't commit the military organization, which was still
weak, until the strike movement became generalized. Formulate
clear demands: Down with the despotism of the commissars, free
elections, continuation of the Revolution. Discriminate carefully between the masses' legitimate revolt against rule by decree and their
weariness, their despair and counterrevolutionary bitterness. Don't
give ourselves illusions: perhaps the masses are not yet ready for a
new upsurge.

Fanny nodded approval. —Who do we send to the Great
Works? Kiril, with his firm moderation, based on self-assured
strength, his intuitive understanding of the feeling of crowds, his
temperament of a forty-year-old worker little inclined toward
empty gestures and phrasemongering? Better Goldin, with his intelligent passion, his eagerness for exploits. You have to throw a
man into certain assemblies as you would throw a torch into dry
wood.

❖

"The meeting is called to order," said the dictator.

A dozen people were seated around the big green table. Bare
walls painted white, bright lights hanging in frosted glass globes;

faces, silhouettes, papers on the table, everything sharp with the stark bright clarity of an operating room. Karl Marx, flowing beard, vague Olympian smile, framed in black, a red ribbon on one of the upper corners of the frame. . . . The windows open over the river, at present undistinguishable from its banks in the whiteness and the fog.

Agenda: (1) the situation at the front; (2) supplies; (3) the Wahl Factory affair; (4) the situation at the Great Works; (5) nominations. Present: eleven names. Excused: two names. The recording secretary fills in the blanks of a form divided into two columns: Reports heard, Decisions taken. The catastrophe of Narva is recorded here, following Fleischman's laconic report, in terms as incomprehensible as the scientific names of diseases are to the laymen in a hospital room. "Make note of the negligence in Transport and the incompetence of the leadership. Replace the political cadres in the Xth Division. Intensify agitation among the troops. Demand that Supply deliver fresh equipment within the week. Give Comrade Fleischman the responsibility for carrying out the measures decided."

Maria Pavlovna, in a black blouse, a high collar, an elderly schoolteacher's complexion, old-fashioned pince-nez glasses with tiny lenses, and a severe mouth, had only one word to say about the nominations. "I'm against promoting Kirk. He's been a Party member for only a year." (Since the night before he and his sailors smashed open the gates of the Winter Palace.) His nomination was set aside. Garina, tiny, wizened, her glance amazingly young, infectious laughter constantly lurking in the depths of her eyes, a round nose, hair always a little wild, also had only one word to say—about the Wahl Factory:

"At the end of the resolution, instead of 'We will not hesitate to use compulsion,' put: 'We will not hesitate to use the most energetic pressure. . . .'"

And she explained, giggling in the ear of her neighbor, Kondrati:

"For in reality we no longer have the means of compulsion."

The men all looked drab in this operating-room lighting, with two exceptions: the President—prominent head, blue cheeks, abundant hair, the well-sculpted yet slightly flabby features of a young Roman emperor or a Smyrna merchant, a deep voice which ran to falsetto when he got excited, an appearance of heaviness, non-

chalance and mastery, fatigue and intrigue, established greatness
and hidden mediocrity; and the committee secretary, Kondrati—light
complexion, golden curls at his temples, a fine-featured yet rugged
face, Scandinavian blood and Mongol blood. All interchangeable:
around this table, in this city, this country, at the front, before the
task and before death itself; each head here being but one head of
that eleven-headed being (this evening) called the Committee,
each merging his intelligence and his will with those—anonymous,
impersonal, sovereign, and superior—of the Committee, each knowing himself to be powerful and invulnerable through the Party yet
insignificant and defeated in advance without the Party; each refusing to exist for himself other than through the fulfillment of a
prodigious will in which his own will was lost, a useful drop in the
ocean.

"Whom do we send to the Great Works?"

A single head inside eleven skulls weighed the problem ma-
turely. Osipov? He was there, chin in hand, with the long face of a
seminarist or a convict. Osipov had led the proletariat of the Great
Works into battle during the great decisive days. No, no, too
idealistic, too inclined toward self-sacrifice, incapable of understanding the masses when they sink, discouraged, back into the passive desire to live in peace, even if it is barely living. . . . Rubin? A
good organizer but too hidebound. Kondrati? Too early. . . . If
things go really badly, to prevent or see through a disaster, but not
before. Garina? A woman wouldn't be right for the job; and in any
case her subtle theoretical mind made her a first-class propagandist
but a very poor agitator. Saveliev? Worn down by the workers'
problems, tormented by scruples ("Look at what the worker eats
since he took power!"), capable of losing his head. No, no. . . .
Several voices said:

"Antonov."

Antonov. Naturally. Nobody could be better. What a voice, Antonov! Made for covering the tumult of a railroad station. And character. Stubborn. Not intelligent. Not stupid. Disciplined. Not many
ideas, guts. Vulgar. Tactful.

"Antonov. You give him his instructions, Kondrati," said the
President.

The rest of the meeting was taken up in reality by intrigue.
Kondrati's coterie was contesting for some positions against that of
the President, whom they suspected of trying to squeeze them out.

A confused argument in which no one said what he was thinking took place over the nomination of some district secretaries. A compromise was finally agreed on: the positions were shared. A slight advantage for Kondrati.

"We're making progress," murmured Fleischman.

Osipov voted mechanically with the others, for at every vote unanimity was re-established. We've come to that, he thought. The Great Works against us! Hemmed in by hunger, picking up all the old weapons of power . . . What can we promise these workers if they no longer want to die for the Revolution?

6

Cold winds blew in from regions where absolute winter reigned—passing over the pearly steppes of Lapland, over the lakes and dark forests of Finland, over the border of Karelia harrowed with white trenches and mantraps—and dissipated the Baltic fog. Perfect clear days followed. The air was so transparent that the laws of perspective seemed somehow altered. Looking across the Neva, you could make out the tiniest details of buildings, the silhouettes of pedestrians, the forms of sphinxes brought over from Memphis and erected on the edge of the river by emperors, only to witness after four thousand years the fall of new empires. The slim white columns crowned with statues and the tall golden spire of the Admiralty stood out at the hub of deserted avenues stretching out toward stations oppressed by shimmering silence. Trams with gray swarms of passengers clinging to their sides moved slowly over the bridges through the infinite light composed of the pale, pure blue of the sky, the gold of a cold sun intellectual in its clarity, and reflected snow. Looking out through the windows of the old Senate, where anemic scholars were sifting through the archives of the Czarist Secret Police, we contemplated the iridescent white square, dominated by Falconet's bronze: the Emperor Peter, draped in Roman garb, rearing his horse on the edge of a precipice overlooking the future or the abyss. . . . And, farther on, the university embankment lined with neat old houses—red, white, and yellow—which reminded you of an archaic Holland.

"Look out," Professor Lytaev said to me, "and preserve the memory; you are more likely to live through these times than I am. The air of Venice does not possess this transparency, for the activity of men disturbs it, and the heat rising from the old stones makes it tremble. Nothing trembles here, the air is crystal. No smoking chimneys, no busy tumultuous plazas. I have only seen such transparency and calm on the high plateaus of Mongolia. That is where I came to understand why the Chinese artists are able to draw such pure close horizons."

All this beauty was perhaps the sign of our death. Not a single chimney was smoking. The city was thus dying. And, like shipwrecked men on a raft devouring each other, we were about to fight among ourselves, workers against workers, revolutionaries against revolutionaries. If the Great Works succeeded in carrying along the other factories, we would witness a general strike pitting the populace of the dead factories against the Revolution. It would be the revolt of despair against the stubborn, willful, organized revolt which still had hope. It would be the fervid and unthinking treason of some of the best, ready to ally themselves with the famine against the dictatorship because they couldn't understand that the faith of millions of men can also die for lack of bread, that we are less and less free men, more and more, in an exhausted, besieged city, an army in rags whose safety lies in terror and discipline.

*

Low crooked wooden houses, each leaning a different way, lined both sides of the alley. Plants were visible in the windows. The alley seemed wide because the houses were so small. It could have been a street in an ancient town had it not ended in a red brick wall surmounted by tall, blackened glass panes, broken in places. A few paces on stood a chimney, black against the sky, just turning blue. The light was getting brighter, objects began to stand out more and more sharply from one instant to the next. At the corner of the street, huddling against the old, blackened wood houses, you could see a long line of women. Even before the first blast of the whistle, they stood there. They were waiting for the bread for which they had waited long hours in vain yesterday outside under a blizzard. The shutters of the store at last opened when it was broad daylight. Did these women's eyes derive any joy from this marvelously open sky, from the perfect sharpness of forms, lines, and colors, from the soft, nuanced sparkle of the snow? "What beautiful weather," murmured some voices. "Yes," bitterly answered

others, "but are they going to keep us waiting a long time again?"
Hours passed despairingly. They discussed the news, their troubles,
rumors, ideas. . . . "Hey, remember before the war the price of
eggs?" —"He beats her, I tell you, she's a martyr. Patient as a saint."
—"So they requistioned his house, and the flour, and everything.
There's nothing left. Nothing but to go out into the world like a
poor wanderer, my God, my God . . ." —"If the English come,
you'll see. Everybody who raised his hand for the Communists even
once will be hanged. . . ." —"Everybody, then?" —"Yes, everybody,
everybody. . . ." —"Do you remember nice old fat Mikhei Mi-
kheich . . . ?"

Communal Bakery No. 60, near the Great Works, occupied the
former shop of that nice fat old fellow, who some said had been
killed by his workers and whom others claimed to have seen in
town, looking important, with a briefcase under his arm. In his
place, behind the bare counter, in the cold airless store where the
odors of badly cooked bread, dead rats rotting under the floor
boards, and bitter sweat fermenting under sheepskins mingled,
stood two skinny clerks, who took ration cards, cut off one square
tab, and heaved a hunk of black bread as soggy as clay into gnarled
outstretched hands. One woman suddenly burst into tears: "Someone stole my card, someone stole it. I had it right here a second
ago. . . ." The women who were already on their way out with
their bread gathered around her, the others brushed past, pushing
and shoving, the precious paper with the stamp of the Commune
clutched in their fists. Eddies of unrest moved through the line.
"What? What?" The anxiety spread from one person to another.
"Citizenesses!" cried one of the clerks inside. Those waiting outside
saw a despairing group flowing back toward them. "There's no
more bread."—"When will there be any?"—"I haven't the slightest
idea," said the clerk, who now stood in the door wiping his nose
with his fingers. "Go ask the commissars." The store remained open,
empty, for the two boys had to put in their hours. They sneered.
"What can *we* do, little citizenesses? We're no different than you."
In the background, over the bare counter, hung a red calico banner
covered with white lettering:

THE WORKERS WANT
BREAD, PEACE, AND FREEDOM

◆

The Great Works was spread out over miles of snow-covered work yards, all the way from the workers' quarter to the sea. Drafts of cold air whistled through the skeletons of its workshops. Piles of tip-trucks lay on their backs near old twisted rails which looked like tangles of petrified snakes under the snow. Still loaded flatcars covered by white carapaces, small locomotives forgotten on sidings, and piles of scrap metal lay strewn about this desert. The chimneys, nonetheless, still intermittently belched forth some astonishing black smoke. Life was concentrated in a few shops full of an odor of soot, cold oil, and neglected metal. Arc lamps hung like big pale moons; gray daylight filtered in through high dirty skylights in whose broken panes jagged patches of blue sky appeared suddenly. The muzzles of the 70-mm. cannon seemed to be pointing out through them. Drive shafts spun with a tired sound like out-of-breath hearts. The men on the job were lost among the machines, reduced to a sort of insignificance, pursued by cold and hunger, right up to their workbenches, heartsick at the emptiness around them.

"They call this a factory?" they said. "It's more like a cemetery. . . . We don't know who the hell we are any more. We're no longer workers: starvelings, worthless beggars, good-for-nothing goldbricks, slobs, that's what we are. . . . Some of these men dismantle the machinery to make cigarette lighters. Others steal brass wire to build themselves rabbit cages. Some steal coal, machine oil, kerosene. Some of them never even held a job before doing that kind of work. Look what's become of us. Terrific."

Groups would swarm, working furiously around the locomotives in fits and starts. They were the same men. They stole like the rest of them. They nursed a dark fury against themselves, against fate, against the commissars, the entente, everything which, by killing the factory, was killing them. They sent delegations to the President of the Soviet of People's Commissars of the Northern Commune. Gaunt proletarians in old boots full of holes wound through the narrow halls of Smolny like exhausted soldiers. Inside the dictator's huge office, surrounded by rugs, leather-covered furniture, shiny telephones, and walls covered with maps showing the blood-red line of the front drawn around the Republic, a cowardly timidity overcame even the most vehement among them. What to do? The fronts are there. No bread, paper money, peasants refusing to deliver grain. Hold out, hold out, or die, by God! But didn't we just say precisely that we can't hold out any longer? . . .

"Sit down, comrades," said the President quietly.

The delegation broke up, dispersed onto the sofa, too far away, onto armchairs, too soft. The men remained fiercely silent, embarrassed.

"So, things are going badly?"

An old man who had marched behind Father Gapon in 1905, face wrinkled like a Chinese mask, stood up to regain his confidence and finally burst out:

"Bad? Impossible! No way to hold out any more. Everybody's going under. The factory doesn't look like a factory any longer."

The President also stood up, attentive, knowing all, knowing too that it was necessary to listen all the way through, then to show the maps, give out the figures, promise, telephone to the Commune —and that, in the end, there was absolutely nothing to be done. (But you can always hold on for another hour, another day, another week; and perhaps that hour, that day, that week will be the decisive one.) He answered in a low voice, very different from the one people were used to hearing at big meetings. He talked about starving, ransomed Germany, about Liebknecht's fresh blood, about the revolution ripening in Europe. . . . Which of these men would come to his aid? What was the composition of this delegation? They had told him that it did not contain any adversaries, just non-Party members, one or two sympathizers . . . Who?

His man was revealed in a rather young, heavy-jawed fellow who spoke in a studied manner, the way they do at meetings. The working class would fight to the end! Every man would do his duty for the International! As long as the food supply improved; and the factory received the special rations they had been promised for a month. . . . What he said sounded strangely false—even though it was profoundly true and necessary to say it—you could feel he was lying in telling the truth. ("So you want to get yourself promoted onto the Factory Committee. . . .")

The same day the women went home without bread, after waiting all morning in front of the bakeries, a Council of Delegates, whose identity was secret, plastered some rather well-printed

leaflets on the walls appealing to the proletarians of the factory to
take their fate into their own hands. The strike was in the air. The
news went out in every direction by telephone from the various
Committees. Out of 3,700 registered workers, less than two thousand had begun work at seven o'clock. The chief mechanic, Khivrin,
went over to the manager's office, his cap over one ear, a cigarette
in his teeth, and announced in a nasty voice that his machines
weren't working any more. "Some kind of breakdown. I can't figure
out. Send over the engineers." He announced this as if it were good
news. Groups of Mensheviks and Left SRs had held secret meetings
during the night.

"Let's get this over with."

*

A thousand men filled the workshop. A platform with a piece
of rail for a balustrade was raised above people's heads. The Assembly Committee was seated at one side, around a slightly raised table
covered with red cloth. Timofei rang the chairman's bell. "Kuriagin
has the floor." The meeting had already been going on for two
hours, dragging and chaotic. The secretary of the Communist cell
had been hooted down. "Give us bread! Bread! No speeches! We've
heard all your bullshit before." As he was stumbling down from the
shaky rostrum, some big guys had grabbed him by the shoulders
and shaken him. He looked thin and defeated in his military tunic.

"Say it! Tell us you didn't phone the Special Commission. Go
ahead if you dare."

Timofei, who was delighted by the incident because it heated
up the atmosphere, had controlled the tumult with his long outstretched arms and his emaciated face.

"Don't get excited, comrades! We're the strong ones!"

Kuriagin succeeded in dispelling the anger of these thousand
men by telling an awkward, embarrassing story, saying all the
wrong things, and relaxing them by making them laugh. He told of
his trip to the countryside near Tver and how his three sacks of
flour had been seized on his arrival home. His buddies assumed he
had been on sick leave.

"Eat-it-all-by-yourself! You bastard!" cried a voice.

The epithet seemed to stick to this red-faced sweaty loudmouth, who was floundering through a tirade against imperialism. Timofei was suffering. A thousand men and not one voice! So much suffering, so much revolt and not one voice! The arc lamps hanging from the metal skeleton of the roof cast a gloomy light over the thousand heads, some covered by old fur hats and others by shapeless caps. Hard faces, bony noses, ashy complexions, soiled garments: this was in appearance the same human mass (yet poorer, shrunken somehow) as during the February Days when the three-hundred-year-old autocracy crumbled under their pressure (because then, as now, there was no bread in these neighborhoods; only people somehow lived much better in those days); the same mass as in July, when they poured through the city like a flood ready to carry everything away; the same mass as in October, when Trotsky's voice swept them on to the conquest of power. . . . The same, and yet not the same; altered, inconsistent now, disoriented, without heart: like an old acquaintance known for his firm jaw, determined gait, and direct way of speaking who suddenly appears spineless, flabby, shifty-eyed, and tongue-tied when you meet him after an absence. Timofei bit his lip. This crowd is spineless. The best among them have left. Some are dead. Eight hundred mobilized in six months. Not one voice. Naturally. Leonti had a voice and, what is more, a head; they say he died in the Urals. Klim is fighting on the Don. Kirk is head of something. Lukin, what happened to Lukin? Timofei could still visualize these veterans standing in this very shop, three or four ranks of men, successive generations who had come up and disappeared within a year. Gone. At the head of the army, at the head of the state, dead: heads riddled with holes, lowered into graves in the Field of Mars to the sound of funeral marches. The Revolution is devouring us. And those who remain are without a voice, for they are the least courageous, the most passive, the followers, the ones who . . .

"Enough! Enough!" someone shouted at Kuriagin. "We've seen enough of you. That's it."

Timofei didn't know how to speak to mass meetings himself. His pale blue eyes fogged up as soon as he mounted the rostrum, and all he could see ahead of him was a whirling, pulsating mist which lured him like an abyss. His voice was too weak to carry far; his thoughts came out in tight formulas that didn't make complete sentences; people's ears were still straining to hear him when he had already finished all he had to say; and since his mind was very sharp, he seemed to lack the breath to make a speech; he resolved every problem he posed before the audience even heard it.

Everything seemed lost to him, when a door opened at the rear and Goldin entered. Timofei, relieved, rang his bell vigorously to get the attention of the restless, murmuring audience.

"Put a time limit on the speakers!"

Timofei pretended not to hear. This was surely not the moment! He rose.

"Goldin has the floor."

Some hands clapped. A strident whistle blast sounded and then broke off sharply. Head, fists, shoulders shook awkwardly. Goldin seized the piece of rail before him with both hands—the cold felt good on his palms—and took possession of the rostrum. He leaned out toward the crowd, his head hunched into his shoulders; his glance sought out people's eyes, held them for a moment, like a black flash, moved on, leaving a burning trace behind. His hot voice exploded, impassioned from the start.

"Do you remember, people without bread? How we drove out the Czar and his little ones, the ministers, the generals, the capitalists, the police? Tell me!"

"We remember," replied a choked voice.

"When was that? Say it! Yesterday!

"What we could do yesterday, we can do today. What is the Revolution? This Revolution which shoots the bourgeois, conquers the Ukraine, makes the wide world tremble? —The Kremlin? Smolny? Decrees? People's Commissars? Come now!" His huge blazing mouth split into a wide grin at this idea; and this infectious smile, which vanished instantly from his lips, spread from mouth to mouth, illuminating each man's soul with the clarity of his thought. "The Revolution is us! You and me! What we want, the Revolution needs. Do you understand?"

Then a thundering apostrophe:

". . . You, out there! You who manufacture laws and decrees!"

(Men were beginning to feel powerful. They were coming out of their torpor, electrified, awakening to new dreams of exploits.) "The Ukraine is in flames. Its fire will never go out. We don't even know what the power of the people is yet! But it must not be emasculated by laws and decrees. We fear neither privations nor sacrifices; we will overthrow those who would snuff our fires. We demand workers' freedom, decentralization, equality of all workers, individual provisioning, fifteen days' paid leave for every worker to go ask his peasant brother for food! What we demand we are strong enough to take. . . ."

A roar rose in the hall under the steel-beamed roof. Hands applauded frantically. Showers of cries exploded around this dark, bony, shaggy-haired man in a black blouse whose long sinuous hands were kneading the steel bar. All that remains is to put the general strike to the vote, thought Timofei. . . . Two newcomers were pushing their way through the crowd toward the rostrum.

*

Arkadi sat down on the steps so as to be able to keep his head above the crowd without, however, being too conspicuous. He immediately tried to pick out the faces of outside agitators among the crowd of faces. He found none, which amazed him.

Antonov climbed ponderously up the rickety wooden stairs. His thick neck topped off by a small, squarish, ruddy head emerged above the crowd. At first he was taken for a worker in the factory.

"I want the floor."

His powerful sonorous voice carried all the way to the back of the hall.

"Comrades . . ."

"Hey! You don't have the floor yet," interjected Timofei.

Goldin shrugged his shoulders. Antonov appeared to bow to the will of the chair but his heavy presence on that platform already defied it. Waiting patiently to be allowed to speak, he studied the audience. His narrow gray eyes searched out expressions and gestures; he could practically read the words on people's lips. His impression was favorable. He became much more self-assured. The chair decided that it was impossible to prevent him from talking: the crowd wasn't sufficiently worked up. So he started in again:

"Comrades!" He wisely skipped the usual salutation "in the name of the Party Committee." "It's obvious that"—and his thick red neck, his broad shoulders under heavy furs, his huge stonecutter's hands resting on the railing emphasized his point—"the condition of the working class is becoming intolerable. . . ."

A vague murmur of approval came from the back rows of the

audience. Son of a gun! So they finally noticed! You better believe it; it sure is intolerable!

". . . We're starving. The bakeries haven't distributed bread for three days. It's a disgrace! What good are paper salaries? We all have pockets full of rubles, but something to eat would be much more to the point. The road blocks set up to prevent individual supply-hunting have done more harm than good in many cases. . . . Things have got to change! They will change if we have the will. We didn't make the Revolution in order to end up like this."

No one knew any more if he was talking for or against the strike, for or against the government. He was repeating the previous harangues almost word for word, but in a more orderly form. Sure of himself now, his voice coming strong, his torso erect, he denounced hunger and poverty along with these thousand men. Goldin blacked in checker squares in his notebook. What a demagogue! he thought. The mistake was to give him the floor. . . .

"This morning the Executive Committee decided to call upon you to form new supply detachments, on the basis of five to ten men for every two hundred and fifty, and prepared to leave within three days. There's wheat at Saratov. Go take it! Don't lose an hour."

Heads moved in all directions in agitated confusion: conflicting winds blowing through wheat before a storm.

"The Commune is sending you four boxcars of provisions: canned goods, sugar, rice, and white flour: supplies taken from the imperialists by the glorious Workers' and Peasants' Army."

(—"What?"—"What did he say?"—"Four boxcars?"—"Rice?"— "Yes, rice and canned goods, you hear!"—"Listen, listen!")

"Tomorrow, this very evening, you must organize teams to handle the distribution. . . . Make sure that not a single pound of rice gets stolen by the bureaucrats and profiteers!"

(—"When are the cars arriving?"—"Let him talk!"—"No interruptions!")

". . . I said tomorrow! But there has been talk of a strike from this platform. Comrades, seven locomotives and thirty cannon are being repaired in your workshop. Each day's delay in delivering the locomotives adds to the famine. Each day's delay in delivering the cannon increases the danger. Where is the fool who can't understand this? Let him show himself!"

Antonov took a breath. His temples were damp with sweat. He

tore open his collar, popping the buttons. Triumphant—with those four carloads of provisions behind him—standing erect, he defied an invisible enemy in the hall:

"Let him show himself!"

He threw back his sheepskin-lined coat, showing himself dressed in a faded blouse with a hole at one elbow, identical with these men. He knew it was necessary to bawl out crowds that might get away from you, to shout into their faces the things they would like to shout at you, to identify with them—against them—through anger and invective. Now was the moment to bear down.

"There are cowards, slackers, swine, traitors, tools of the Allies, henchmen of the generals, scoundrels who think only of their skins and their stomachs, who want to stuff their bellies when the whole beleaguered Republic is hungry! Let them remember that proletarian bullets have been cast for their heads!"

Having proffered a threat at the end of his diatribe, he stopped short, concluding rapidly with an affirmation which nearly brought on applause—he could see it:

"But I swear, there's not a single traitor among us!"

Arkadi listened with admiration. Antonov pushed his advantage to the limit:

"Did you know that this week we discovered fifty rifles in the cellars of the Church of St. Nicholas?"

(They were old ceremonial weapons which had been placed among the tombs at the time of the first Turkish campaign.)

". . . that Allied agents are planning to blow up the Kronstadt forts?"

(They would have liked to; but the only evidence of a plot was the self-interested report of a double agent.)

". . . that the Special Commission has just discovered a new conspiracy?"

(The Special Commission was, it is true, looking for this conspiracy.)

*

The meeting was ending in confusion and defeat. A worker read out the text of a resolution in a rasping voice: ". . . the powerful hands of the proletariat will mercilessly crush . . ." Always these clichés, thought Timofei. Boosted onto the shoulders of two

men whom the human waves rocked gently, he shouted: "Workshop
B is meeting separately"—for it was necessary, despite this debacle,
to try to tally those men who were still dependable. Goldin led the
way.

The night was about to waylay them on the border between
the hubbub and the silence when a bearded giant with blue-veined
neck and temples came running up to them, gesticulating. You
might have thought him drunk. Bare-chested, teary-eyed, he held
up a pair of black hands like hard roots—ready to grasp anything.

"Look at us!" he shouted. "We're like dogs. The belly's empty,
they growl. Throw 'em a bone, they shut up. Look at me, comrades,
little brothers. I'm like that too. Don't hold it against us, little
brothers, poverty made us this way!"

He clung to Goldin's lapels with both hands. His despair was
like rage. His powerful clouded eyes were like ponds whose bottom
has been disturbed, as he stared into the dark eyes opposite him.

"And yet," he stammered, suddenly releasing his grip, "if you
knew what they have done, these hands. If you knew what they are
still capable of, comrade . . ."

For a brief instant all that the three men could see in front of
them were those two hands: dreadful, yet trembling with fatigue,
hands which appeared to be charred.

7

Arkadi awoke late, at sunset. Scraps of blue showed through a sky closed in by white and leaden clouds scuttling off to the west. A difficult case had kept him sitting up until dawn opposite silent, tight-mouthed Maria Pavlovna, whose glance was direct when it fell on you, yet evasive when you tried to catch her eye, and that brute Terentiev, with his fat blond face and his disgusting way of licking his chops and of pulling his upper lip back over his bright red gums when he laughed. The file on the Schwaber case had been passed on from one hand to another. Terentiev indicated the examining magistrate's conclusion with the black-rimmed nail of his sausagelike finger: "guilty and dangerous." But what if they were telling the truth, these Schwabers? The father, the mother, the older son and daughter all stubbornly gave the same story, which sometimes seemed strikingly sincere and at other times like an absurd denial in the face of the obvious. The spy had lived with them. They had passed on letters to third parties, received messages for him, lied to cover his indiscretions, kept a suitcase containing his code. They insisted they knew nothing about it; that it was all simple; that they had thought they were dealing with an ordinary, rather pleasant man. Who were they? None of the three judges had ever seen them. Arkadi pored over their signatures with a strange inner tension. Under hers, the girl had written, in a schoolgirl scrawl: "I swear before the Virgin that we are all innocent, Olga Schwaber." This evocation of the Virgin made Terentiev's lip curl.

"So," he said, "that would make four coincidences!"

"Four coincidences," repeated Maria Pavlovna with raised eyebrows.

"They were duped," said Arkadi.

"One coincidence per head: nineteen years old, twenty-one ('student at the Institute of Technology, Catholic'), forty-four ('graduate of the school for the Daughters of the Nobility, religious, monarchist'), fifty-three ('noble, *rentier*, former landlord, member of the Constitutional-Democratic Party . . .')." Rich religious nobles, "class enemies throughout every fiber of their beings," wrote the examining magistrate. "By the way, who was the magistrate?" "Zvereva." "Ah, yes, that ugly little woman—still young, always well dressed, zealous."

"But still," replied Arkadi, "the suitcase with the code, without which there would be no case: they brought it out themselves at the end of the search. Babin was ready to leave, without having seized anything."

Terentiev broke out in a deep loud laugh:

"But that was their ultimate ploy! They were convinced we knew everything from Procope. How do you explain Procope's report?"

"Procope is an interested party."

Here Maria Pavlovna broke in. Her voice was thoughtful, almost distant:

"Procope is a swine, that's true. But up to now he has always been a reliable agent. And he is supervised by Zachary."

"You know very well that Zachary is a bigger swine."

It was the eleventh case to be judged that night. Dawn showed at the window. Maria Pavlovna said:

"I'm calling for a vote. Terentiev?"

"Death."

"Arkadi?"

Arkadi stared down at the blue-covered file and felt the weight of two pairs of eyes pressing in on him: one glance was sensual, mocking, revolting, like a rude nudge; the other cold, severe, sad; detecting, perhaps in his indecision, a sign of weakness, of nervous fatigue, of unconscious revulsion against the task. The word was wrenched out of his mouth before he was fully conscious of it and fell onto the file like an invisible seal:

"Death."

"Death," said Maria Pavlovna impassively.

"I'll sign."

Terentiev countersigned.

It was over, the inner nightmare subsided. Maria Pavlovna proposed adjourning the next cases until Wednesday's meeting. They rose. Terentiev, apathetic again, was now nothing more than a big red-faced slob with sparse, nearly colorless eyebrows. He appeared to droop slightly, staring out the window at the white roofs and, in answer to Maria Pavlovna's friendly inquiring glance, he murmured:

"My youngest boy has scarlet fever."

Arkadi, before going home, wandered for a short while around the vast deserted square, bathed in a strange, extremely pale blue dawn glow. The great calm of the stones, the snow, and the dawning day seemed to enter him through every pore. Like the cool of the water when the swimmer dives in, his skin burning. Reassured, he thought: Tomorrow I'll go see Olga. Then he realized that a coincidence of names had weighed on his powers earlier. Olga. He thought about her as he got into bed in his messy room where Daghestan weapons with beautifully etched silver scabbards lay tossed on the divan. Olga. He had only to close his eyes and she was present. This was a different freshness than that of the dawn in the square: a bland freshness as calm and luminous as the late afternoon sun reflected on the windowpanes.

*

Olga clapped her hands when he entered.

"I knew you would come today. I knew it! See, I was waiting."

She placed her hands on his shoulders, looked into his eyes, and said:

"I woke up at four o'clock last night. I felt you were thinking about me. Tell the truth: did you think of me at four o'clock?"

It was too dark for her to be able to detect the somewhat forced smile with which he answered, believing he was lying:

"Yes."

Olga clapped her hands again.

"I knew it! I knew it!"

He held her off with a gesture as she was about to throw herself into his arms. She could see his smile better. She felt his suppleness and his toughness. His soul as strong as his muscles, whose least movement had a masterful precision. He dropped himself onto the divan, crossed his legs—his high boots glistened—and said:

"Let me look at you, I feel so good."

"I'll make some tea," she answered.

She was happily aware of the red glow of his cigarette in the semidarkness. She loved to move about in the invisible light of eyes following her from the far end of a dimly lighted room. Nowhere in the world could anyone ever give this man a greater feeling of calm, a more secure rest, a surer joy. She knew this. And the warmth of his gaze resting on her, soft at first, then imperious like a magnet, enveloped her wholly, imparted new suppleness to her movements. Somewhere, deep inside, her whole being cried out that this was an immense happiness. When she was sure that he couldn't make out her face, she laughed silently with all her pretty teeth, with her depthless, shining eyes. Then she shut them for a moment, motionless, content with the single thought: He is here, ravished in delicious anticipation of hands ready to touch her.

She was tall and lissome, glowing all over with the multiple luster of her eyes, whose long golden lids were always blinking as if to veil the brilliance of her gaze, of her sleek hair in which a touch of sunlight seemed to be captured forever, of her slender neck. Arkadi smoked. This female form filled his eyes and, far beyond his eyes, his mind, which forgot itself. And slowly within him a wild heat came into being.

For her he emerged from a fearful shadowy region of which it was terrible even to think. There reigned a law of blood, incomprehensible yet necessary, since he was fulfilling it; he who was so pure, so strong, so calm after the mysterious labor of his nights. (She had only tried to question him once. He took her head between his hands: "Not a word about all that, my dove. Never. We are making revolution. It's a great, great thing. . . ." Olga repeated: "A great, great thing." Those words were engraved on her mind. Whatever she learned, whatever anyone told her, she repeated them to herself to regain her confidence. There was a great deal of silence between them . . .)

"I promised Fuchs we would see him together. He has drawn a huge map, imagine . . ."

"Let's go," he said joyfully.

Arkadi was feeling light and vibrant, as when, at eighteen, in his village of Adjaris-Tskhahi, he would bound into the circle of clapping hands, one hand on his hip, the other on the back of his neck, with his dagger held tight at his waist, and dance—lighter, nimbler, and with greater endurance than anyone else.

*

The visiting card tacked to the door of the neighboring room read:

Johann Appolinarius Fuchs
Artist

Under the *ancien régime,* old Fuchs had lived rather well by his modest talents. The best dealers knew their way to his studio. His works could be found in the homes of patrons of the arts. Rasputin had liked them. He was the originator of those bathing girls with airy gestures who moved in or out of the waves as if offering themselves to love, wearing just enough to be more naked than they would have been entirely nude, borne on the light, smiling and sensual. He had spent twenty years painting them over and over again, aware of his mediocrity and good workmanship, conscious that the shoulder which he finished off with a last touch would hold the eye and kindle, in older men, certain furtive sparks whose appearance he watched for, amused, in the prudent gaze of his visitors. "Ah, *signore,*" he would say to himself, rubbing his hands together, "this too is an art."

Even today, in this humble little room where a few carpets and some unsalable knickknacks in the worst of Viennese taste barely recalled better times, ex-dealers, ruined naturally, living off illicit trafficking, still sometimes came to ask him for "a red-haired bather, something *à la* Rubens, you understand?" for a mysterious client. —For, on the other side of the river, at the end of an empty street, in a vast frozen apartment, an aged man who, in order to feed the last of his great Danes, the only living being he had left with him, was selling his ex-mistresses' old-fashioned dresses, was waiting anxiously for "the red-haired bather *à la* Rubens" as formerly he waited for a living woman.

Fuchs, who had been busy painting the emblem of Labor surmounted by a figure of "Revolution" with the straight nose of a Greek goddess for the flag of the porcelain makers' union, immediately changed easels. He painted from memory now. One of his

models had had precisely the Rubens complexion, but he had seen
her for the last time back in '17, stouter and sunburned, wearing
the uniform of the Women's Battalion whose sorry end at the hands
of the sailors on the night of the victorious insurrection is now
legend. —Another, a thin brunette who used to pose for his Sevil-
lanas, walked the central prospect every night, between the Fon-
tanka Bridge, guarded by its noble horse tamers, and Caravan
Street. She was often alone on that little-used sidewalk. On the
other side you could see the red, rectilinear façade of Anichkov Palace, its corner topped by the delicious golden bulb of its chapel.

Fuchs accosted her as she strolled along, kissing her hand a little further up than necessary. She lived in a little inside room on the
top floor of an ordinary biggish apartment house. The furniture was
covered with worn lace. Pictures of young officers, leaned against
empty cologne bottles. She still had rather clean underthings, which
she herself washed in the kitchen; she didn't remove her high laced
boots to make love—that would take too long, on the other hand,
she was good at spurring her males gently above the calf. . . .
Fuchs rather fancied this Lyda.

A knock at the door. Fuchs quickly turned the Rubens-skinned
girl to the wall. Olga and Arkadi filled the room with a virile grace.

Arkadi, completely relaxed, a friendly smile revealing his fine
teeth, scrutinized the fussily attentive old man. Short in stature,
small-featured, a white goatee like an old faun.

"This comrade," said Olga, "is interested in your chronicle of
the Revolution . . ."

"I'm thinking of the future," said Fuchs seriously.

Each day he would go out and get the newspapers, which was
not an easy task since very few were for sale. Sometimes crafty and
cautious like a thief, he had to peel the freshly posted pages off the
walls, a risky undertaking. He studied them. It was his favorite job
each day, the one which gave meaning to his daily existence. He cut
out clippings, underlining with a ruler and red and blue pencils the
significant parts of his chosen passage which he then pasted into the
large pages of his monthly classifiers.

Fuchs had to stoop to retrieve his clipping books from a trunk.
Olga and Arkadi exchanged identical amused smiles. The little man
stood up again and said, all of a sudden:

"The greatest happiness for a man is to live during a great
epoch."

"That is true," said Arkadi.

"That is true," repeated Olga more quietly.

". . . even," Fuchs continued, "if it's hard, even . . ."

Three minds stopped short on the threshold of something repeating that uncompleted "even . . ."

"That is true," said Arkadi in the serious voice he used for passing sentence at the Special Commission.

"Here's my new map," said Fuchs.

Europe was divided between two colors, white and red. Red Europe was spilling over into white Europe. Red pincers encircled the Mediterranean. Italy, still white, was crisscrossed with red arrows; red arrows in Morocco, Algeria, Tripoli, Egypt—red arrows!

"The arrows," Fuchs explained, "indicate revolutionary movements which have not yet triumphed."

Red countries covered the whole east, from the mouth of the Pechora on the White Sea to the gates of the Crimea, to Odessa, reconquered from the French and the Greeks, to Daghestan, divided down the middle by a border of blood. The red countries, each bearing its date, spread out to the heart of Europe. Bavaria, a Socialist republic since April 7, 1919. Galicia, Soviet republic since April 25, 1919. Hungary, Soviet republic since March 22, 1919. Serbia—Serbia cut into the Balkans like a tooth—Socialist republic since April 14, 1919. Asia Minor pushed forward its red head like a snub-nosed pachyderm: Turkey, Socialist republic since April 19, 1919.

"Look here," observed Arkadi, "the island of Crete is red too."

"There has been a telegram from the Rosta Agency!"

Red arrows were exploding in Germany. Scattered red arrows were pointed at Paris, Lyons, Copenhagen, Rotterdam, London, Edinburgh, Dublin, Barcelona.

"How beautiful!" exclaimed Fuchs.

Arkadi answered:

"I don't think Bavaria will hold much longer. They say Toller has been killed at an outpost."

Fuchs flipped through a stack of clippings.

"What about this?" he said triumphantly.

Istanbul, April 27. The Executive Central Committee of the Moslem Revolutionaries of Turkey, Arabia, Persia, Hindustan, Algeria, Morocco,

and Constantinople announce with the profoundest joy that the Re-
public of the United States of the East will soon be proclaimed in Con-
stantinople.

The struggle is being carried forward vigorously. A soviet revolu-
tionary corps of 2,000 men has been formed in Odessa.

The Turkish Consul at Odessa
Akhu-Ato-Bakh-Eddin

Arkadi burst into laughter.

"Your Akhu-Ato-Bakh-Eddin looks like a joker to me. I think
. . . I think the wisest thing would be to have him locked up."

"Really?"

J. A. Fuchs's eyes went back and forth from his visitor to the
map, whose veracity was suddenly being undermined. "So you
think I should erase all of this?"

"All of this" meant the red arrows piercing Mediterranean
Africa from Suez to Casablanca.

"No. No. There's no doubt about the revolutionary ferment in
the colonies. See the Manifesto of the Third International."

When his visitors had departed, Fuchs wrote (in pencil so as to
be able to erase it later) in the corner of the map, in neat little characters:

"*Cf.* Manifesto of IIIrd Intern."

They had only a few steps to take to be back in their room. But
even before, in the dark corridor, as Olga turned toward Arkadi to
say, "He's a character, isn't he?" she felt his masculine breath
against her lips, and he did not answer. He enveloped her waist in
an iron grip. She melted against him and it was as if he was carrying her away toward an unknown happiness.

❁

Arkadi could never stay long. His nights of work began early.
He departed, leaving behind him, in the room still full of the odor
of his cigarettes, a cloudy wake of joy, confusion, and strength; but
in that wake Olga's soul and flesh felt emptied. A strange desert of
worn lips and slack nerves . . . She dozed. The bell rang twice.
"For me! . . . Who could it be?"

She felt, as the tanned young soldier entered, a mixture of
surprise and unease:

"You? You? How is it possible?"

Nonetheless they kissed each other's cold cheeks.

"Little sister, I'm exhausted. I've come from Rostov, the long
way round. Makhno's men took me prisoner on the way. I told them
I was practically an anarchist. They only took my fur coat and a
thousand rubles. No importance."

". . . You're a soldier? A major? . . ."

On his shoulder, a red star.

"No. Yes. Whatever you like. How's Mama? Can I sleep at your
place? Is this house safe? My papers aren't in order."

". . . not in order? Why?"

"You wouldn't understand, little sister. Don't worry about it.
Where do you think I could stop for a few days?"

"I don't know, Kolia. Maybe at Andrei Vassilievich's. Or at
Professor Lytaev's."

"How things change, little sister. My name is now Danil. . . ."

He sat. He drank the tea which Arkadi had not touched. How
mature he had become. His hands were those of a worker. As Olga
listened to him laughing and talking her uneasiness grew.

"I'm dirty, huh? What you smell on me is the peculiar odor of
trains. Yet I've washed. Four weeks on trains, little Olga. And what
trains, you couldn't imagine. No windows, smashed in on every side,
stinking like pigstys. . . . I even rode on the roof! Listen to this
one, little sister, you'll laugh. In Kharkov, in a little hotel full of fat
bedbugs (they were fat from their habitual diet of government
officials), I ran into some Frenchmen coming from God knows
where, an old socialist crank, Durand-Pépin, bringing us his 'life's
work,' a complete outline for the organization of the new society. . . ."

The idea made him laugh so hard that he had to put down his
teacup and bend over, choking.

"He wanted to teach rational culture to the Ukrainian peasants
by showing them little colored pictures. . . ."

Olga laughed too, infected. "When he saw that the peasants
were more interested in stopping trains at night to rob the passengers and hang the Jews, he declared he had to leave for home right
away because of his heart disease. But they made him a member of

a non-existent Academy, and gave him a set of aluminum cookware, so he stayed. . . . And his pretty niece, little sister, was worried whether she had enough dresses to appear in Kharkov society! Kharkov society! The biggest collection of bandits you could ever find. . . ."

8

His papers, beautifully done, read: Danil X——, company commander in the 1st Kuban Regiment, sent to the center by division headquarters to procure maps of the field of operations. Signed, for Regimental Commander Shapochnikov; Adjutant Shutko. The misspelled words were there, too, and they had a good laugh over them. They authenticated a document better than any seals. . . . His real mission, typewritten in code on a piece of silk, without any spelling errors, was sewn, along with other messages, in the lining of his tunic collar. He was also carrying, at the bottom of an apparently untidy pocket among shreds of tobacco and bits of string, a precious little ball of crumpled paper.

As soon as he left the October Station, which everyone still called—thank God!—the Nicholas Station, Danil rediscovered the city, magnificent after so many devastated villages and provincial towns through which had passed endless hurricanes of cavalry, bombardments, epidemics, and the terrible chill of executions. The third-class waiting rooms spilled over into the corridors, and the station halls were like a nomads' camp. The masses of people living there were so compressed that aisles formed of themselves between the piles of bodies sitting, lying, and squatting on shapeless bundles, which were less shapeless than the half-sleeping forms of the people. Through the acrid brown air you could see mothers suckling their squalling children; mothers with flaccid breasts, cradling sallow children with inflamed red lids closed over their eyes and greenish scabs clinging to their tiny heads among the patches of gold or black hair; mothers singing lullabies to put to sleep these little bits of flesh who clung to life with such inexplicable power, singing lullabies whose rhythm was so sweet that their voices, embit-

tered by anger and unfathomable sadness, rekindled, amid all that
squalor and animal stench, some ember of charm. There were
bearded peasants who had been waiting for weeks for God knew
what train. Others seemed to be waiting for their neighbor,
delirious with typhoid fever, to die; but every time they got near
him he would recover enough of a glimmer of consciousness to
swear, with vile curses, that, Name-of-God-of-Holy-Name-of-God,
dirty bastards (and so on), they'd never take him to the hospital
station alive; he knew all about those miserable hospitals, Name-of-
a-Name-of-God, full of dirty sons of bitches who thought of nothing
but stealing the boots off poor sufferers. Thus he would settle his
account with that sacred thing called life—which so many great
poets have sung—right here. His perspiration-soaked head was
thrown back over his sack (flour and salt), his body curled up in
the manner of sleeping animals or the young of humans sleeping on
the maternal breast. He drooled and groaned in his last agony. His
neighbors, a whole family from Kaluga with gorgeous grimy children, poured boiled water into his mouth three times a day. "He's
got to drink, poor man!" said the wife. "Ah, how the Evil One tor-
ments him! Lord have pity on us!" The father carefully pushed
away the hairy, louse-infested head which he sometimes found loll-
ing against the thigh of his oldest daughter, thirteen-year-old Maru-
sia, asleep with her rag doll clutched in her arms. —"What beautiful
boots!" observed the sick man's neighbors, promising themselves to
remove them when he died, so as to keep the damned city folk from
taking advantage.

The nauseating atmosphere in the darkness suggested a cave of
primitive men. Sixteen dialects were spoken there: Polish, White
Russian, Karelian, Mari, Mordvian, Bulgarian, Finnish, Chuvash,
Tartar, Ukrainian, Georgian, Kazakh, Aissor, Gypsy, Yiddish, German. The Gypsies—those horse thieves!—were universally regarded
with mistrust (but where were the horses?); they jealously guarded
their corner over which reigned a beautiful dark gold girl and a
magnificent bearded man who must have been a bandit. They sent
their old witches and ragged little girls out to tell fortunes in the
market places. People whispered that they robbed the crypts in
cemeteries. —In that crowd you could buy salt, lard from Little
Russia, salt butter marvelously preserved in indescribable rags,
grain, rifles with sawed-off barrels and stocks for easy concealment
under one's clothing, identity papers. At night the men mated

joylessly with their women: sounds of stirrings, and pantings—procreations of misfortune, for the future. One out of a hundred survives, but who can know if he is not the one millions of men are waiting for? Never, since the mass migrations invading the old Slavic cities surrounded by palisades of pointed sticks, had such crowds been gathered in such misery—and within each heap of mortal beings, the eternal will to live!

Danil moved toward a door at the far end of the encampment. There, a tattered calico banner proclaimed: *He Who Works Does Not Eat,* for they had cut out the negation *Does Not* from *He Who Does Not Work.* Danil smiled with satisfaction. *Agitation Bureau. Travel Orders. Registration.*

"Where from?" a black leather man barked at him.

"From Armavir."

"Orders?"

A green stamp crashed down on his orders. Good.

"The situation out there?"

"Could be a lot better."

"Same old story, eh?"

The man yawned.

"Four dead from typhus in the main waiting room since yesterday. One hooligan smothered under his blankets by his pals, near the lavatory."

From a poster on the wall above, a soldier in a scarlet tunic and a sort of pointed cloth helmet (whom the artist had drawn to look like the Chief of the Army) pointed an imperious hand and face toward every newcomer: *Have You Enlisted in the Workers' and Peasants' Army?*

"Are they enlisting?"

"They enlist. Especially the young ones. The army eats, you see. And then they keep the boots and the rifle, and go over the wall."

❀

The vast circular plaza was nearly deserted. At the far end, near the low domes of a little white church, it opened out into the central prospect, empty of vehicles, extending in a straight line into the distant haze. . . . Vagabonds in dirty rags wandered about in front of the station dragging little sleds behind them. The dirty fog blurred the outlines of objects. A sledge stood waiting hitched to a black horse with protruding ribs. Danil saw a well-dressed sailor emerge from the station, disdainful of the impoverished throng, carrying a red leather briefcase with a silver monogram; a woman was on his arm, dressed in a cloth coat with a wide mink collar, but wearing light-colored high suede boots and a woolen shawl around her head like a peasant. This couple pushed its way brutally through the throng. Emaciated women, worn to the very soul, turned on them with envious looks. "Go ahead and act haughty, sailor's girl, we know what you are!"

"*Ira, Iris, Odaliska!*" cried a shivering urchin wrapped in an old soldier's coat.

His dark fingers proffered two packs of cigarettes and a little box of candy to the passer-by. Next to him, a stiff, skeletal old lady in an old braided hat, both her hands stuffed inside a hairless muff, offered three cubes of sugar, in a saucer attached to the muff.

"How much, madam?" Danil asked her.

As she answered she looked only at the passer-by's hands, for customers would sometimes try to swipe a third of her merchandise in one quick movement.

"Forty."

As Danil moved on, he heard the urchin say to the old lady:

"Open your old peepers there, Grandma, and take a gander. You didn't see many men like that in the salons of your booge-wazee. That's Egor, you know. The one who escaped."

Danil turned around quickly. The sledge was already sliding off, carrying away the sailor and his companion. She looked toward him for a brief instant, and Danil saw that she had long, well-shaped, slanted eyes whose warm caressing brown glance was like a ray of sunlight filtering through closed shutters. In the middle of the plaza, on a huge rectangular granite pedestal, sat a square-shouldered, square-bearded emperor, massive from boots to neck, cap screwed down heavily over his bovine brow, fist on one hip; he slouched heavily in the saddle, astride a monstrous beast with a lowered brow, and seemed to contemplate, while digesting his dinner, a world forever limited, while his horse, untroubled, stared into the abyss below. The weight of their power implied an unlimited impotence.

The train from Moscow had been about six hours late. The afternoon was fading. Danil walked up Nevsky Prospect, on which he hadn't set foot in a year—of course, since the day after his arrest.

Czar Peter's city, he thought, a window opened on Europe. What grandeur is yours, and what misery, what misery. . . .

Nobility and grandeur still showed through the rags and tatters. Laundry hanging from dirty windows right on the main boulevard. Windows broken to allow for the passage of the chimney pipes of little iron stoves, spitting out their puffs of dirty black smoke against the façades of buildings. Mud-spattered shop fronts, crumbling façades, shopwindows full of bullet holes and held together with tape, splintered shutters; watchmaker's shopwindows displaying three watches, an old alarm clock, and one fancy pendulum; unspeakable grocery stores; herb teas packaged to look like real tea, as if there were still fools so stupid as to be taken in by these labels, tubes of saccharine, dubious vinegar, tooth powder— brush your teeth carefully, citizens, since you have nothing to use them on! —A nasty joyful feeling awakened within Danil.

Ah, what they've done to you, Czar Peter's city, and in such a short time!

Here had stood the Café Italien, the Salzetti quartet; to the right of the entrance, on the mirrored corner, the prettiest prostitutes had sat smiling out with painted eyes from under their gorgeous hats; some of them spoke French with a funny accent and played the *Parisienne* even in bed. . . . Half the metal shutters were lowered, the pretty white door smudged with black under the press of dirty hands. "*Headquarters, IInd Special Battalion, transferred to Karl Liebknecht Street. "Consumers' Cooperative, 4th Children's Dining Hall.*"

Danil pushed open the door, but all he could see through the herring fumes and the darkness were some broken mirrors. Farther along was the street of women's hat shops: *Marie-Louise, Elaine, Madame Sylvia, Sélysette,* aristocratic names taken from novels or the *noms de guerre* of courtesans. It had been a charming street, inhabited morning and evening by pretty errand girls and elegant ladies. Now sinister, piled high with snowbanks.

Here's Léger's, the goldsmith. Why in the Devil's name have they stuck their bearded Marx in here? (A piss-colored plaster bust, ghostly behind the half-frozen window.) "*Club of the Poor People's Committee of the 1st District.*"

Not a single car. And yet what a beautiful city it still is! The Alexandra Theater showed its noble colonnades. Anyhow, *they* didn't topple the tall silhouette of Empress Catherine in court dress holding the scepter; but some idiot had scaled the bronze figures and attached a red rag on the scepter—a red rag which was now blackened to the color of old blood, the true color of their red.

The tattered elegance of a slim brunette appealed to Danil. She had the eyes of a sad gazelle; her voice was more common than her appearance. Danil took her arm. They walked up the dilapidated street of the hat shops.

"What's your name?"

"Lyda."

In her narrow little room on the sixth floor of a big white house there were worn lace doilies on the furniture. Pictures of young officers were leaning against empty cologne bottles. For months this man had not embraced a pretty, willing woman with clean underwear, lying on a bed with proper sheets. The narrow iron bed with its gilded balls reminded him of another such bed; but one which had been covered only by a pink, badly stained mattress with holes in it, in that pillaged villa on the outskirts of Krasnodar, where a stale odor of rot oozed up from the cellars which had nonetheless been carefully boarded shut. Dunya, a little Cossack girl with warm dry skin, used to come there to meet him, barefoot, naked underneath an old red sarafan with blue flowers. The window was wide open to the soft nights with thin showers of shooting stars. The cool marble hall: vague anxiety of doors ripped from their frames. The voices of buddies, drinking nearby at the Georgian's tavern, burst in with snatches of the dirty songs which the drunken squadrons sometimes sang at the top of their lungs as they trotted into conquered towns whose silence resembled that of cemeteries.

> Where, where, where do we get the clap?
> From Seraphita, Se-ra-phi-ta!

"All my white eagles are blennorrheal!" said a jovial colonel.

Linked to this memory was a taste of fresh watermelon in the mouth.

"You won't mind if I don't take off my boots?" asked Lyda. "See how long they would take to unlace."

He nodded, no, distractedly. Other images rose up into his consciousness, emerging from depths thick with slime heavier than stones. Even the frenzy of the next moments failed to drive them away. Lyda saw a terrible, absent young face, closed off in an inner convulsion, driving into her, and she was afraid. At last the big male body, with its animal armpit odor, sank down next to her, emptied; but no peace returned to that face. "Where do you come from?" she asked to break the silence.

"From the south."

He talked in snatches, little by little, into the air. Us. Them. Who? The Reds? The Whites? In war they're all the same: brutes. Listen to this. What an awful memory: they captured this man in a secret room hidden between the walls. A member of the Committee, understand? They tied him to a stake, in the square. The crowd was watching, calm, like him, thinking he was going to be shot. A thick rope was passed around his head; then, from behind, it was slowly tightened, like a vise, with the help of an ax handle. Then only, the man understood; in a desperate effort, he nearly broke his bonds; his neck strained and turned blue with the struggle. The rope tightened heavily around his forehead. "Slower," cried fat Shutko, steady in the saddle, albeit drunk. A curious fellow, Shutko: he could sit his horse perfectly even when he was unable to stand. . . . The skull broke open like a nut, the rope was red, the body collapsed into its bonds, like a limp sack. An uproar broke out in the square. Everyone ran, the long piercing screams of the women scared the horses. . . . "My horse . . ."

"You were there?"

Lyda was reminded that she was naked, naked in front of a man who had seen these things, and that the traces of this man's arms and lips, the seed of his flesh, were on her, in her: it was as if she suddenly felt soiled with blood, brains, body fluids—a dizzying physical revulsion. She reached for her coat and covered herself with it, shuddering, her eyes wide open, no longer brown but black.

＊

If, on the third landing of this stairway, behind a door like any other, the leather tunics appeared—"Your papers!" "Hands up," whatever they say—it would be all over, irremediably. All. Every step thereafter would be a step toward . . . toward what? Better face it, or you're no good for anything. Toward a revolver held in a monstrous fist in the grim light of a cellar which you enter naked, shivering a last shudder. It took *them* to think up that one: undressing you. *They* are shameless. *They* don't hesitate to commit any

disgrace. —Clothing is precious, of course. And are our saber executions in front of two-foot-deep trenches dug by tottering prisoners
any less abominable? Less. Our bullets are precious. The sabers
glittering in the sun recall the massacres of antiquity. . . . And
what if there is no sun, phrasemaker? Danil was still arguing with
himself in front of the door which was about to open onto his fate:
the end of an adventure or the end of everything.

The rites unfolded simply. Ask for Comrade Valerian: Ameri-
can-style mustache, fleshy nose, close-cropped hair. Say "Prokhor
sent me." Once inside, add: "Allow me to light a cigarette," and,
getting out the cigarettes, drop a wad of crumbled newspaper.
Wait.

Valerian carelessly flicked the wad into an ashtray, which a
moment later he carried into the next room. Then he reappeared
smiling, having matched up the two fragments of a newspaper
headline on the open pages of a book.

"Is it true that Kazan has fallen?"

It seemed likely. On the black stock market the value of shares
had been rising since the fall of Perm and the defeat of the workers'
councils of Bavaria. The rumor of Lenin's assassination, followed by
a denial, had recently enriched some smart operators for a few
days. Shares in *sociétés anonymes,* although fallen into the triple ano-
nymity of illegality, emigration, and anonymous death in prisons,
still persisted in representing the value of nationalized factories,
long-pillaged inventories, and phantom capital. Gamblers with less
to lose than those who commit suicide outside casinos still placed
bets at each new rumor, on the sticky cards of the Civil War.

An idea cut through Danil's brain like a knife. We are spilling
blood and these people are speculating on every battle, on the firing
squads and the hangings, on . . . And, since he had to answer himself at every moment, he finished out his thought: —but *they* don't
even know how to speculate; they pillage.

He made his report to the Three: Valerian, the Professor,
Nikita. The samovar was humming on the table, which was spread
as for a feast.—"How many trains, did you say?" The Professor was
repeating his question; he was a little deaf; gold-rimmed pince-nez,
the heavy features of an aging billy goat. Could this asthmatic bu-
reaucrat be one of the leaders of the liberation movement here?—
"How many airplanes did you say?" Wasn't he just asking these
questions to give the impression he understood? They might be the

sign of infantile incomprehension. What importance did he attach to these uncertain figures? Just a moment before, the Professor had mentioned "the Yids" in a voice thick with scorn.

Nikita, close-shaven, with a high smooth forehead and porcelain eyes, was smoking as he took notes. The Three spoke little, but Danil learned a great deal. An Esthonian regiment had passed over to the Whites. The fleet on Lake Peipus as well. Other great blows would soon be struck: a fortress—another fortress—a regiment—a heavy cruiser . . . Valerian was examining old railroad maps, on which rivers, as blue as fresh ink, and the straight lines of tracks stood out against the white background.

Then, by the Professor's way of inclining his wooden face with its prematurely detached chin and sharp nostrils over Russia, Danil discovered in him an ancient hidden power which must make him precious to the others. He understood that the figures fell necessarily into place in his mind the way crystals form around a first crystal. No doubt, no hesitation, no error was possible for this man. No sophism could influence him. No truth other than his own. Danil thought: If I were to cry out to him: "Look at what they are doing, look at what we ourselves are doing. Here's what I saw. I saw a man's head split open under the cord. That form of execution has been extinct since 1650! Are we really any better than they are?"— he would merely reply in an absolutely neutral voice: "Second Lieutenant, I believe your tunic is missing a button. Be more careful of your appearance." And this would be more crushing than any vehement reply.

"We have them at bay," the Professor concluded.

"No bread. No metal. No combustibles. No cloth. No medicine. In the north, the Americans, the English, the Serbs, the Italians. Here, the Finns, the Esthonians, the Whites. To the east, the Supreme Commander. To the west, the Poles. To the south, the Whites. Us—everywhere: in the army, in the fleet, in the economic councils, in the cooperatives. Behind us, the Powers. With us, the people, all who are not the dregs of the ignorant masses. Us, the only hope.

"They nationalized the notions business. You stand in line for seventeen hours in four different places to get your seventh and final piece of paper: a ticket good for four spools of thread. And when you get to the store there is no more thread because the last of the stock has been stolen during the night, ha, ha, ha! —Do you

know why they made the mails free? Because it cost too much to
print up the stamps!

"*They* instituted a free food program for children, but small
coffins are at a premium on the market and there's a line at the
cemetery! —And how *they* ape us! In their trenches the soldiers no
longer salute their officers with 'Your Honor,' but they cry out in the
same voice, by God, 'In the service of the Revolution!' Jolly service!
Every night groups of men desert by fleeing forward toward the
enemy, who has bread."

The conversation had become animated. The Professor was
explaining to Nikita that when order was re-established there would
be a ticklish problem facing jurists. Which laws to apply to the ring-
leaders? Common-law crimes, sacrileges, *they* have plenty to answer
for; but in their case the exercise of power has created a new juridi-
cal situation. Usurpation . . .

Valerian began to laugh:

"Martial law, by God! The fewest possible formalities."

The Professor raised his wooden face, the two sides of which
were multiplied into geometrical reflections in the lenses of his *lor-
gnon,* and shook his head slowly from side to side.

"The State is based on the notion of right. Regicides, parri-
cides, and the sacrilegious have a right to the safeguard of the
laws. According to Roman law . . ."

Nikita thought about forests. Last year he had walked for five
weeks through the forests of the Dvina, sometimes following the
trails of great hungry bears through the fresh snow, listening to the
wolves howling at sundown, resting under the pines in the awful
cold, building himself a fire as a rare treat (a dangerous treat, for
fire could attract man), learning how to devour the raw flesh of
wolves and crows. The silence of the forest was so immense that it
seemed to cover the whole earth, to blot out all memory; the pines
under the first snows seemed in turn white, dappled, blue, dark,
darker than night, depending on the hour and the light. The sounds
of flapping wings and indistinct animal cries, of broken branches
falling, of faint breathing, lingered momentarily and vanished, leaving a sharp, delicate imprint on the man's soul like the snowy
footprints of an emaciated old wolf who passed by a while ago with
his tongue hanging out between sharp fangs, making his own mysterious way through the woods, through the cold, through hunger
toward his prey or toward death. The man stooping attentively over

his trail knew trigonometry and recited André Chenier's poems—
which he knew by heart—to himself in clearings. On the seventeenth day, in the middle of a mortally cold frost, with only seven
cartridges left, Nikita saw lines of smoke rising straight up over
gray huts squatting like moles on the Russian earth. He turned back
with hurried steps, skis sinking into the soft deep snow. Better to
stretch out alone beneath one of those ancient pyramidal pines
sparkling with diamonds under the rays of the moon and die in
peace, of slow exhaustion—better this end than encountering man.
And yet he did encounter a man, being unable to avoid him, and
the encounter was a fortunate one: they came upon one another,
inexplicably, face to face in the middle of the forest, two rifles, two
wary instincts overcome by surprise, sniffing each other out at a distance of twenty yards like two beasts of the forest. The other man
was a forgotten old woodsman who knew nothing about the war,
nothing about the Revolution, nothing of the death of the Czar,
nothing about anything. Every summer he traveled one hundred
versts to the northwest, to a Komi village, to get powder, brandy,
and matches. Arriving home, alone as always with the silent female
who slept at the back of his hut, he would drink for days on end.
During these times he would talk out loud, volubly and disconnect-
edly, dreaming, attempting to sing but remembering only the opening words of the Lord's Prayer—"Our Father who art in heaven"—
and snatches of a sad prison ballad—"Open up the prison door for
me. . . ."

The female, too, her spirits warmed by the alcohol, would
begin singing languorous lullabies in her Komi language. Then they
would fall asleep huddled next to each other on the beaten earth.
The door of the hut was open to the green vastness. Birds hopped
in and out. Red squirrels plumed with magnificent tails came to
stare with their bright little eyes at the strange disarmed sleep of
two human beings. The man had been living this way—nameless,
ageless—for years. He barely knew how to talk any more. He didn't
know what a newspaper was. The sight of a lighter impressed him
so much that for an instant Nikita feared he might kill him from
behind as they slid along single file on their skis, just to possess this
marvelous object which could give birth to fire at the flip of a
fingernail. But this solitary figure had lived away from men too long
to think any more of striking his own kind. He tamed squirrels. He
derived great joy from spending warm afternoons frolicking with

these intelligent little animals. "So intelligent," he declared, that
thanks to them he still retained the idea of intelligence. From him
Nikita learned that he had come the wrong way. Snenkursk, the
British outpost, was still distant by twenty days' march that way, toward those constellations, then following the course of the river:
watch out for bears . . . In these forests you needed to get your
bearings by sextant, as on the high seas. Nikita went back the way
he had come. Now he no longer knew whether it had been a nightmare or a rare burst of sunlight in his life.

9

Egor, lying on his belly crosswise on the big bed, considered Danil, straddling a chair in front of him. Egor was wearing a blue blouse belted at the waist by a silk cord and a pair of long sailor's trousers. He was beating time on a pillow with his feet, which were clad in simple red leather Turkish slippers. His head appeared enormous. Nose sniffing for a fight. Wide, fresh-looking mouth, high forehead topped by blond tufts. A sort of intoxication, which was not due to drink but rather to an inner restlessness pregnant with storms ready to break out, hovered under the surface of his glance, in the sharp curve of his mouth, in the quick pulse of the veins of his neck.

Danil, seeing his expression harden into that of a high-powered gambler about to stake his bet, sensed an obscure danger approaching. He had come to ask this bandit for arms, munitions, money for the Green partisans hiding out in the forests.

"Your Greens," Egor said heavily at last, "are too green. Understand?"

Golden candelabra standing on the piano threw the saffron light of twelve candles into the room. Open tins yawned up from the deal table. There was black bread, bits of dried fish spread out on crumpled newspaper, cigarette boxes full of butts, and little crystal glasses decorated with vine-leaf tracings. Discarded cigarette butts studded the floor on every side. Rifles were stacked against the back of a brocade armchair over which a long black silk stocking lay like a serpent. An enamel washbasin full of toilet water was standing on the white marble mantelpiece. The windows, boarded up on the outside and hung with Bokhara rugs on the inside, gave no clue as to whether it was day or night. Seen from

without, the big dead house must seem abandoned. The red seals of
the Special Commission covered the doors. The only way in was
through deserted, disreputable back courts or through a secret
opening in the wall of the neighboring house.

"No," said Danil. "You . . ."

Egor stared into space. His feet beat the pillow more rapidly.
He was groping for an idea as, in a fight, he would have groped for
something to throw—a glass, an inkpot, a knife. In a different voice,
he called: "Shura!"

Shura entered. Noiselessly she appeared at the foot of the bed,
a woman wearing a long silk Turkoman dress with wide red and
blue stripes.

"What?"

"Take off my shoes and socks. Quick."

He continued to tap his foot nervously against the rug which
covered the bed while she removed his slippers and silk stockings in
heavy silence. A bare foot, red, with flat toenails, buried itself in the
pillow. Egor withdrew behind his eyes. Danil felt vaguely chilly.

"Anything else?" asked Shura, who seemed to be unaware of
the presence of another man three feet away. She had a thickset
face, broad through the cheeks; eyes which slanted toward her temples; thick painted lips whose crimson suggested a scream crushed
against that mouth; black hair plastered down on both sides of her
forehead; bare arms. She was from Asia.

"Cognac."

He swallowed the liquor in one gulp.

"Anything else?"

"Sit there."

Seated on the side of the bed, the woman at last turned a soft
glance on Danil. Egor seized her knee in a grip like a pincers.

"Do you see," he said to Danil, "how I hold this knee? I felt like
grabbing you by the neck that way. You would have removed my
slippers, you would have poured me a drink, and if I had spit in
your face you would have wiped it off without a word. Some of
them even smile when I do it to them. Enough! Remember that
Egor is in a good mood tonight. You picked a good time to come
and tell him lies to his face. I know what your Greens are worth. To
hell with them and you too. Now, let's drink. Pour, Shura. Not those
glasses . . ."

A little crystal glass shattered somewhere across the floor.

Shura filled some tea glasses with cognac. Her profile revealed a tall form, bizarrely striped, a bare arm, smooth and tawny, and a low Chinese brow under jet-black braids. "You drink too!" Egor told her. She drank slowly with one elbow lifted the way teamsters drink in cabarets. An ambiguous half-smile creased her face. Danil saw warm golden sparks in her pupils. Perhaps it was only the reflection of the candles. Egor resumed his monologue.

"What were you Greens doing when I was taking the Palace? I may well have been the first man in there, rifle butt forward. You can still see the mark of my rifle on the wall paneling. I shot Paul I in effigy. You can still see the holes in his white breeches. That's where I aim. You don't like that?"

"It's all the same to me."

"Ah, very well. I took Pavlograd; me, do you understand?"

The dull anger building up inside him vanished instantly, carried away by a sort of fond merriment.

"What's your name? Danil? Listen, Danil, I set fire to Pavlograd prison. *That* was a pleasure. . . . Hey, Shura, do you remember back in December, the way we worked in the square at night? That was another good time."

On those nights their jolly band moved into a huge square bounded by a half moon of buildings whose windows suggested blind eyes. The arch of Army Headquarters, surmounted by an invisible four-horse chariot, opened like a triumphal gate into a deeper darkness. The breeze blew up a snowy powder which suddenly began to sparkle, suspended within the limits of visibility, when the broad straight beam of a searchlight rose over the Winter Palace. This huge luminous sword cut uselessly through the polar sky. At the bottom of the square, the old Foreign Ministry building bent sharply toward Cantors' Bridge like a cardboard stage setting. The gang proceeded to the foot of the tall granite column, erected in memory of a forgotten victory, in order to saw off the bronze grillwork. The copper was excellent! The fences were offering a good price for them. Egor had also thought of stealing the Turkish cannon planted muzzle down at the corners, but they weren't offering enough for them. The lights were burning in the windows of the militia a hundred yards away. A few good pals were inside. —Egor yawned.

"Danil, you can go tell your people that Egor says, 'Up your ass.' He's with the Revolution, Egor is. Not the commissars' Revolu-

tion, but his own, his very own, which still has some good days and
fine nights ahead of it. Pour him another drink, Shura, and then to
hell with him."

Danil left. Shura walked ahead, carrying a candlestick. Huge
shadows danced noiselessly around them. The young woman drew
the light close to her lips, whose irritating red was like a scream.
The flame went out, the cold night blew in with a sudden glitter of
starlight.

"What stars!" said Danil in spite of himself.

"What stars!" murmured distinctly the irritating lips which had
just disappeared behind him.

Stormy chords banged out on a piano were exploding somewhere like an underground symphony.

✱

Egor crossed the room, his hips rolling slightly, gesticulating.
And, speaking aloud, he muttered, "Yes, yes, yes . . ."

Yes, I took Pavlograd. I set fire to the prison. A little orange cat
was caught in the guardhouse. So we dashed up the smoke-filled
stairs, Brik and I, and we pulled the poor animal out of the flames,
yes. And then I worked a whole morning behind the wall of a little
station—but what station! what station?—shooting the officers who
had surrendered the night before. How tired we were afterward! I
swam across the Dnieper. They had killed Brik. What was the name
of that nice old *mujik* who fed me, dried me, dressed me, hid me? A
funny name, a mare's name . . . We crashed two locomotives
together to block the right-of-way. That was at Matveevka, yes.
What a magnificent thing that was, the crash of those two machines, the speed, the momentum, the power, the screaming boilers
and that explosion—black, red, white! I jumped out of the cab just
in time, yes. The precise second! I felt the hot breath of the
explosion on my back, yes, yes. I almost felt like hanging on. . . .
Me, me—us—yes, yes, yes.

Suddenly he thought:

If they had hold of you now, you'd get a bullet in the back of
the neck and it would be all over for you, Egor.

He cried out in the middle of a lengthy yawn—the yawn of a
caged beast.

"Shura, I'm bored. . . ."

Half consciously he opened the piano. His head was ready to explode, it was so full of things. How to say them? How to silence them? What to yell? What to smash? He struck the keyboard with both hands, seeking deep rumbling notes, unleashing wild chords, a raging battle, a fantastic storm mingled with inarticulate melodies, ecstasies, and sobs.

❋

With the firm tread of a drunk he walked down the long dark corridor toward the women's room—the "Bitches' Barracks"—which was at the end. Whispers were audible through the half-open door.

"Didja hear that?" asked Dunya-the-Snake?

Katka-Little-Apple sighed:

"That's Egor going off his rocker. I feel bad for him, poor Egor, with those restless eyes. Oh, Manya, Manya, he feels the end coming, I tell you, and I feel sorry for him, really sorry. . . ."

The three women were probably squatting as they always did on pillows around the little stove. Between the two young ones sat old Manya, wrinkled hands under the candle spreading out toward solitaire cards: Manya reeking of old age with the eyelids of a century-old lizard and an obstinate furious will to live—eh, why go on living, old witch? Egor would have wanted to grab his own life full of red strength and wring it out in both hands like a discarded rag and throw it in the face of . . . in whose face, for Christ's sake?

Old Manya's answer filtered out of the room along with a faint ruddy glow:

"Don't worry about him, Katka. Men are all swine. Spit on them. And then, he's got his Shura. Too bad for her. God bless her."

Egor smiled, relaxed, his shoulder blades flat against the wall, his body heavy.

"Manya," interjected Dunya-the-Snake, "tell us about Nice."

"Another time. Those were different times, my girls, the good old days. . . . But we manage to take care of ourselves, don't we? Do you know what Tata is doing? She can't sleep with the commissars, not with a broken nose and a voice like an old worn-out shoe. But she found herself a racket. She undresses little kids. 'Here, little boy, come here. I've got something interesting to show you. . . .' —She takes the kid by the hand, all sweet and nice, and leads him into a hallway. Two slaps across his little face and Tata collects his coat, his hat, his gloves, a good day's work."

"That turns my stomach," said Katka. "Poor little kids."

"They're gonna croak one way or another," said Manya softly. "These days."

"And anyway," ventured Dunya-the-Snake, "if they're the kids of the bourgeois, too bad for them."

"Shut up, you stupid little Agit-Prop. You know that big building they're putting up over on the canal? Well, a whole gang of kids is holed up in there, with Olenka-the-Runaway as their chief. What do you say to that? Ah, now there's a somebody for all her thirteen years. Looks like a little lamb; sweet, well-mannered and all that, but cunning. I'm sure she's the one who killed that little boy by the Oats Market. You know what they thought up? They catch cats, they eat them, and sell the skins to the Chinese. . . . They also work poorboxes in the churches and ration cards in the food lines. . . ."

"Tell us about Nice, sweet Manya, tell us about Nice," begged Dunya.

Egor moved away noiselessly, his head bowed.

✱

It was very late when Stassik arrived. Icicles clung to his burgeoning beard. His old soldier's coat was stiff with the cold. They sat across from each other leaning on their elbows and drank tea and cognac. Stassik brought the latest issues of the *Tocsin* published in a Ukrainian village during the passing of a singing army which moved in carts—a machine gun and an accordion in each cart—under black banners.

Egor glanced at a headline:

Resolutions of the Special
Conference of the Confederation . . .

More resolutions, more organizations, more conferences even under these midnight banners! Egor drank, and this last swig of burning liquor seemed in a strange way to sober him at the same time as it made him entirely drunk.

"Put away your papers, Stassik," he said. "I don't want to see them. I'm not a believer. All I know about is one thing: the melting snows, the great spring waters, the flooding rivers carrying along granite-hard ice blocks, dead dogs, last year's garbage, old planks . . . It's a flood, understand, and we're all rolling down to the sea; ah! how beautiful it is to be carried along and to carry off everything before you! A block of ice, that's what I am. I've got to crash into arches and bridges. I've got to hear the barge hulls resounding under my blows."

"And afterward?" said Stassik.

"Afterward, I don't give a fuck. Put away your pamphlets, Stassik, I don't believe in them."

He took another drink.

"I'm bored, Stassik. Do *you* believe?"

"In what?"

"In what you say."

Egor's head felt heavy, ready to fall. He was holding it up with both hands. Wouldn't it fall anyway, roll across the floor, bounce up like a great soccer ball and smack its brow against the black and white keyboard, there to unleash storms and perish? Stassik, sitting stiffly, black and white, black beard and white skin like the piano keys, was certainly not drunk. Stassik's hands lay flat on the table, sharp and clear amid the general disorder. He answered with words as blunt as deeds.

"You've got a child's brain in an athlete's skull, Egor. 'Believe' is an old word, Egor. I *know*. I know that man will be free on a free earth. I know that we will be killed long before that. I know that we will be forgotten. I know that the future will be magnificent. I know it's time to begin."

"Yes, yes," cried Egor, "you're right. I believe, too, Stassik."

He burst out laughing.

"So long as we're killed beforehand. Are you sure about that?"

"I'm sure of it," Stassik answered gravely.

Egor thought his forehead had hit the keyboard. A splendid storm thundered around him. He was smiling, ecstatic, into an immense certainty. Like the sun over the Baltic in July, bursting through the clouds and making waves of light ripple suddenly across the sea. Certainty. He was searching for something in this chaos, as he had been searching in his memory across this seascape: the near-forgotten name of a woman.

"Stassik, do you want some money for the organization? Take."

The money was in the drawer of the table. Tea had spilled over the stacks of bank notes, which were mingled with dirty postcards. Stassik began methodically to sort out the dry bills.

10

Danil lived in a maid's room at Professor Lytaev's. Evenings, before going to sleep, he read love notes that had been left in his night-table drawer by a brunette. Some of them were formal, written on paper decorated in the upper corner with colored flowers: "Dear Mademoiselle Agrafena Prokhorova, Allow your most obedient servant . . . ," ending with a contorted invitation to a birthday party. "With respect, your sincere perpetual admirer . . ." The writing was that of one of those public stenographers who used to keep stands in the market places.

When Danil came home early enough he would find two old men absorbed in their spoken meditation before a window which was still milk-white. The tea in the glasses took on a tint of wine; Vadim Mikhailovich Lytaev was saying:

". . . Peter's mount has got back into stride. Russia is beginning her revolution again. After Peter, she drifts slowly back into her past again. The Czars only borrow two things from the West: uniforms and money. Behind their false front the old Russia subsists: superstitious, bent under the yoke, floating her huge rafts down the Volga with the same songs as in the sixteenth century, still dragging the wooden swing plow through the fields, building the same houses as a thousand years ago, getting drunk the same way, Christianly celebrating pagan festivals during Easter, making love to fat, painted women and beating them from time to time, deporting or immuring heretics . . . This old country is still there, deep down, under a thin layer of burning lava."

The historian, Platon Nikolaevich, answered:

"That is so. And the lava will cool. And when the lava is cool, the old earth by its fermentation alone will crack open the thin

layer and once again push its old, eternally young green blades into
the sunlight. Ashes make good fertilizer. After each era of disturbances, Russia begins living again according to her inner law like
the plants which spring back after a storm. This land 'where Christ
trod on every clod of earth' binds her wounds and continues her
mission, which is neither that of the West nor that of the East, but
hers alone. Even in these disturbances, which are alike from one
century to another, old Russia remains faithful to her law . . ."

"Platon Nikolaevich! This year, while Lenin was speaking in
the assemblies, they burned a witch alive a hundred and eighteen
versts from Moscow. Two hundred and thirty versts away, in order
to protect a village from an epidemic, naked virgins were harnessed
to a plow, following a custom which may go back to the Scythians,
and dug a furrow around the fields and dwellings. We are darkest
Asia. We can only be pulled out of ourselves by an iron fist. Peter is
the model and precursor of the Revolution. Remember this: 'Con-
straint makes all things happen.' He founded industries, ministries,
an army, a fleet, a capital, customs, by means of edicts and executions. He gave the order to cut off the beards, to dress European
style, to open this window on Europe in the Ingrian swamps. The
earth was bare, but he said, 'Here will rise a city.' He caned his
courtiers, drank like a trooper, and ended his life full of suspicion,
doubt, and anguish, smelling treason everywhere (and it was everywhere, like today), trusting no one but his grand inquisitor, thinking even of striking the Empress. And he was right. He left a
country depopulated in places, bleeding and moaning under the
effort, but St. Petersburg was built! And he is still the Great, the
greatest, because he hounded the old Russian, even in his own son,
because he wrenched this ignorant, passive, bloated old country
around toward the future the way you pull up a restive horse with
bit and spurs. I hear an echo of his edicts in today's decrees. All this
can even be expressed in Marxist terms: the rise of new classes."

Platon Nikolaevich resembled Lytaev in a multitude of con-
trasts: in his immobility; in his face, which was as full as the other
man's was sharp; by his faith, which was as solid as the other's was
anxious. The mold of a face mask resembles the face because it
reproduces its harmonies in reverse. . . . Platon Nikolaevich answered slowly, for they spoke to each other mainly in order to
affirm a living thought which, though expecting nothing from men,
still felt the need for the ephemeral finality of expression.

"No, Vadim Mikhailovich; Peter, like the people in the Krem-lin, is only an accident—perhaps a necessary one in the accomplishment of certain developments—in the history of Russia. It is Alexis who is right against Peter, just as Christ on the cross is eternally right against the eternally vanquished Anti-Christ. Peter is only great to the degree that in spite of himself he becomes the instrument of a cause which is not his own—when he renews the reasons for living of the old Russia he attacks. This time of troubles will end. The southern Slavs, who have remained healthier, closer to the soil, will recreate order and unity in the faith against the sick cities. We are passing through a sort of dark age and we will be reborn. And we will once again bring light to the West."

"The question," said Danil, "will be decided by the sword."

"No, by the spirit."

It was their common thought, so much so that of the two historians neither was quite sure who had answered.

"But what is the spirit without the sword?"

"But what is the sword without the spirit?"

Danil saw the same indulgent irony in the eyes of the two scholars. He looked at the books lining their shelves, old books full of facts, of ideas, of things so useless when it is a question of bread, of lice, of blood. In the drawer of a mahogany secretary manuscripts lay sleeping. History: that vile scholar's lie among whose printed lines not a drop of spilled blood can be found, where nothing remains of the passion, the pain, the fear, and the violence of men! He felt a kind of hatred for these two old mandarins who knew so many dates and theories but hadn't the least idea of the stench of a sacked town or the look of an open belly full of fat green flies over which poppies droop their heads.

"Dostoyevsky . . ." began Platon Nikolaevich.

"I don't read him. No time, you understand. The Karamazovs split hairs with their beautiful souls; we are carving flesh itself, and the beautiful soul doesn't mean a damn thing to us. What is serious is to eat, to sleep, to avoid being killed, and to kill well. There's the truth. The question has already been decided by the sword and the spirit. A sword which is stronger than ours, a spirit we don't understand. And we don't need to understand in order to perish. We will all perish with these books, these ideas, Dostoyevsky and the rest; precisely, perhaps, on account of these books, of these ideas, of Dostoyevsky, of scruples and of incomplete massacres. And the earth will continue to turn. That's all. Good evening."

✿

The days got longer, heralding white nights. The snow melted
on the steppes, revealing patches of black earth and pointed yellow
grasses. Streamlets ran in every direction, babbling like birds. They
glistened in every fold of earth. Swollen rivers reflected pure skies
of still frigid blue. Scattered bursts of laughter hung in the woods
among the slim white trunks of birches. Specks of dull silver
seemed to hang in the air. The first warm days were tender, caressing. The pedestrian in the damp streets offered them his face and
his soul. His glance clung to pretty white clouds which passed
above like cares carried off by a great gust of confidence. The
charm of life revived with the little children playing on street
corners; it hovered over an empty square above a horse carcass devoured by stray dogs. The animal's skull emerged, a fresh ivory color,
from a burrow of melting snow. Shreds of hairy brown skin, laundered by the frosts, clung to the crushed rib cage. The five little
golden onion domes of a rococo church pierced the pale sky, azure
turned white, but an airy white of limpid freshness. One could no
longer believe that there was still war, death, hunger, fear, lice. The
river, immensely free between its granite banks, carried along huge
blocks of ice. They moved downstream with soft crunching sounds
from northern lakes toward the sea now reopened to the lapping
waves, to the living lights beading the foam, to the warm Gulf
Stream breezes which, starting from Yucatan and the Floridas,
passed over the Atlantic, the fjords of Norway and the plains of
Sweden, and came to rest on our icy shores. Atop the golden spire
of the Admiralty Building a tiny gilded ship, as light and distinct as
an idea, sailed through the sky. The colors of the red flags revived.

The first buds opened in the gardens. Then there was an
explosion of fresh green foliage over the rivers and canals cutting
through the city. The pleasure of life, suddenly recalled, had an
acid taste. The evenings were cold under skies tinted steel blue as
from the distant reflection of huge icebergs. There was no more
night; dusk dragged on gray, blue, mauve, ashy, pearly, brighter
and brighter, to midnight. The sky glowed white until sunrise, cap-
tivating every glance, at the end of the sparkling canals, through
the black arching branches, above the heads of century-old riders
holding in their rearing horses. . . . Couples roamed the river-
banks. The sky poured its brightness down on them, the river en-

compassed them with solitude. They met with ghostly smiles. They paused before rotting barges abandoned by the boatmen last autumn when the river transports were nationalized. Soon they would be dismantled to make firewood; it would be a rough job. The Poor People's Committees were struggling bitterly over possession of these hulks.

A blond adolescent girl with deep blue eyes shimmering like rivulets of melting snow questioned her lover, who wore the ragged uniform of a vanished academy:

"Will you come help me?"

He whispered yes as he kissed her ear, for she had given herself to him on one of these days, naïve and willing, bewildered and feverish, in a cozy nook of this rotting barge; the stale smell of the river pervaded the silvery gray of the endless evening. The waterlogged planks yielded under their footsteps. The waves lapped the hull with a dull hissing sound. They had come there out of curiosity, unmindful of their joy since their joy carried them along. She had nearly fallen into a dark square hole at the bottom of which the water was lapping. "You see! You see!" he said, alarmed. She laughed. "If you had to count every near miss!" They found themselves suddenly alone. Nothing but the vast empty sky over their heads and the watery ripples below, reflecting the sky through a wide gap in the disjointed planks. "How nice it is," she said, offering him her lips, and the idea came to her simply that in love you have to give your body; it has to hurt and you feel a little ashamed, but you have to, with eyes closed and lips entwined, and you shudder with happiness afterward just thinking about it. . . . But how do you do it? The books don't explain it very clearly. —"I don't know, I'm all embarrassed, forgive me, do what you will with me, I love you, I love you . . ."

Now her rosy petal-shaped lips mingled ordinary things with important preoccupations:

"We'll set aside a provision of wood for the winter. . . . Listen, I want to become more conscious; tell me what to read."

❋

Another couple. She: close-cropped hair under a brown leather cap which gave her small head a sporty appearance; gilded temples and eyebrows and gold-flecked eyes. He: a soldier, the red star incrusted in black leather over his brow. She had just left the Dis-

trict Committee, he had come from the political bureau of the 23rd
Regiment; they met on a bench in the Summer Garden, a few steps
from the Dutch House built by Czar Peter as a temporary residence
while this city was emerging from the swamps and forests, with
wooden sidewalks running along muddy streets, huge empty tracts,
and parks which were in reality the edges of the forest. The graceful gestures of Dianas and Artemises hovered beneath the trees.
The severely wrought grill of the garden stood out black against the
great pale light of the north. There flowed the river.

Their handclasp was firm. Without apparent tenderness.
Nearly the same height, the two breathed the same strength. Her
eyes followed the hopping sparrows as she said:

"I've been thinking over the theory of imperialism. You were
right the other evening. All you have to do is read Chapter Four in
Hilferding. But on the problem of freedom I'm the one who's right.
Here . . ."

She pulled a sheaf of notes out of a pamphlet whose colored
cover showed a globe of the earth covered with chains broken by a
red lightning bolt dropping from the Milky Way.

"Marx writes: 'Value transforms every product of labor into a
social hieroglyphic. . . . For those who exchange their products,
their own social action takes the form of the action of objects,
which rule the producers instead of being ruled by them.' They
believe themselves to be free because they are subject to the action
of anonymous objects and not to men. They believe themselves free
because they see no master over them. But 'the reciprocal independence of persons is achieved through a system of universal material
dependence.'"

"That is valid for the past. By becoming conscious of necessity
we become free. Read Chapter XI of *Anti-Dühring*. By its understanding of necessary historical development, the proletariat, accomplishing what must be accomplished, passes from the realm of
necessity to that of freedom. Read Chapter II and Part III."

"Let's go," she said. Standing, he put his arm awkwardly
around her shoulders and, in a quieter voice:

"Xenia!"

She knew what he was going to say, but with what words? She
waited for these words and it seemed to her that her chest was
bursting with joy.

"Xenia, we are necessary to one another, and we are free because . . ."

They kept silent until they reached the part of the garden where a great porphyry vase stands on a gray pedestal. Only there did he dare to ask her with awkward detachment:

"Will you come, Xenia?"

She nodded *yes,* simply, and, so that he wouldn't see the joy laughing in her eyes, looked into the distance toward the varicolored bulbs of the Church of the Savior on the Blood. In preparation for this nod, she had spent a long time this morning washing and decking herself out in fine linen, hesitating whether to take along the vial of French perfume. Was the use of these luxuries invented by the depravity of the rich not unworthy? Yet the District Committee distributed perfumes impounded by customs to the women activists with the most important jobs. She made up her mind on the basis of this specious argument: it was not a luxury but a matter of hygiene. Wouldn't he be angry at this bit of refinement in her? But how he breathed in the fresh smell of her bare arms. . . .

They were leaving the garden. An auto, having passed them, stopped short. A high-booted man with a revolver at his side ran to meet them. Ryjik was only three paces away when Xenia recognized him.

"You're taking a stroll? You don't know what's going on? Come over to the department right away. Everyone is mobilized."

Ryjik climbed back into the car. Only there did he feel, as one feels a bullet only the instant after it hits you, what a sharp jab had pierced his heart at the sight of that couple. Sprawled on the greasy old upholstery of the Ford, instead of thinking of the Revolution he thought that he was too old and that it was irreparable.

11

The 1st Esthonian Regiment went over to the enemy on May 24. The 3rd Infantry of the Second Brigade turned traitor on May 28. This 3rd Battalion, accompanied by the brigade commissar, Rakov, was bivouacking in Vyra. A former guards officer, himself a Communist Party member, backed by a detachment of soldiers, had all the Communists arrested at dawn. Rakov defended himself alone in a thatched hut, fought desperately, and saved the last bullet for himself. The other Communists were massacred. Five women in nightgowns were shot in a damp field. A general arrived in the morning. After the killings, the men had taken an hour to remove their red stars and sew on nationalist cockades. Then they paraded behind the band for their new commanders like troops in a military tableau. A few days passed. Below Gatchina, at the gates of the city, a regiment opened the front. Hastily called reinforcements gradually filed up, without ammunition, without food, without shoes, without clothes. An inspection team was sent out from the Hill Fort, which rounds out the Kronstadt defense perimeter on the south side of the Finnish Gulf, and made a most reassuring report: "Conscious and disciplined garrison, no sign of mutiny." It was necessary to feed the starving troops, the huge, restless factories, the population decimated by typhus and cholera (which the newspapers were under orders not to mention). The announced supply trains never arrived, either because they had never left or because they were stopped by the starving cities along the way. The Council of Defense unofficially authorized requisitioning of food in the surrounding countryside. The peasants armed themselves with scythes, unearthed old machine guns, brought sawed-off rifles out of hiding, and chased away the detachments of workers when they didn't disembowel the agitators during the night. The priests announced the end of the Anti-Christ. People gathered at evening vigils to read appeals from the White Army, which promised order, peace, respect for property, punishment for the Jews, and handouts of white bread. Round white loaves brought back from the front passed from hand to admiring hand. Lists of suspects to be denounced on the arrival of the Whites were drawn up in every village. Anyone who had accounts to settle with a neighbor made sure his name was set down. The Greens controlled whole regions. They obeyed a single headquarters, manned by trained commanders. These deserters, who refused to fight for either party, and, being neither Whites nor Reds, took the color of the forest, their refuge, had managed to form an army as regular as the others and tended to coordinate their actions with the Whites against the Reds, since the former were still stronger. Four thousand Greens occupied the Velikiye Luki region. There were probably 15,000 in the region around Pskov. They engaged in full-scale battles. Naturally they executed the Communists.

Enemy aircraft flew over Kronstadt, dropping pretty glistening bombs ringed with red copper. Huge white flowers of explosions burst out of the ground and in the May sky. A big British submarine attacked some Red torpedo boats on June 4 and was sunk. Fifty men in Davy Jones's locker—Olde England—and among them jolly Ted, who sang so merrily to a Negro melody:

> *"Every ship will go to the bottom*
> *Sixty fathoms deep!*
> *Who gives a damn! Who gives a damn!"*

The incident was completely hushed up. It spoiled the Lord High Admiral's breakfast one morning. The city learned mysteriously that the Hill Fort, Fort Gray Horse, and Fort Obruchev had gone over. The breeze carried gasps of cannon fire in from the sea.

Alongside the little white posters announcing free rations for children appeared brief placards signed by the head of internal defense. OUTLAWED—*Under Pain of Death—Will Be Shot Without Trial.* Death crept into every dwelling. Men bowed their heads before these fresh placards, sensing rifles lowering slowly over them. The commander of the place, surrounded by telephones, called his staff assistant in to report. Comrade Valerian—peppery mustache cut

American style, fleshy nose, close-cropped hair—aimed a frank gaze into the eyes of the commander ("pretty clever, nonetheless, for an ex-machinist promoted to non-com after fifteen months at the front") and recited:

"Two cruisers returning enemy fire at the front. The Communist battalions are confined to barracks. The Committees of Three and of Five of the Evacuation and Destruction Services are in permanent session. The aircraft factory can be destroyed in seven hours. I will supervise that operation personally."

*

A note bearing the seal of the Central Special Commission brought news of the greatest gravity. The Counterrevolutionary Center Right organization could count on 146 confederates in the city, organized in groups of five, and a thousand sure sympathizers. These forces could be mobilized in a single night. According to a plan marked with blue circles seized during a raid in Moscow, the organization planned to occupy about twenty strategic points from within as soon as the Whites outside were ready to threaten the city directly. The Regional Committee of the Center Right was allegedly presided over by an older man, known as the Professor, perhaps an actual professor (*check university circles and the former Academy of Theology*). An intercepted letter indicated that an emissary had arrived from the south with important messages and was still in the city.

File No. 42, the Center Right Affair, was in the hands of Comrade Zvereva, a rather ugly little woman, always well dressed, under the supervision of Special Commission members Terentiev and Arkadi. At two in the morning, as Zvereva was getting undressed in front of the mirror, as was her custom, caressing her flabby breasts with a distracted smile, the telephone on her night table began ringing insistently:

"Hello! The President here. You're not in bed? Can you come over here, Room 12?"

Never before had the President spoken directly to Zvereva. She snapped to attention, overwhelmed by self-esteem mingled with anxiety. This narrow-eyed, broad-hipped little woman, tormented by desire, pride, and scruples, saw every man as a male, didn't know how to give herself to any one of them, and lived haunted by carnal hunger. She powdered herself quickly but lightly, so that it wouldn't show, checked the finishing touches on the imperceptible dark lines lining her eyelids, hesitated a moment between her black dress with the straight pleats, which made her look thin, and the military tunic she put on for interrogations, but decided on the dress. She was sorry she didn't meet anyone in the long red-carpeted hallway, for no one could have failed to realize from her mien that affairs—secret affairs—of the highest importance still occupied her at this hour of the night.

The President was wearing an old smoking jacket, worn at the elbows. Thick strands of pearl silk hung from the collar of his broad-checked shirt. From close up, his head appeared very large and swollen. He had puffy eyes with thick lids, and a little pink pimple on the edge of one nostril.

"Sit down, Comrade. You're in charge of the Center Right Affair? Well, what about this plot?"

His voice was low and casual, as was his glance, which wandered around the little white sitting room. He had the air of someone getting on with a bit of unimportant business. The chandelier was burning, although it was broad daylight on the square outside, where an equestrian statue with a winged helmet was visible.

"All right. Get this case moving. You know the situation. Bring me a detailed report on Monday at four o'clock."

Zvereva bent forward, her eyes shining, happy to shake that flabby hand. "Very well, very well. It will be taken care of, Comrade."

She put on the uniform tunic which molded her figure and ran to the Commission. The great palace-lined square was immense at that hour of the morning. Every paving stone stood out with perfect sharpness like a piece of inlaid parquetry. Footsteps rang out. Their echo was strangely loud. A group of Communists, doubtless on their way to a house-by-house search, turned the corner. A sailor walked at the head, talking animatedly to a working girl in a white kerchief. Then came an old man in a sport coat, a cigarette dangling from his lips and a rifle slung over his shoulder. A couple of young men brought up the rear. Zvereva was struck by their apparent gaiety. Rosy hues spread across the sky above the huge gilt dome of St. Isaac's. A magnificent purity descended over the city.

The electric lights were nonetheless burning at Commission Headquarters. A few decrepit trucks, some motorcycles, and a black limousine were lined up at the entrance. Two soldiers passed Zvereva in the stairway; they were leading out a tearful old lady whose hair had come undone. At the end of a hall there was a mound of typewriters piled one on top of another. Some were upside down like huge crustaceans lying on their backs, showing the bizarre mechanism of their bellies. The odor of phenol floated in the air; a wounded man emerged from Room 25 and made his way toward the toilet, leaning on the wall for support. Through the window Zvereva noticed white coffins lined up in a courtyard. She opened the safe and took out File No. 42.

Almost no hard facts. The Central Commission didn't know what it was reporting.—A decentralized organization. A first-class double agent had failed to get beyond the lowest echelon. He only knew three men, who were as ignorant as he was—two ex-officers, a druggist, and their group leader, whom he thought it would be useless to arrest: he was too firm a character and wouldn't spill anything unless he were put to torture. Zvereva had suggested the latter method to Terentiev, who passed it on to the Commission: in vain, prejudice was too strong. —What else? At most two new pieces of information might be placed in File No. 42: the report of another informer who, on the say-so of his mistress, a prostitute, announced the presence in the city of a young officer recently arrived from the south where he had witnessed horrible executions of Red prisoners. The description of this officer was fairly precise. His name began with a D. A denunciation signed by "Johann Appolinarius Fuchs, artist loyal to the Revolution," gave details which agreed in every particular, obviously taken from the same source. "D: Damien, Daniel, David, Demid, Denis, Dimitri, Dosifei . . ."

Arkadi, consulted, smiled at the name of Fuchs. "Have the group we know about arrested tomorrow at the latest. I will sit in on the interrogations. Try to find this D., even though the information doesn't seem very solid. No lead should be neglected. Send his description to every reliable man on the House Committees, and get it out to the leaders of the house-by-house search patrols."

12

"It's the end. Kronstadt in flames. The regiments are going over to the enemy one after another. The city is living on hay. No anesthetics at the main military hospital! While you were busy talking about the society of the future, you have slipped to the very bottom of the pit. The soldiers don't want to fight any more, do you understand? *You* dream of self-sacrifice because you are the daughter of a bourgeois, raised on bourgeois idealism, on that stupid idealism we cultivate so well and which teaches you to turn around and strangle us with innocent eyes and clear consciences. . . . Get yourself sent to the front, you little fool; go tell those flea-bitten *mujiks*, those Ivans, those Timochkas, those Matveis who have been fighting for five years against the Germans, the Turks, the Bulgarians, the Austrians, the Czechoslovaks, the Poles, the English, the Serbians, the Rumanians, the Japanese, and against other Matveis, other Timochkas, other Ivans, conscripts just like themselves, go tell them they should go on living like this for another two years or ten years, without bread or shoes, in order to bring socialism to the world! And that when they have to dig a bullet out of Ivan's thigh they won't be able to put him to sleep for lack of chloroform! And that when winter returns he'll freeze like his brother froze last year. I've seen frozen corpses stacked like firewood! All Ivans, Timochkas, Matveis, fair or dark, with broad noses like young Tolstoys."

Xenia buckled her belt with clenched teeth. The sky was heavy with a cheerless light. At the back of the room under the icon (before which, when Xenia was absent, a little red lamp was kept burning) her mother pretended to sleep, lying on the couch, her face against the leather. Andrei Vassilievich continued his mono-

logue in a low voice; his words, muffled in his beard, sounded like
an incantation.

"Your Revolution is a corpse. There's nothing left to do but cart
it away."

Going out after eight in the evening without special permission
prohibited. Mandatory guard duty at the doors of dwellings. Mandatory labor. Mandatory surrender of all arms, even processional
ones (it would have been too easy to invoke processions), within
twenty-four hours under pain of death. Telegraphed order from the
President of the Revolutionary War Council prescribing the es-
tablishment of lists of relatives of former officers serving with the
Red Army, these families to be considered responsible for the loyalty of the officers. Arrest of hostages. Special surveillance of automobile and motorcycle traffic. House-by-house searches. Identity
checks. Arrest of suspects. Division of the city into internal defense
sectors. Mobilization of Communist battalions. Death penalty for
speculators. Death for spies. Death for traitors. Death for deserters.
Death for misappropriators of public funds. Death for spreaders of
false reports. Death.

"Andrei Vassilievich, they just posted a list of seventeen men
who were shot. I read Aaron Mironovich's name on it."

She saw Andrei Vassilievich's image reflected in the glass over
a large picture of a child (her portrait as a little girl). She wished
never to see it again, after having said these words. This trembling
bearded specter had dark holes in the place of eyes. His hands
clenched his collar like someone being asphyxiated; his necktie,
always correctly adjusted, was pulled to one side; he looked like
that same Aaron Mironovich whose features had been reflected so
many times in that same picture frame.

"Enough!" said Xenia sharply to herself in the stairway. The familiar image of a potbellied, bearded Jew with an unctuous smile
floated in front of her, unsubstantial and persistent. His convulsed
smile faded into a pool of blood. Xenia stopped in the gray stairway, her hand tightly clutching the banister. Her throat was
parched. She made a great effort to think coldly, clearly. We are in
the right. I want what must be. I will do what must be done. It was
a relief for her to add mentally: Whatever that may be and whatever the outcome.

It was two in the morning. In the ashy white street the forms of
sentinels appeared at intervals in doorways. A militia-woman paced

up and down at the corner, her rifle barrel planted straight against
her shoulder. Xenia felt hostile glances spying on her. These were
enemy houses. The faraway gasps of cannon vibrated almost imperceptibly in the cool air.

   . . . The Timochkas, the Matveis, the Ivans are perfectly right,
poor souls, not to want to fight any more. It is their Revolution that
we are making; it is to end war forever that we are fighting, that
their blood must still flow. They suffer, they want to live, they have
their eyes wide open and can't see what human necessity bows
them. We see for them, but the law is too hard, they rebel against
us, they flee. Their weakness turns against them. (Thus, in Leonid
Andreev's play, crowned Hunger, who reigns over the poor, pushes
the plebs to revolt, then betrays them and bows down to the rich,
for she is always in any case their servant.) The Ivans don't know
what history is. Nonetheless history pushes them forward, drags
them along, grinds them down, pulls them by the millions out of
their thatched huts to the sound of the tocsin, of mobilizations, piles
them into cattle cars, puts repeating rifles into their hands (hands
which guided wooden plows or turned over haystacks with slow
movements consecrated since the peopling of Eurasia), throws these
human masses against Europe in Prussia, against Asia in Armenia,
parades them through French port towns and scatters their bones
in Champagne, lines them up—Ivan, Matvei, Timochka—alongside
helmeted Senegalese, turbaned Sikhs, and Tommies with pipes in
their teeth, against methodical Germans whose leaders are all doc-
tors and who go into battle wearing piglike masks preceded by
waves of gas. . . . Who will save them if they don't save themselves? Who will guide them if not us? Tomorrow, if we are
defeated, they will become brutes again. They will give back the
land. They will be hanged, whipped, and mobilized. Newspapers
and schools will be founded to teach them that such is the eternal
law. They will be lined up, like mechanical soldiers, in the squares
of workers' cities, and when the red flags appear the Ivans will
shoot.—They will shoot at *us*, who are *them*.

✱

   The ranks were forming in front of the District Committee, a
princely little town house now stuffed full of files, typewriters,
machine guns, and armed men sleeping on straw mattresses. There

were jostling crowds around the secretaries' desks in rooms hung in
white silk dotted with cornflowers.—"The comrades from the Meyer
Factory, second company, in front of the church."—"Kostrov Factory and waterworks people across the street."—"Stack your arms,
at ease!" An astonishing calm reigned over the activity of this
anthill in the square.

The district commanders—a man in black leather, an old
woman who seemed radiant because of her halo of white hair, and
a stocky man in a jacket and cap with cartridge belts across his
chest—approached the special company. Men and women of all
ages stood there in formation. Most of them were poorly clothed. A
few soft felt hats. Caps pushed flat across the backs of heads.
Women workers in overcoats with kerchiefs tied around their
heads. A few pince-nez. Some detachable collars. An artist's mane.
Hands resting on rifles.

"Squad leaders fall out to the right."

Xenia followed the movement and found herself in a crowded
courtyard. Three gilded domes surmounted by finely wrought open-
work crosses—the cross victorious over the prostrate crescent—
stood out against the deepening blue of the sky. The stones had a
bright sheen. The crosses floated through a singular serenity. People's faces looked concerned; there was little talking. Everyone
signed and received his papers in the corridor. *Warrant: Instructions
for house-to-house searches. Descriptions (secret).*

"Give special attention to the dwellings of intellectuals."

"X., military man, aged 22–24, chestnut hair, medium build,
thick eyebrows, laughs easily, habit of folding his arms across his
chest, Muscovite accent, recently arrived from the south. Long scar
on outside of left wrist. First name begins with D."

A tall old workman with dirty linen, yellow skin, and some
wasting disease whispered into Xenia's ear:

"Seems like we'll get half a pound of bread and a herring. I
guess we'll develop a taste for these searches, eh?"

Kondrati appeared standing on a chair. His voice rang out in
the crystal crispness of the morning air as sharply as the three
crosses standing out against the sky above his head.

". . . disarm the enemy within. Order, discipline, firmness . . .
Our sailors are launching an assault on the Hill Fort at this very
moment. . . . Decisive days . . . The proletariat . . . We will hold
on, we will hold on; woe to those who . . ."

"Some of them are bums. In my squad yesterday one little guy swiped a gold watch from a lawyer's place. I had him searched. I smashed his face in, personally. You should have seen how he thanked me, afterward."

"And the watch."

"In the fund for the wounded. I don't give a damn for the bourgeois, you see."

"Remember," hammered Kondrati, "the thirty thousand who died in the Paris Commune! Remember the fifteen thousand who died in the Finnish Commune! Remember the three hundred who were hanged at Yamburg! Not one of us, not one . . ."

Xenia left, carrying bread and herring for her people. The squads were assembling on the square in an apparent disorder which was the birth of order. In hers, Xenia found a sailor from the *Vulture*, a tired woman worker of about thirty with hair gracefully arranged in a cluster behind at the back of her head, a sullen redheaded young soldier with a big mouth, a flat nose, and jutting brows whose name she asked and who answered "Matvei"; and two young workers from the Meyer Factory, both beardless, one with a deformed shoulder and a limp. This group went off through the empty streets. The sailor smoked in silence. The soldier carried his rifle by the strap, muzzle down; the strap was made of rope anyway. The woman worker said: "Four hours? We won't be finished before seven o'clock." She explained: "I'd like to be home in time to feed my husband. He's a non-Party member, but a good worker—what a life!"

∗

"This is the place," said Xenia. The sleeping house was not expecting them. A white cat with red markings dived into a cellar at their approach. In the sky, rosy shadows were warring with turquoise hues. A splendid day was rising over the city, the estuary, the sea, the forts, and the enemy columns on the march. A very old man stood guard at the door of this big house with windows dead behind drawn blinds. On this June morning he stood muffled in an ancient greatcoat which had turned green at the shoulders. His wizened face, elongated by a goatee, was half hidden in the fur collar.

"They should have left him in his mothballs," joked the worker with the limp.

Hands in his pockets, the privy councilor from apartment 26 waited to be spoken to. The smaller carnivores have that same watchful, sharp, hateful look when taken by surprise in front of their lairs.

"Come on, open up," ordered the *Vulture* sailor, "you know who I am."

"Kindly present your warrants," answered the privy councilor without emotion.

Xenia showed her paper. Seal of the Special Committee of Three. Valid for six persons. —"Good. Enter." When they had passed, the old man shuddered. Inside the courtyard, the squad divided up into three couples. Xenia took the soldier, Matvei, with her.

They knocked on doors among hostile shadows. They knocked at length, for the people were either sleeping or pretended to be asleep out of anxiety. At last bare feet ran toward them down the corridor. Fearful voices asked, "Who's there?" They answered imperiously, "Open up!" Iron bars and chains were lifted, bolts were pulled back. Keys grated, and they entered. The bad air inside caught in their throats after the vivifying crispness of the clear night. The relative misery or comfort of these dwellings was soon patent to these intruders—a sailor, a woman worker, a young hunchbacked man, Xenia. . . . Here, sleeping in a camp bed, lay a skeletal man of about fifty with a smooth skull of old copper. Huge unlaced shoes gaped up from under the bed; on the window sill a hotplate, a potted cactus, a vial of poison: a skull on the label. The man resembled that skull. "Who are you?" "Physician attached to Typhus Clinic No. 4." Papers in order. "Excuse us, citizen." "It's okay." At the head of his bed, a little icon, a very old Virgin with Child dressed in sculpted silver, painted by the first master miniaturists of Palekh. In the next rooms terrified women, a mother and a daughter with long tresses hanging over dressing gowns, trembled as they revealed their treasure: sixty pounds of potatoes in the bathtub. Then, in the living room, while their papers were being checked, the lymphatic daughter raised her blue-tinted arms to adjust her hair, and guarded her diamond-studded earrings which were lying on a shelf.

Matvei stood motionless among the rooms, curiously considering the unfamiliar objects. They paused for breath in a stairway that smelled of wine. A sepulchral silence hung behind the door they had just knocked at. All Matvei said was:

"Let's get this over with."

At around five o'clock in the morning they arrived at Professor Vadim Mikhailovich Lytaev's. Danil, smiling, arms folded across his chest, stood in front of a wide-open window interrogating Matvei, who was now weighted down with an old cavalry saber seized at the apartment of a paralytic old lady on the floor below:

"How's it going, little brother?"

At that instant Xenia, who was about to leave, remembered a phrase she had read or heard, a long while ago, long before the lassitude of these hours and the blue splendor of the sky in this window. An important phrase nonetheless, which characterized someone: "The habit of folding his arms across his chest." Who, then? Kondrati, perhaps. Xenia was struggling against a sort of intoxication resulting from nervous tension, tiredness, and a vague sense of physical well-being instilled by the more and more iridescent glare of the morning light as the sun rose higher in the sky. —Kondrati, his fresh complexion, his wheat-colored hair, his orator's mouth with its healthy teeth;—and the three svelte onion domes floating high above that tribune's head. He was unaware of them as he spoke, his hand outstretched; but the sky, deeper than any thought, and those brilliant crosses nonetheless hung over him, as necessary as his gesture, necessary in fact to his gesture, for there is no such thing as chance. We move through life without ever knowing all the riches, all the power, all the beauty, which lies around us.

"What a fine morning coming up," said Matvei in the dreamy voice of a prisoner. "It must be nice in the fields right now."

Danil let out a big jovial laugh. "You bet! Listen to those birds!" They heard them peeping, thousands of them, in the garden of the school next door. Xenia, too, listened for a moment. Then she briskly held her hand out to Danil—"Good-by, Comrade!"—nodded farewell to the Lytaevs, whom she glimpsed in the next room, a really nice old couple, and left.

Behind her, Maria Borissovna Lytaeva said:

"How nice she was, that little Communist. I felt reassured as soon as I saw her. Aren't you coming back to bed, Vadim?"

"No. This unexpected visit has done me good. And it's really morning already. My head is full of ideas, I'm going to write. Try to go back to sleep, Maria."

○

When the searches were completed Xenia decided to drop by at the Committee in order to prolong her walk through the city in the burgeoning light. New vistas opened before her at every street corner. A pair of crouching red lions spread their fiery gold wings along the entrance of a delicate bridge suspended by cables over a bend in the canal. Farther on, the green freshness of trees burst forth bathed in transparent shadows. The white columns of a little palace were mirrored in the canal, their outlines undisturbed by the shimmering water. A single white cloud floated in the sky of that water as if above the city.

When we are dead, thought Xenia, when everything is finished, perhaps a similar cloud will pass through a similar sky at this very spot. What eyes will see it reflected in this water, eyes that will have known neither war, nor famine, nor fear, nor anguish, nor night patrols, that will not have seen man strike down man? I can't even imagine it. I can see nothing of that future. I am like a man emerging from a cave. The light at the mouth is dazzling. He cannot see the brilliant landscape before him. I must learn. Perhaps I will be able to glimpse the world out there when I know enough. I will learn if I live.

But must I live? We must smash everything. Purify everything by fire. I saw fear trembling a little while ago in an old woman's eyes when I entered. I felt pity. I crushed my pity like someone crushing a worm into the earth after a rain. The highest love excludes pity. Make way for men, old woman; men are rising up! The workers are changing the world just as they demolish, build, forge, throw bridges across rivers. We will throw a bridge from one universe to the other. Over there: the black and yellow peoples, the brown peoples, the enslaved peoples . . .

Words no longer followed her thoughts in their ineffable flight. The shimmering crosses of the churches attracted her eyes. Old faith, we will break you too. We will take the Crucified One down off the cross. We want people to forget him. No more symbols of humiliation and suffering on the earth, no more blindness; knowledge, the clear eye of man, the master of himself and of things, rediscovering the universe afresh.

From the mouth of a pink street surged trucks, bristling with bayonets. They came bounding out, shaking the ground, jolting and pitching over the broken pavement, huge meteors made up of a human mass and a heavy tired-out machine fed on the filthiest oil. Each carried sixty broad chests washed by the sea air, sixty heads ready to burst open like futile pomegranates under a hail of shrapnel, sixty heads readier still to plunge forward, death and victory in their eyes, sixty rifles topped with glistening steel like cold rays of light, nine hundred cartridges belted across warm stomachs and male chests. The ribbons attached to their black sailors' berets danced around their heads. The silence continued to tremble long after these meteors had disappeared.

Xenia listened as the intense clamor of the passing masses of men and machines subsided within her. The same will that carried them off on their inevitable trajectory toward obstacles and dangers kept her walking, alone, her task completed. The same imperious soul coordinated every gesture, repressing weaknesses, stifling hesitations, reducing all forces to a common denominator, enlisting man in a sort of legion which was much more flexible and impassioned than any army. Stay at your post, do your job; we are multitudes animated by a single thought, which is the very law of history discovered by the surest science. We are accomplishing that which cannot not be accomplished. Still greater masses are behind us, whose dim consciousness we embody, who think, will, and act through us and who cannot act otherwise. If we go under, the laws which regulate the development of man will not be modified because of it; the same struggle will continue to set the same classes against each other; the same conquest will be prepared for tomorrow. The waves can take centuries to undermine a cliff. Anyone who understands the process of the slow movement of continents, although he cannot predict which particular effort of the waves will give the final shove to the rocks loosened by seepage, does not doubt that the cliff must crumble. Each of us, and you, too, Xenia, is only a droplet participating in the sweep of the waves; a droplet in which, before it dissolves, is reflected a whole vast strip of landscape, skies, rocks, ground swells, powdering spray, rainbows.

How clear it all is, when you think it through. I am glad to be a mere drop in the wave which is beating against old overturned stones here. I consent to everything. Here I am.

At the Committee, the stale smell of cigarette butts filled the messy rooms. The man on guard was sleeping, his rifle between his knees, seated on a step of the great marble staircase. Stuffed bears snickered on the landing. Ryjik, alone, was pacing back and forth in front of the windows, which were open onto the sun-filled garden. They saw the joy in each other's eyes.

"The fort has been retaken," said Ryjik.

And he opened his arms; he never knew how it happened, but he took her in his arms and their mouths met joyfully. Then he asked—in order to dissipate the growing embarrassment between them, the blush rising to the top of his head along with the desire to slake his thirst totally in that spring of joy:

"No suspects?"

"No," she said, "no."

Her childish brow wrinkled; her whole face screwed up in painful concentration. "Yet it seems to me . . . yes!" She fished the identification sheet out of her pocket. ". . . laughs easily, habit of folding his arms across his chest, Moscow accent, first name D. . . ." —"How could I have? . . . Ryjik, we must telephone right away."

13

"I can do without everything," Comrade Zvereva would say, in a voice full of unction, "except flowers. Don't laugh at me," she would add, "I have such a sad life!" The blue files were piling up on her little worktable between a vase full of azaleas, the telephone wired by direct line to the Special Commission, and a portrait of Rosa Luxembourg in the dark oval of an Empire frame: gold fillet and bows. Sometimes, friendly and familiar, she would telephone the director of the former imperial greenhouses: "You haven't forgotten all about me, Jacobsen? Yes, yes, my dear friend, send me some flowers tomorrow." Jacobsen, slack-faced, crippled with rheumatism, took his cane and headed for the desolate greenhouses. Only a small section was still kept up, and this with great difficulty: in winter he had to deprive himself of fire at night out of love for a few rare plants. In the damp warmth of a gallery defended with unsung heroism, he found the only man remaining at his post, silent Gavril, agile for his seventy years, who had created many masterpieces in his long life as a horticulturist; Gavril, who knew all the varieties of roses, whether they came from Bulgaria, Italy, California, Japan, or the Indies, and who had invented some new ones of his own. "Gavril Petrovich, *that woman,* you know who, is asking for more flowers." The two men considered each other for a moment with sadness. They alone had survived the disaster of the most beautiful greenhouses in the Empire, in Europe—perhaps in the world!—visited in 18—— by the Crown Prince of Japan, who was amazed to find an extremely rare family of chrysanthemums there. . . . They no longer, even in summer, crossed the threshold of the closed galleries, exposed to murderous winter, containing Indonesian ferns, Brazilian lianas, thin palm trees from Ceylon, dead

and still in the polar cold and still standing, tragic to look at like
the corpses of children. "Very well, I'll go over again," muttered
Gavril. "What must be, must be. Poor us." —"Poor us." At that moment Jacobsen noticed among the little red pots some tiny buds of a
tender feathery green, growing around a yellow grain. "What! You
were able to save them, Gavril!" Gavril's gnarled hand caressed the
little pot lovingly.—"It wasn't easy, Iakov Iakovich, but look how
well they're coming along." Heads bent, they contemplated the tiny
buds together. But the harsh breath of the outside world brought
them up short. "Iakov Iakovich, our fish are dying. . . ." Jacobsen
expected as much. "It's not possible!" —"They're dying of hunger,
Iakov Iakovich. They closed down the German's shop; seems he was
speculating. The aquariums in his window are full of little dead
angels. It breaks my heart! Yesterday I climbed every flight of stairs
in the Commissariat of Public Education. I waited four hours to get
in to see the member of the collegium himself. I told him like that,
right to his face: 'You've got to feed my fish. You nationalized them,
you've got to feed them. I'm an old proletarian myself, understand?
I'm telling you my scalares are dying already; my pantodons . . .'
He showed me the door, Iakov Iakovich, that's what things have
come to."

Jacobsen proposed:

"What if you spoke to *that woman* about the fish, Gavril Petrovich?"

Old Gavril trudged through the streets for a full hour bearing
four pots of nearly white hortensias which he carried on a plank
suspended across his chest by a thick strap around his neck. People
watched intrigued as the silk-paper-covered flowers went by. They
brought back memories of galas, weddings, saints' days, other times.
Where did they come from? For what happy people?

When Gavril arrived, Comrade Zvereva was in fact happy. A
note from headquarters informed her of the arrest of two of the
wanted suspects from File No. 42: X, first name Danil, discovered at
Professor Lytaev's with papers which were probably fake. "The Professor!" What a master stroke for her first big political investigation.
What long faces some of her colleagues would pull when they saw
her handling this case. She could hear those hypocrites congrat-
ulating her in advance, and she answered them, full of austere detachment: "For me, you see, there are neither big cases nor little

ones; there is only the service of the Party." That would shut their mouths, all those neophytes who think they're so great just because they're examining magistrates of the Commission. She would make her report to the President that very evening: "I got the case moving, as you requested. . . ."

Gavril found her in an excellent mood. Evidence of a sumptuous luncheon—Gruyère cheese, salami, real tea—arrested the old horticulturist's eye. So they were true, eh, the stories they told about special rations set aside for those people. After all, they are masters.

"Gavril, you're my best friend in the world. But your hortensias are simply marvelous! And how is Jacobsen?"

That bitch would never think of offering him a cup of tea, though she might be able to guess he would be thirsty in such hot weather! And for months he had drunk nothing but slops of an ersatz tea made of carrot scrapings. Poor us. Gavril sighed. The countless wrinkles of his face seemed begrimed with damp earth. His eyes shone out of it like the dark elytra of tiny coleoptera.

"I have a big, big favor to ask you, Comrade Zvereva, and for Iakov Iakovich, too. . . ."

(. . . You have to know how to say no. We've not sentimentalists. Duty first. Say no politely but irrevocably. Don't go thinking that I'm easily moved just because I'm a woman.) Comrade Zvereva's winning smile melted slowly into an expression of austere distance.

"Go on, my friend."

Gavril felt a sudden chill. He felt like grabbing his cap off the chair where he had thrown it and beating it without saying another word; but it was a matter of life or death for his scalares and his pantodons.

"Well, my fish are dying . . ."

A warm smile illuminated *that woman's* glance.

"Really? Your fish? And what can I do about it, Gavril, my good fellow?"

The seeds, the flour, the earth, the worms that were needed existed in the German's shop, which was closed. The German was in flight or in jail. The shop under seals. All that stuff was going bad. And the fish were dying. Zvereva, delighted, noted the details: the address, the department. "Well, I'm going to save those fish of yours. This very day the German's store will be opened for you, Gavril, my good fellow. . . . I'll get on the telephone this instant, you'll see!"

She loved to insist on imperative orders or requests over the telephone. There are, you see, people who are born organizers: those who know how to make others listen to them, to handle the levers of authority, to give precise instructions. There are also other types, anarchic and romantic temperaments, whom, all things considered, the Party needs only for a time.

Gavril walked home with a high heart. Trucks bristling with shimmering blades jolted along huge bouquets of black torsos with glowing heads. Hands waving their berets on the points of bayonets: dark tulips borne by straight stems of heavenly blue. Hair flying, mouths clamoring, eyes flashing quick bright glances. A chorus of powerful voices mingled with the motors' roar:

> *"We will unfurl*
> *Labor's red flag*
> *Across the world!"*

Gavril realized that these men were returning from a victory. For the first time, his joy was in unison with theirs. He crossed himself, for it was in front of the Kazan Cathedral. "Let it live, let it live after all, our starving Republic . . . when the war is over, the greenhouse will come back to life. Maybe we'll see it, Iakov Iakovich. . . ."

❋

Kirk lived in Room 218, Frumkin in 311, Arkadi and Ryjik way upstairs. The President of the Executive occupied the best suite on the second floor. A nest of cables ran through a hole in the wall next to his door. Kirk seemed out of place among these more or less interchangeable men. Kirk loved only revolution, energy and, secretly, outlaws. He had come to know them on the highways of America when, himself a tramp, he had bummed his way across the States from north to south and from south to north, following the seasons, spending winter in Florida, spring in Manhattan, and the summer on the shores of the Great Lakes. You slept at a buddy's, in the woods, in gardens, in barns, in jail (some of them aren't bad). The loggers' strikes, in those days with one-eyed Big Bill. That was nice work! He still bore their scar, over his right eyebrow, which was thick and brown, split in half by a pink line. His big round eyes took easy possession of things, jostled people, and forced their reserves with careless, good-natured ease. "What will they do with me after they drain me dry?" he asked, propping both booted feet on a chair.

His wide mouth split into the constrained smile of a man who has made a bad deal and knows it.

"What will become of me when there are new uniforms for the whole army?"

Zvereva was admiring herself, something she always did. She never failed, when at home, to sit so that the big looking glass returned her slightest gestures bathed in silvered, mirrored purity. Hysterical, thought Kirk. A whore's temperament; and that snout, like an evil nun for a Maeterlinck play . . .

She answered: "You will serve the Party, Kirk."

(. . . Not for long, though. Semi-anarchist, not a real proletarian, a lumpen-proletarian rather, newcomer to the Party, ready to criticize everything, calling the leaders' portraits "little holy pictures," casting a chill over the table of the Executive by declaring the President's last speech "horribly boring, and completely wrong as far as the figures are concerned!" —She could easily see herself interrogating him one fine day, with him accused of having a hand in some stupid adventure of the third revolution. . . .)

(. . . Orthodox, of course, to the tips of her nails. Flat on her belly before the President's slippers;—but tomorrow, if Kondrati's clique takes over, pfui, it'll be "Comrade Kondrati this" and "Comrade Kondrati that" every time she opens her mouth. Where does she get her flowers? I'd bet she gets a special ration at the Executive with cocoa, hazel nuts, and condensed milk taken from my wounded. . . .)

"Some people," said Kirk, "make revolution like getting kicked in the ass. The garrison on the Obruchev front, hearing what happened at the Hill Fort, arrests the Communists, debates for hours whether or not to shoot them, and locks them in a cellar, so as not to compromise themselves, while waiting for orders from the Whites. We take the hill. I telephone the sons of bitches: 'Ten minutes to surrender, no conditions.' They pull the Communists right out of the bunker and stick their officers in. What shits!"

He spat a heavy glob at the blue carpet.

"By the way, Comrade Zvereva, the Committee has directed me to work with you on the Center Left case."

Zvereva took this blow without batting an eye. She knew you had to swallow many affronts before being able to inflict them in turn.

*

The arrest of the five Center Right confederates accidentally brought about that of a stranger known only as Nikita, who refused to answer when interrogated. He was kept closely watched in a special cell at the Commission. He was obviously a man of exceptional endurance. Kirk observed him through the peephole, stretched out on the floor, eyes closed, with his arms behind his head. "He won't talk." But, sewn inside the collar of Danil's tunic, they had found a scrap of paper covered with ciphers. Bobrov got it directly from Zvereva. Bobrov was a little man of about sixty, neat, meticulous, dressed exactly as if he continued to report to his office in the Ministry of the Interior every morning. He lived with a Lutheran matron and two ugly little girls supervised by a German nanny. The fall of the Empire and of two governments had changed none of his habits except the route of his morning walk, during which, in winter, he wore the same fur-lined coat and, in summer, the same black, silk-lined, lightweight overcoat and well-brushed, pearl-gray derby hat, perhaps the only one still to be seen in this city. Witty and apathetic, he occasionally smiled at himself along the way; his white sideburns, hanging down on both sides over a China silk necktie on which gleamed two tiny riding crops, in gold, gave him the air of an old roué in an operetta. He had long preserved this "Parisian" elegance, which he had picked up in Vienna around the high-class bordellos. For a little distraction, as a supremely disinterested spectator, he would read the first lines of wall posters along the way: *Mobilization of Workers; Obligatory Registration of non-workers called upon to Execute Public Works; Peace to Religionists!* When a poor devil in an engineer's cap walked next to him for a moment in the street murmuring: "Ruined civil servant, twenty-four years of irreproachable service, two sons killed at the front, four months in jail; I haven't a stone to rest my head on, like the Son of Man!" —Bobrov stopped, slowly opened his billfold and pulled out a wad of rubles, the price of a half pound of bread, which he considered to be a Christian alms. He gave only to extremely clean beggars you could imagine coming from the former bourgeoisie. Under the dictatorship of the proletariat, as under the *ancien régime*, secret directives kept him free of all cares. The furnishings and arrangement of his office, in a building next to the Commission, had remained nearly identical for twenty-five years; he had personally seen to it that nothing changed when they were moved from the quarters of the Political Police. They consisted of colored cartons, pigeonholes, file cabinets, card indexes, dossiers, alphabetical records, charts, complicated number systems, thick annotated volumes, literary classics, *Lives of the Saints,* sheaves of newspapers, photograph albums. The *Secret Codebook* of the British Navy neighbored with Gogol's *Dead Souls.* There were several useful editions of Lermontov's great poem, *The Demon.* Bobrov deciphered the most carefully coded texts. He possessed the key to all the locks of the mind. He divined miraculously, reading "I. 81. V." at the head of a cryptic rune that the key was to be found in Volume I of the 1873 edition of Lermontov's *Works,* on page 81, in verse V of *Mtsiri.* He knew the favorite first names of terrorists, the false initials most frequently adopted by people whose names began with a K, the codes preferred by lovers, madmen, assassins, blackmailers, secret agents, great idealists, world organizers. They would bring him a postcard with the following lines, written under a view of Lake Constance (white sails, lake hotel, mountains): "Splendid weather, wish you were here, Linette"; he would translate: "Check received, sum insufficient, Agent 121"—and it would be true, he could have demonstrated it by the yachts on the lake, the number of windows in the hotel, the indentations of the mountains, and those of the postage stamp. Under the *ancien régime* the chiefs of the police used to introduce him into the residences of important ministers for highly special services; they would personally act as go-betweens with the procuresses attached to the imperial family to get them to reserve him skinny, depraved little girls, which he would painfully deflower every month, on the twenty-fifth, from five to eight o'clock. Under the new regime, special couriers brought him envelopes sealed with five red stamps; Comrade Zvereva herself made sure that he received a food ration more opulent than that of the members of the Executive Committee and which could only be compared with that of the President. If the memory mechanism of his brain had not been reduced to a purely technical function, he might remember having deciphered the cryptograms of the illegal Central Committee exiled in Cracow for the police in the old days. Now he deciphered those of the former ministers exiled in Danzig for the Central Committee. Their systems were not profoundly different.

It took him little time to penetrate the meaning of the following line: 21.2. 2. M. B. G. 4. H.O. 6.2.4. 60. 2. R. 11. A. 4. M. 9. 10? 4. 2. R. 9. S., which should be read: "Kaas, 8 Avenue of the English, reliable." Moreover, he remained convinced that the encoder had made two mistakes. What he feared most in the subterfuge of others were irrational complications due to error. Before subsiding into an astonishing imbecility which bordered on genius each day without ever attaining it, he had dreamed of writing a *Treatise on Error,* where stupidity and the multitude would be revealed as the only invincible enemies of the human mind.

Thanks to him, Kaas, who was strangely like him, was arrested. An unlucky businessman, the files of the former Political Police presented Kaas as a double agent. As soon as he was seated face to face with Zvereva—Kirk studied him from profile—his tremulous voice reeled off a prepared speech:

"Citizeness. The admirable vigilance of the Special Commission has convinced me of the justice of the great cause of the proletariat. I confess that I have conspired, but as a loyal adversary of the dictatorship and through a profound mistake. I no longer have any desire but to rectify it by lavishing the proofs of my repentance on you. I was to have occupied an eminent position in the government of the counterrevolution; I am ready to reveal to you all the threads of the conspiracy, beginning with the names of the thirty members of the League of Resurrection."

The sickly creature was playing his last card with an intelligence sharpened by so much fear that he seemed on the point of collapse. He kept his hands beneath the edge of the table so that their trembling should not be seen. But his whole head was trembling.

"I know your organization quite well. You are Kirk of the Public Health Commission, the Economic Council, the Metals Management, the Special Supply Commission of the Seventh Army . . ."

"Citizen," said Zvereva, "that's quite enough. The Commission will find ways to put your sincerity to the test."

14

"Imagine Zvereva face to face with Kaas, a puppet in a goatee, impaled by a phenomenal attack of gas, stinking of treachery—of every imaginable kind of treachery—like a dung heap smells of shit! And behind them the chubby shadow of Bobrov, self-satisfied and satisfied with us. We pay him well. If we get hanged tomorrow, there'll always be someone around to pay *him* well. The idea that Zvereva would probably be hanged from the same limb as us is hardly any consolation, you see. I don't give a damn about bad company beyond the grave; I know that the gallows has a way of making quite suitable and perfectly historical heroes out of rather insipid spawn. But that female, under any regime, will simper in front of mirrors, have her own car, and put caviar on her white bread when the stokers down at the Great Works are getting their special milk ration only on paper. I myself am ashamed to speak in front of them, understand, when I see their bony faces and sunken cheeks. Me, I eat at the Executive table, and then I go, make them pretty speeches. 'Gotta hold on, comrades! Hold on, hold on, hold on!' They know it as well as I do; but *they're* starving.

"I tell you, these Zverevas will make themselves indispensable under any regime until man is completely transformed. We're having a good crack at it, it's true, assuming we win. Can't you hear her purring, one well-shod pad on the running board of the Renault: 'The speaker from the Central Committee spoke so well! These four hours went by like nothing. Comrade Artem has a great future ahead of him.' Have you noticed the flair she has for always being on the stronger side? She's never been seen voting with a minority. When difficult questions come up, she isn't seen. But as soon as a more or less stable majority has been formed, you discover that she was in it the day before, that she's one of the oldest of the old, well within the line. When I think about it, I feel like spitting: the same effect as the lousy plugs we used to chew on board the ships of the Blue Star Line. . . .

"You see, old pal, those types infallibly land on their feet. If the Republic holds out, Zvereva will bury us all. We'll end up tripping over some insoluble problem and falling on our faces, assuming nothing worse happens to us. We'll say stupid things, we'll do them! You are capable of getting yourself killed to set an example. Me, I'm capable of telling the most authoritative speaker of the most influential majority of the C.C. to go take a walk. I'm capable of voting alone, *against!* —So that, in the long run, the common lot will fall to us, it's in the nature of things, it's even good. Our type is necessary: we are not negligible. But your Zvereva will outlive us, old pal.

"Bobrov too. Or his young. Kaas, perhaps. For after all they can't shoot that bastard now. He's needed. He's precious. He has become a factor in our interior defense system. The best workers' battalion can be sacrificed in a fourth-rate operation at the front; Kaas cannot be sacrificed! All these vermin whom we are using, whom we are making work for us, who are necessary to us, who carry out a million tasks with us, necessary ones, I know—won't they end up by devouring us? Aren't they gnawing away at us as they obey us?"

Kirk stopped talking. He had before him the dry face of Osipov, who was leaning back against a tree trunk. In the distance the countryside was emerging from the mist.

"Devoured or not," said Osipov, "the important thing is to make ourselves useful: to do what must be done. In that sense, no one can harm us. It is already an achievement that these vermin, the Bobrovs and the Kaases, are in our service. Their natural destination is basically to serve the wealthy classes. Today they serve us. Afterward, we will try to rid the earth of them; first, let's win. All weapons are good. Don't take me literally: all weapons are not good at every moment. All means do not lead to an end; an end demands specific means; the choice of weapons depends on the objective of the struggle.

"Zvereva gets on your nerves too much, my friend. She's not that important. Somebody's got to compile dossiers, go through denunciations, interrogate people like Kaas. Who should it be, if not her? Beings of another stamp choose different tasks. We don't have many men. We are a few handfuls. Millions of men, the most mightiest masses ever, are behind us—and there are only a few of us, mortal men, susceptible to influenza, susceptible to fits of conscience (much more serious, that, watch out for that one, no laugh). The Party is becoming contaminated, you say? It's inevitable. Remember the entrance of the anarchists into Ekaterinoslav? They were carrying a big black banner with these words: 'No Poison Is More Deadly Than Power!' That's pretty true. It's also a poison we need. They've used it against us from time immemorial without knowing it's a poison. We know it. We want to suppress it. That's progress. Speaking of the anarchists, behind the banner rode Popov on horseback surrounded by his bodyguards, a dictator like any other, a dictator in spite of himself, missing all the cues in his part.

". . . In the long run we'll see. Not you or me, of course: the working class. I'm optimistic for the long run; as for the present, I have my doubts, I'm even rather pessimistic. I'm not sure we'll survive the winter. But I'm certain we have time, a half century, a century perhaps. The mechanism of the world is exposed; it's easy to see how it turns. That is our strength. We are pushing in the right direction. Perhaps we'll be swept away; that direction will be no less the right one for it.

"Our mistake is in thinking too much about ourselves. We say *I, me,* every minute. We have that mythology of the ego in our blood; it's not our fault. We haven't yet discovered what the new place of the individual is in the age of masses. A place which is certainly very great and almost insignificant at the same time. On this point of the front, from these trees to that cottage over there, we three, you, that fellow sleeping there, and I, can make the two hundred men dug into this trench hold out a few more days—and those few days could be enough to save the future and this point of the front could be just the place where the victory is decided. Thus, we are great, we count. I think of the places where I have held on in my life: in '05 at the underground printshop, in '07 in the combat organization, then in prison; then on the Irtysh where we were only five, in exile, with Sonia, who was losing her mind—we had to hold onto our reason and our strength, not lose all hope. That was the hardest. Sometimes on summer nights we would go out onto the steppe and light bonfires, which were strange holidays for us; I used to jump across the fire with the secret desire of falling into an abyss. I kept my reason, you see, it still works. Then—the Great Works in '17, what days those were, brother! Prodigious days! Where were you? At La Chaux-de-Fonds? Where's that? Oh. —Then the inner-party struggles, for or against the insurrection; there are times when everything depends on voting a resolution in a committee, for if you let the occasion slip by, the enemy won't let it slip by. And since committees depend on organizations, everything depends on each of us, you have to fight for every conviction. . . ."

"That, Osipov, is why there are good organizers who juggle with votes and imagine they are doing a great service to the Revolution when they have put together a fake majority on paper. . . ."

"Let 'em do it. You can fool one man, one hundred men, for a time with lots of printed paper, and by blinding yourself; you can't fool classes locked in struggle; you can't force events like forcing a door. You see that each of us serves, that he is great. We, too, are great. I can't see your face in the dark, but I know you're not smiling. Yes, you're great too, in spite of your hemorrhoids, your doubts, your pointless rebellions. You hold down your corner, you'll hold on as long as you can. . . . But, my friend, if we weren't here, this morning, the Committee would have sent others who would have done the job just as well. If I hadn't been the prison librarian, the politicals would have found another, wouldn't they? We are not necessary. Think of those who have died: Sacha, Bokin, Vlassov, Gregor, Fugger, just among us, just in one year. Yet we're holding on without them. Among the men sleeping there, several are per-haps nearly as valuable as we and could replace us. And if the working class lacks men, if, when the time comes, the man who is needed doesn't spring up at the head of the masses, understand! in-carnating the millions who are hesitating, feeling their way, keeping quiet, if that man doesn't spring up, if those men don't spring up in the necessary numbers, it's because the proletariat is not ripe enough to conquer. Let them go back down into the mines that belong to others, then, let them take up the harness again, let them get drunk, let them fight for others. We'll either be dead or we'll continue. We'll know tomorrow or the day after if things must go that way.

"Kirk, the question is that of the proletariat. As it goes, so goes the Party, so goes the Revolution. We're pretty solid for the mo-ment. I have confidence in the workers' grip."

"Me, not so much. If you called a real vote in the Great Works without checking on who raised his hand, without them feeling we have the upper hand and the resolve to pass over, what a mess that would be!"

"It's therefore necessary not to call them to vote. They know that they're hungry and that they're worn out. We know that the best among them have left. We are at a time when votes are no longer appropriate. Do people vote on a ship which is taking water? They pump. And the captain must crack the head of any man who cries: 'Every man for himself' because he wants to live, too, like everyone else. The Great Works just gave another forty-eight men for the special mobilization in the south. That's more than a vote."

"We eat better, that's true. Sometimes I feel ashamed of it, too. What do you want? It's the law of armies that those in command eat better and are less exposed. Our privileges are rather modest, admit it. Do you have a spare pair of boots? . . ."

"No, but Zvereva, with her car glued to her ass, has a closetful. The Zverevas were behind the decision to divide up the stock of the Select among the female activists holding the highest positions, dammit . . . while half the female workers at the Wahl Factory go barefoot. . . ."

"I tell you our commanders are still worth more than all the others. A question of human material. After all, let the pigs get fat off the backs of the working class, just as long as it holds out. The working class has more time than the pigs. It will deal with them quite easily when it has conquered half of Europe—which we need to keep from suffocating. . . ."

Someone stirred in the half darkness where the shapes of trees were beginning to take form. Wisps of fog marked the bed of a river.

"And that guy sleeping there," said Kirk, "another faceless, mindless man, an X, Y, or Z, the type who gets lost on a street corner. You should have heard him the other night; Goldin asks him: 'After all, what does it mean to make revolution?' And our Antonov answers, without a moment's reflection, like an automat returning your money when it's out of candy: 'Carrying out the tasks assigned to me by the Central Committee.' Ha! That's what it's all about for him: memos, instructions—'order for Comrade Antonov to nationalize the Titov Manufacturing Co.,' without which he'd probably walk right by the place without even thinking of it! What if those orders became stupid? What if somebody got hold of the great seal of the C.C. and no one noticed it right away?"

"Your suppositions go far. I'm glad the battalion can't hear you. You yourself would arrest the man who formulated them out loud in front of these men. Antonov isn't wrong. He's a voice. He doesn't know how to think by himself, but he knows very well what the Party thinks. He's worth more than Goldin, who thinks too much, thinks only by himself, gets high on his thoughts and tries to comprehend, rediscover, and reinvent the world because he's a poet, because in the end he's nothing but a romantic muddlehead and rather dangerous to have around when safety depends on order, method, and cohesion. The cohesion of a class, even in error, can be stronger than the isolation of a few men, even with the highest degree of clean-sightedness—provided the error is not one of principle. History has not forged nor men invented a better instrument for struggle than organization; you know that as well as I do. But there is no weapon that doesn't get rusty, no instrument that doesn't bend one fine day. Whoever lives will see. If the proletariat has sufficient resources within itself—and it will have them, I will answer for that, as soon as we're on the banks of the Rhone instead of being on the banks of the Narova—neither the cream-skimmers nor the adventurers will be able to outflank it. If it's not yet able to pick up the world on its shoulders and carry it away, is it by disdaining its best weapon that it will be saved from a Bonaparte? And then, old friend, the Bonapartes did their job well for the bourgeoisie. Who knows if the proletariat won't need them?"

Osipov seemed to take fright at what he had just said. His hand, a shadowy hand, moved through the opaque air seeking a dead branch which was hanging and snatched it. The branch snapped. Then he went on, with a calm little laugh.

"One should not, even in thought, cling to rotten branches. I would only accept a Bonaparte in the firm intention of shooting him one day in recompense for services rendered. Because . . ."

They both remained silent for a long moment. A vast rural landscape, bristling in the near distance with anti-cavalry spikes, was taking shape around them.

"Because," Kirk finished, "we haven't come to start the same old story all over again. Or it wouldn't be worth it, no. . . . It would be better, for the Revolution, to perish and leave a clear memory. Blood? Blood is never completely lost."

Osipov was practically shouting, even though his voice remained low:

"No, no, no, no! Get rid of those ideas, comrade. They've been beaten into us with billy clubs, I mean with defeats. No beautiful suicides, above all! They were invented by literary folk, who don't commit suicide either beautifully or any other way. A philosophy of the whipped. No more of that! We're here to stay, by God! to hold on, to work, to organize, to use everything to the limit including dung. Dung is also necessary. And then if we break our necks it will be something great, I grant you that, on the condition that we strike our pose before history with epic grandeur, et cetera. To live, that's what the flesh-and-blood working class wants, that great collection of hungry people behind us whom we seem to be leading and who in reality are pushing us forward. Whenever there is a choice—give up or continue—they continue. Let's continue, let's get into the habit of living."

❀

All of a sudden the sun came up. A rooster crowed. The white clouds opened up, magical waves of gold rippled through the pale grass. Osipov was sitting at the foot of an apple tree. Kirk picked a green apple off the ground, took a bite, and tossed it into the distance with a side-arm twist learned in his twelfth year.

"Right!" he cried. "Let's get into the habit of living. A good habit, brother. Ah!"

He felt like frolicking around the green like a colt. Osipov was smoking, eyes off in the distance, lips half open in a smile which gave the tortured oval of his face an almost childlike appearance. Had it not been for their uniforms and the undefinable weight of the years somewhere behind their thoughts, the two men might have thought they had returned momentarily to that borderland between childhood and adolescence where life is new with each morning.

"I think," murmured Osipov, "that I'm about to be appointed to the Special Commission."

"My friend, I've got a beautiful case for you. A whole factory stolen—land, buildings, machinery, twenty-seven workers (none of them worth much of anything), including an assistant manager! I just discovered the key to the mystery, imagine. It wasn't nationalized, because it wasn't under any administration. Just disappeared, what!"

The sleeper lying near them shook his covers. Antonov's ruddy square face, planted with rust-colored whiskers, appeared illuminated by a warm blue gaze. A hundred yards away, men were coming out of the trenches. A famished-looking soldier dressed in a shapeless tunic, whose walk seemed lopsided under the weight of the heavy wooden-holstered pistol slapping his hip, made his way toward the three envoys from the Committees. An oversized cap covered his narrow head. He might have been only a kid, even though he was as wrinkled as certain old peasants. "There's Parfenov, the battalion commissar," said Antonov. "A little guy from the Wildborg Print Shop." Osipov brought him up to date in a few words: "No relief for a week." (He should have said two.) "No clothes or ammunition for four or five days. Can you hold?" The ageless little man had a slightly crooked, pointed nose, hollow cheeks in which the bones seemed about to push through, and parchmentlike lips. "We'll try," he said.

In front of the men, who were assembled on the edge of the trench—140 dirty faces—it was Antonov who spoke first:

"Comrades! The Third International . . ."

Osipov sat at the orator's feet, taking notes: "2nd Battalion, 140 men: workers, 8; employees, 4; peasants, 103; undetermined social origin, 15; returned or recaptured deserters, 40. Commander and four men gone over to the enemy at our arrival. At the first meeting, shouts of 'Down with the Civil War! Boots!' Lacking clothing: all. Rations: all. Boots: 27. Low on ammunition." He hesitated when he got to the question: *Morale?* Above these 140 heads which had surged out of the earth and were still contaminated with the earth, Antonov was throwing out clear phrases, hammering each one home three times in order to implant them in every brain. The Allies relentlessly set on killing us, all-powerful and yet powerless; Germany, where your brothers in Hamburg—the largest port in the world—are winning victories; the world on the point of exploding in a 1917 vastly more powerful than ours; peace, which we are proclaiming, peace which we will impose through victories and insurrections in every country; the land, which we are holding onto, the land, which the generals and their train of bankers, landlords, and traitors are trying to take back from us ("but all these hungry dogs will break their teeth . . ."). The sharp words, cracked out, sometimes like pistol shots, sometimes like a flag snapping in a strong breeze. Pent-up angers changed into a cold exaltation: friendly snickers and stubborn glances were drawn like magnets toward the orator. As soon as he had stopped speaking, someone who had been waiting for that moment cried out:

"We have no underwear, we're being eaten alive by lice! So!"

And another voice rose up:

"Is it true that the Soviets of Hungary have fallen?"

"They have fallen," barked Antonov. "Long live the Soviets of Hungary! Hurrah!"

His two fists and his throat tossed out the cheer for the vanquished like the news of a victory. Scattered voices echoed him, sought each other for a moment, and finally came together:

"Hurrah!"

It was the very rumbling of the earth from which these 140 soldiers had emerged. Most of them didn't know there was a Hungary. They thought they had heard of an unknown victory. They were greeting, in this, the hope of deliverance. They're right, thought Osipov. And under the heading, *Morale,* he noted: "Satisfactory."

15

The last fine days of autumn passed, swept off by such a wave of events—all fatal, for they all either brought death, kept it at bay, warded it off, or insured it—that their very succession became a kind of calm. Thus, under a constant clatter of machinery, there arises a kind of silence in which man listens to his heart beating, smokes his pipe, and dreams perhaps of his wife in a waking sleep.

The harvest had been brought in in the countryside. It was being hidden. Tillers who had fought under the red flags with their old scythes buried their wheat and sounded the tocsin at the approach of the Anti-Christ. Others, their sons, with red stars sewn into their old Imperial Army caps, arrived to search their barns. Workers, fearful of being stoned, harangued village elders. They were men caught between hunger, hatred, discipline, faith, war, fraternity, typhus, and ignorance. Around the edges of this bizarre continent, like feverish ant heaps, moved armies which melted into bands and bands which swelled until they became armies. In the land of blues and yellows—peaks and sand dunes—a non-com transformed into an ataman had railroad workers thrown into locomotive boilers alive. But, a son of the people, he gave the daughters of his old generals to his exasperated soldiers. From armored trains the blind eyes of cannon peered out over steppes once overrun by Gengis Khan's archers. Gentlemen with immaculate bodies daubed with cologne, wearing perfectly laundered underwear under the uniforms of the Great Powers, gentlemen who didn't know what it meant to sleep in the open with lice at every hair and a good chance of getting killed the next day, watched the Russian earth pass by through the windows of Pullman cars. Their orders were dated Washington, London, Paris, Rome, Tokyo. They had Gillette razor blades, enough money to pay the old Chinaman of Irbit for the favors of his most heavily rouged, courtesans, enough prestige, wealth, arrogance, gleaming shirt cuffs, to humiliate and reduce to oriental obedience an entourage of penniless, ignorant, intriguing ministers watched over by camarillas of officers, and generals, admirals, supreme governors who still exercised their profession with a modicum of competence; they had ideas as polished and well rounded as their fingernails: ideas about barbarism and civilization, about the Jewish plague, about Slavic anarchy, German gold, Lenin's treason, Trotsky-Bronstein's madness, about the inevitable triumph of order, which means being able to go to one's club or café and to take hot showers.

They brought along cases of canned goods: Amieux sardines, tuna, beef from La Plata, Prince's herring; and when they decamped at the sound of rifle fire coming too close, in an auto jolting with the breath of panic, under the flag of the Geneva Cross, some yellow partisans, smelling of animal hide and soured goat's milk, picked up these mysterious boxes lacking any sort of openings and turned them around and around in their shepherds' fingers. Their wrinkled olive masks were fixed in terror and joy before the mirrors in the railway car, explaining to each other that it was really them, there, straight ahead—me, you, the one laughing there, that bearded fellow, that's me!—delighted with self-discovery, for they were men of the desert and had never seen themselves.

And then one of them, face to face with his double, laughing at his double, became seized, without knowing it of course, by metaphysical vertigo. I don't want my double to laugh when I laugh! I don't want my double to exist! I want this mysterious spell to be over! He grabbed a stump of a rifle by the barrel and, raising his hand against himself, smashed the mirror with the butt, which was made of a gnarled root. For these were desert men who battled victoriously against the most terrible spells. That man was the equal of Prometheus. He dared to break the chain. He would have dared to steal fire; unless he was merely a brute whose muscles and whose anger harbored elemental forces. It matters little.

They found the sardines tasteless.

What does matter is that the station at Voskresenskoe (Resurrection) has been taken. Telegraph the Revolutionary War Council: a plasterer, a mechanic, a schoolteacher, bone tired and fast asleep in a round tent of motley skins. Telegraph the Kremlin that com-

munication has been re-established. One more chance for safety
(lighter, it is true, than a grain of sand from the plains) has been
added to your side of the scale, Republic. One chance? Voskresenskoe has been taken in Turkestan; Rozhdestvenskoe (Nativity) has
been lost in Siberia. It matters little. Announce it to the press:
"Progress in Turkestan. The valiant partisan army of Ali Mirza . . ."

"Ali Mirza? You know very well he went over to the enemy."

"It matters little. Put: "The Revolutionary Council of the Army
of Red Partisans . . .'"

Deacon Epiphany sings expiatory masses at Rozhdestvenskoe
(Nativity). A meeting at Voskresenskoe (Resurrection) decides that
the station will henceforth bear the name Proletarskaya, which most
of the inhabitants take for a woman's name. Where is Ali Mirza's
head at this moment? Let's keep this unique photo for the Museum
of the Revolution. Magnificent fanlike beard, glasses: you'd think
he was a Western businessman, circa 1890. But those machine-gun
ribbons around his body, that tall turban of the sect, those Tommy's
puttees around spindly legs? Where did he come from? It seems
that the turncoat's head, tongue cut out, was stuck on the end of a
pike in front of the tent of a Cossack ex-non-com (a fine waltzer)
and left until there was nothing but a skull. The drunken ataman
maintained that day that it was the skull of the Bolshevik, Lukin. A
legend grew up that Ali Mirza was still alive. A pseudo Ali Mirza
roamed the desert on horseback and slept in the ruins of Tam-
burlane's forts.

It matters little.

Various bands, all of them liberators, roamed the roads through
the high grasses of the plains in carts weighted down with machine
guns and phonographs. Drunken cavalry raided little Jewish towns
with old white houses leaning low to the ground; not low enough.
And all the women, all the girls down to runny-nosed eight-year-
olds, had venereal diseases afterward. An American woman doctor
went methodically through these horrified hamlets. She promised
medicine and gathered statistics. The medicine never arrived, the
statistics were false. Other pitiless cavalries pursued the first. Four
hundred bands (but why four hundred? it matters little), thirty
armies which were no more than stronger, more organized bands,
two great armies, the Siberian and the Southern, commanded by
real headquarters staffs provided with real artillery, accompanied
by authentic journalists and profiteers, all fell upon the Republic at

bay, blowing the *mort* with every horn, sounding the charge with every bugle. Two lesser armies in ambush were getting ready to leap at our throats. Tanks were arriving from Cherbourg, rifles from London, grenades from Barmen, money from the whole universe. It was the end, the end, the end.

. . . This city at the very limit of this encircled land, this city, prey to famine, at the very limit of the end, lives on with the carelessness of the living! The days are in some respects alike for all the living; days most heavily loaded with glory or death (that will be seen later on, or not, for these are still ideas of the living) are the same as others; and as long as there is sour cabbage soup, as long as the sky is mild, as a streetcar comes by anyway (Hey, they're running today!), as long as you're in a good mood, it's life as usual. "Quite fortunately," philosophized my friend Kukin, "man has no antennae to feel his neighbor's pain." This peaceful harmonica player was in his own way a useful citizen. He was the first in his neighborhood, in the center of town, to have the idea of raising rabbits and chickens in a room; he sold, cheaply, bunnies and chicks born in a great parqueted salon with cupids hanging from the cornices. —Quite fortunately, the wild shrieks of sacked cities were not heard any more than the insignificant little noise of skulls being cracked, production-line style, with rifle butts or mallets, to save ammunition, after the enemy's victories or ours. "If the human species," Kukin went on, "could achieve a collective sensibility for five minutes, it would either be cured or drop dead on the spot." I could never figure out if Kukin was a moron, a crackpot, or something much better. *Harmonica Lessons from 2:00 to 6:00 P.M.; Reduced Prices for Soldiers and Workers.* This notice helped him live. "I've always been a socialist," he declared, "for socialism promises a great future for music. And the harmonica . . ." It was he who told me the news of the events of the twelfth, which he knew twenty-four hours before the Party cadres and three days before the newspapers admitted it.

Conspiracies were hatched, unraveled—spider webs knocked down with ax blows—and irresistibly re-formed. The committees sat. In the name of public safety, Committees who wanted to end the dictatorship of the Committees, in coalition with others who wanted to set up their own, blew up an important Committee in the middle of a session. Our old weapons—fulminate, bomb throwers' valor, tyrannicidal faith—were absurdly turned against us. Committees having fraternal relations with the fratricidal committees repudiated them. This tragedy occurred under red banners. Intestinal typhus was worse. What were people eating? "Tell me"—Kukin shook his head—"how does the Fourth Category live with their twenty-five grams of black bread a day? If it weren't anti-socialistic, I would establish a philanthropic rabbit hutch to feed the last surviving capitalists. . . ."

Sixty-seven spies, counterrevolutionaries, foreign agents, ex-financiers, ex-high officers, monarchistic professors, vice-den operators, and unlucky adventurers were executed following the anarchist bomb attack. It filled two whole columns of 8-point type in the barely legible newspapers plastered on the walls. The southern front was going badly. Sixty-seven? The price in blood of a skirmish. Who among those sixty-seven would have spared us? We knew all too well what was happening on the other side of the front while *Te Deums* were being sung in churches and educated people were voting motions on the return to democracy. We could all see our own names, in anticipation, on similar lists. Did the statesmen of the great nations ever think of the number of this people's children condemned to be carried to the cemetery when they ordered the blockade? The mildest of these ministers (all good family men) had more innocent blood on his neat, downy hands than old Herod, whose villainy had been highly exaggerated and who missed Jesus besides.

"With that kind of logic you could execute anyone. Nobody counts any more. Even the numbers don't count any more."

"You're catching on. It's about time. That's just the kind of logic we need. Today is the twelfth. The question is whether or not the city will hold until the twenty-fifth. If not, every kind of logic will be bad, for *they*'ll be killing *us*. If it does hold, any logic is good. Right now, in order to prevail, we must survive, my friend."

"Well, we don't have much chance of that."

"Do you think so? Then sixty-seven isn't enough. Let's avenge ourselves in advance: that may increase our chances. And then: what else would you propose?"

The last dabs of sunlight on the great dome of St. Isaac's vanished and the summer ended. The beautiful broad river—along whose granite banks the rotting hulks were fast being stripped bare —carried the bacilli of cholera, dysentery, and typhus down to the sea. This river was deserted. The absence of boats created great voids between the bridges. The golden spires rising above the Fortress, the Admiralty, the Old Castle, like old-fashioned court swords, turned pale in a whitening sky. In the Summer Garden the statues grieved over dead leaves; the grill at the gate imprisoned exiled goddesses. The straight streets were a little emptier than last spring, with their pavements collapsing here and there, their flaking façades more leprous, an even greater number of broken panes and shopwindows abandoned as if in the wake of unspeakable bankruptcies followed by auction sales and abscondings. . . . All of that had no importance. Sokolova was dancing at the Little Theater in *The Green Butterfly*. They paid her in flour. The great tenor Svechin was about to make a new appearance at the Opera in *The Barber of Seville*. Tamara Stolberg was playing Vincent d'Indy in the great hall of the Conservatory. You could get up to twenty pounds of potatoes in the market for a worn-out suit of evening clothes; but they wouldn't give you more than five lumps of sugar for a brand-new silk hat. "There's only the circus still buying them," explained the old-clothes dealer. And the circus was about to close: some of the stable boys were contemplating devouring its emaciated lions, who were fed on bread crumbs. Leather sofas attained fantastic prices, for obscure master cobblers had discovered ingenious ways of making boots, high button shoes, and even little high-heeled slippers for elegant ladies out of them. . . .

The Superior Council for Regional Economy was working on reorganizing the management of industry: hence conflicts with the Commissariats of Transportation, Supplies, and Agriculture; friction with the Central Council, intervention by the Regional Committee of Trade Unions, underhanded opposition from the Executive of the city, displeasure in the Central Committee of the Party, deliberations in the Council of People's Commissars, a proposal to convoke a special conference of economic institutions, exasperated complaints from the High Commission for Army Supply, which . . .

Fleischman made a special trip back from the front to draft, in haste, with the Kondrati faction, new theses on the vertical organization of industrial sectors (*cf*. the Resolution of the Seventh Congress of Soviets, Title IV of the Resolution of the Eighth Party Congress, Circular No. 4827 of the Central Committee;—don't forget to quote Engels' letter to Sorge of March 1894) when the event of the twelfth took place.

Rain began to fall on four thousand men. They came out of

their crumbling trenches and crossed over waterlogged fields to seek
shelter in immensely dismal villages. These starving Ivans, Matveis,
and Timochkas saw nothing but absurd horizons all around them.
Winter was coming, snow in the trenches, frozen hands and feet,
hungry stomachs and the poor neglected earth! Virgin Mother of
God, Savior Christ, Revolution, leaders of the world proletariat!
When will all this end? Or is there no one who cares about us, who
understands us, no one to cry to that we have had enough? Some
escaped into the woods. That's where the Greens were. How to in-
vent a new color, no longer be White or Red or Green, no longer
fight against anyone! We have taken the land, declared peace,
shown we have had enough, but it's never, ever over. Some escaped
to the other side of the front, because there was more to eat, it
seemed. Enough of Jewish commissars with nothing but exhorta-
tions to resist on their lips! Let them get killed all by themselves
defending their Kremlin! The people of the soil have had enough,
do you understand? (But they would return, for on the other side of
the front it was worse. . . .)

The White Army, wearing British uniforms, attacked on the
twelfth. The 6th Division melted before it. A few men were killed
fighting desperately in the wet hay, under the rigid gestures of already bare branches. They searched among their corpses for the
dirty Jew in order to spit into his filthy hirsute face. Thus died the
author of a *Goethe's Philosophy*. This time it was really the end; the
city would be taken inside of a week.

It was raining dully. The Professor and Valerian found the situation satisfactory. Kaas was informing. "But," said the Professor,
"the clever bastard is only informing on his own people. He hasn't
fingered any of ours. He's holding onto his trump card, for our
chances are improving. Seems he is even recognizing that old fool,
Lytaev, in my place! . . ."

"Rather imprudent of him," observed Valerian.

"Kaas is never imprudent. He has the excuse of having barely
met me; and I can hear from here, acting scrupulously: 'I think I
recognize him, but I wouldn't be able to testify that . . .' Nothing is
more convincing."

In the comfort of his large, untidy study, under Repin's portrait
of Tolstoy, they were preparing proscription lists. "Kaas's is the
most complete." The Professor resembled a rain-washed Polynesian
idol made of varicolored painted wood. His heavy square chin fell

over an academic necktie—although he was not a professor, naturally. The yellow corneas of his eyes glowed, streaked by tiny red veins. High, bare skull tinted green under the lampshade, bony nose like a triangle stuck in the middle of a petrified face. Several of the sixty-seven touched him rather closely: that's why his absent stare resembled the passive glaze found in glass eyes.

The city couldn't know anything; but an indefinable anxiety wandered through it, pouring out of the rain, carried in by deserters, hawked in the lines by women who had read a manifesto from the Whites. "The hour of punishment approaches. . . ." It was on one of those days that Zvereva made a surprising discovery. The suspect Danil Petrovich Gof was in reality named Nicholas (Kolia) Orestovich Azin and he had been arrested under that name a year before. The object of a clearly unfavorable investigation, he had been released at the time on an order signed by Arkadi, through inexplicable negligence. The suspect's sister, closely watched, saw no one outside of a few aged relatives of no interest for File No. 42; but she did get visits from a military man of extremely Georgian appearance. She went on an excursion with him to Detskoe Selo Park. She was dressed all in white under a big straw bonnet with a pink ribbon; he was rowing. The informer had rented a rowboat and succeeded in passing by this couple several times. He thought he had recognized an influential personage from the Special Commission itself. . . . At this point Zvereva felt overwhelmed by an even greater happiness than that of the love-struck girl in her lover's boat. The precious Kaas revealed that he had long known about an affair between a member of the Commission and a young woman of the upper middle class and had thought of taking advantage of it one day.

The river rolled toward the sea in dull, glaucous green masses. Driving rain poured down on the city out of a dirty white sky. Water streamed through barren fields, coastal moors, forests of pines, and bare birches. Across mud-soaked fields and rough, shapeless roads streams of gray men stampeded toward the city pursued by columns drunk with unhoped-for victory. The new President of the Special Commission got the latest dispatches from the front at three o'clock. The situation was getting desperate. There was a knock at the door. It must be Arkadi. It was.

"What's the news?" he asked, seeing the blue ribbons of telegrams on the table.

"Bad," said Osipov without raising his head.

Arkadi shrugged his shoulders. Fresh troops or the city is lost. But why was Osipov hiding his face? Arkadi waited. He was never afraid. Yet when at last he saw Osipov raise his pale forehead—that blank, weary face, incredibly sad—he felt a vague premonition of some terrible trouble.

"What have you done, old brother?" Osipov said heavily at last.

The words wrenched out of him like blocks of clayey earth breaking loose from the sides of trenches ruined by rain.

"What?"

Osipov rose, anguished.

"What? What? Do you know Olga Orestovna Azin?"

"Yes."

"Did you have her brother released in February?"

They got to the bottom of things immediately, and that bottom was deep as an abyss.

"Well," said Osipov, "I have to arrest you."

"You don't have any doubts about me, I hope."

"I don't have doubts about you, but what can I do?"

Osipov added, nearly whispering, as if to excuse himself:

"The warrant was countersigned by Terentiev."

Him or another . . .

A dull, painful silence made the room grow larger. The ticktock of the clock on the mantel—Cupid and Psyche—wore out seconds void of all content. Arkadi looked through the window at the fine rain streaking an unforgettable yellow façade with thread-lines, broken, yet infinite. And, speaking aloud, as if in a dream, he said something stupid:

"Dirty weather. We ought to have that façade repainted in blue."

"What have you done, my poor old friend, what have you done!" muttered Osipov, perhaps out loud, perhaps to himself. They shook hands.

16

It is admirable and inexplicable the way bad news gets transmitted in prisons, besieged cities, and countries with censorship. In civil war times inhabitants are able to discern in the usual atmosphere of a city the indefinable signs of its doom. The authorities of the moment may very well post announcements that the situation is improving; the inhabitant knows that evacuation will begin tomorrow. He guesses that the first horsemen of the new terror will be seen the day after tomorrow in the withering silence of deserted streets—people with flowers will run ahead of the buglers. . . . Houses will be searched. . . . Suspects with blood at the corner of their lips will move off like automatons flanked by strange-looking infantrymen with huge black sheepskin headgear . . . et cetera. The people of Kiev have known eleven occupations. The people here go about scenting their fear or their anticipation. For our fear is made of others' hope; our hope is woven of their fear. City adrift. The foreign papers, smuggled in and passed from hand to hand with the greatest secrecy (your life depends on it), are saying—according to a dispatch from Stockholm—that this city has been taken. Another dispatch rectifies: "From our special correspondent: the National Army plans to enter in three days." (You read it, madam! The shoemakers will be back in their shops, the banks will reopen, praise God!) The Whites have occupied the old imperial residences, twenty miles away. They have tanks. . . . The price of bread triples at the clandestine market place jammed by two thousand people. Of what value is the paper currency of a revolution about to receive the *coup de grâce?*

Time for action; retreat is no longer possible. A puffy old archivist, having survived for months on frozen potatoes fried in

castor oil, slowly forces open the drawers of the mahogany secretary of the presidency of the Senate, a beautiful piece of furniture
from Emperor Paul's period, but it must be done! His heart beats
like a great bell. The time for daring came so simply. Tomorrow
perhaps these archives will burn, yet the autograph letters of the
great *provocateur* must be saved. He carries them against his skinny
chest, and his halting step in the street is more joyful than if by
some miracle he was twenty again and had delirious love letters to
read over at night. He stifles a silent laugh on his pinched lips. A fatigue party of ex-bourgeois guarded by two women soldiers in short
skirts is digging trenches in front of Trinity Bridge. The archivist
contemplates their slow, probably useless labor for a moment:
women in unfashionable coats clumsily push wheelbarrows full of
wooden paving blocks; the men don't seem to be in bad humor.
"Let them take the city now, what do I care?"

They're stealing the supplies from the Commune, they're even
selling non-existent supplies. Who'll be here tomorrow? Money to
escape, money to hide oneself, money to buy papers, money to betray, money to enjoy and get rich. Procuresses, whose telephone
numbers are passed along discreetly, offer you charming ballet
dancers. A grand duke's favorite? A sentimental one who clings? Or
do you prefer a kinky one? Scattered around the egalitarian city
subsist invisible seraglios where you can enjoy life forgetful of discipline, of assemblies, of the Revolution itself, provided you have
jewels. And what else is there to do but take them, when you find
jewels? Expropriated antiques dealers, who are probably nothing
but looters, offer you precious miniatures: they will always keep
their value, they're easy to hide, easy to carry. You slip over the
border one night, a little suitcase in your hand—guard your little
suitcase well in the dark woods!—and you're *rich!* Ah! Smugglers
who are perhaps nothing but double agents of the Special Commission will guide you into Finland (or into an ambush) for a few
thousand rubles. But where to hide the jewels? Think about it
carefully. In the heel of your boot? Too well known. A good new
one: in the buttons of your overcoat. Under the matches in a match-
box you pretend not to care about. In your anus, as convicts do
it. . . . Men in black leather, like us, standing their turn of guard
duty in the offices of the Executive, sell the supplies of the Commune, and even carloads of foodstuffs that have already been stolen.
The thick face of a greedy peasant ill improved by years spent in

the storerooms of battleships smiles over the miniatures: Paul I
(Kalmuk nose, red-rimmed eyes, and three-cornered hat), a mar-
quess with a bluish complexion, Napoleon. And if the city holds?
Take the kinky one or the sentimental one? The face flushes,
transfixed by a sudden flash of hot blood. Both, Devil take me, I'm a
male, what! and I've a fortune here. . . . Five o'clock. It's time for
dinner at the table of the Executive—the only one where you get a
succulent soup of cured horse meat. Then reports to the President—
"State of food supply?" "Bad. Gromov, this can't continue. . . ."
Gromov is nothing but zeal, frank explanation, and careless proletarian devotion. "Transportation. Those stinking railroad workers
only think about their bellies; all speculators!" "Still, propose something; after all, Gromov!" "I propose requisitions in the market
places. Let's go there army-style." (We will take back from the
market places, to the sound of militiamen firing shots into the air
and the panic of terrified women, the flour and rice sold yesterday
to Andrei Vassilievich for two sprays of diamonds.)

The upper floors of the vast Institute are already empty. On the
ground floor a throng reminiscent of days of uprising gloomily or-
ganizes itself. Are the offices growing empty due to the mobilization
or due to flight? The President hasn't the slightest idea. His step is
listless. He walks down the straight corridor with his hands in his
pockets, like a gentleman emerging from a small café. The doors of
the former girls' dormitories are numbered: No. 82 Party Committee, No. 84 Cadres Assignment Bureau, No. 86 Press, No. 88 Office
of the International. The President enters this last one. In a dark,
bare antechamber made out of deal partitions two young kids, page
boys, are having a wrestling match, stifling their laughter for fear of
being heard by the terrible secretary, who is correcting proofs of a
message to the G.C.P. on the split of the Bremen group. They freeze
on the spot at the apparition of the President. But his big unkempt
head wears a vague smile. The boys suddenly grow bold: "We don't
have any more pants or shoes, look, comrade! Sign us a voucher,
comrade!" Hot dog, he's gonna sign the voucher! "Ask at the secre-
tariat." The President said it! Behind him the kids dance a silent jig:
we'll have shoes!

Spacious white room. The President dictates to the stenographer, a pale blonde. "Workers of the world! . . ." This evening
the wireless will broadcast—*to all! to all! to all!*—the final appeal of
the Northern Commune. In the last analysis we have nothing left

but that voice with which to oppose the squadron blockading the
harbor and which, tomorrow, will disembark flat-helmeted battalions. "British soldiers and sailors, workers and peasants, will you
forget that we are your brothers?" The President paces from one
corner of the room to the other, emphasizing the rhythm of his sentences. The stenographer steals a glance at him as, searching for his
words in front of the window, he runs his hand through his rebellious hair. She is thinking that it's always the same thing, that he
has a handsome face, that she's going to miss the distribution of
herring at the sub-secretariat for Latin countries, that in case of an
evacuation he will surely take her along in the presidential railroad
car. . . .

*

The headquarters of a division moves into one of the railroad
stations. The line of combat is edging into the outer suburbs. The
lines of resistance and retreat for interior defense follow the con-
tours of the canals. Certain intersections will be well defended. The
survivors will retire along the river at the risk of being cut off
twice. . . . Then, dynamite and fire will reign. Kondrati states
calmly:

"We'll blow up the bridges. We'll blow up the factories. We'll
blow up the Executive, the Special Commission, the old ministries.
We'll set fire to the warehouses in the harbor. We'll turn the city
into a volcano. That's my solution."

The President would prefer a different one. His big, bluish
chubby head is glued to the telephone. His muffled voice tirelessly
transmits the bad news four hundred miles away to the very heart
of the Republic. No food supplies, no reinforcements. Enemy
progressing irresistibly. Tanks. Yes, tanks. Troops demoralized, not
very reliable. Conspiracies inside the city. We risk being taken in
the rear. The troops on the northern front will give way at the first
push; let's have no illusions about it. The British fleet . . . That's
what I'm saying: untenable. Evacuation, yes. Avoid useless massacres, save the live strength of the proletariat. . . .

*

The full membership of the Special Commission was sitting, in
accordance with the statutes, to judge the case of Arkadi. Fleisch-

man, nominated to replace the accused, would then report on the situation at the front. Twelve heads in the small oak-paneled meeting room. Osipov presided. The case presented itself with irreparable simplicity.

Zvereva's report, stated in terms of an apparent extreme moderation, ended with a veiled supposition of corruption. Nothing proved that Olga Orestovna Azin had not obtained the release of other individuals besides her brother and had not been paid by interested parties. An ambiguous passage in a deposition by Kaas reinforced this hypothesis. (This odious report had made Osipov decide to withdraw File No. 41 from Comrade Zvereva in order to give it over to Kirk; but some people saw this as an arbitrary measure; the President's coterie, in private conversations which "somehow" got reported to the Central Committee, censured "this singular manifestation of comradeship. . . .")

Maria Pavlovna, sent to Moscow in order to submit the dossier to the big chief, had found herself in the presence of a bony man so overworked that he looked like an old, careworn recluse. His thin shoulders stuck out under his green tunic. He was all nerves, concentrated movement, reserve, reticence, silence. Sharp profile, sharp pointed beard, sharp eyes whose absent stare transfixed his interlocutor inexorably, perhaps on account of its limpidity tempered by inner tension. Nothing on his desk but a great, massive inkwell made of rare stones from the Urals of the color of flayed flesh veined with blue violet, presented by the proletariat of Ekaterinburg, "executioners of the last autocrat, to the inflexible Sword-Bearer of the Revolution, our great and dear——" No ink, naturally, in the beautiful closed inkwell, for the big chief signed his decrees with a fountain pen, a gift from the Quaker journalist, Mr. Pupkins. Maps of the front. Under the life-sized portrait of Karl Marx, between two windows, a bizarre panoply: masses of weapons made of huge nail-studded roots; gnarled clubs hanging at the ends of hunks of rope; mutilated rifles with sawed-off barrels and amputated stocks; a sort of deformed cannon—a metal tube inserted in a tree trunk; and, on a square of Bristol board a typed inscription: "Liquidation of the Tarasov Gang—Tambov district, February 1919."

The chief opened the file. Zvereva's report. The interrogations of Olga Orestovna Azin and Arkadi Arkadievich Ismailov (Arkadi was given his full name, which distanced him even further). The statements of the two defendants corresponded so closely that it appeared they had carefully agreed on everything in advance. The accused woman declared having been convinced of her brother's innocence at the time. Arkadi had believed her. A month later she became his mistress. On this last point, it had been difficult to drag precise details out of her. A secret denunciation emphasized the fact that the investigation, arbitrarily removed from the hands of Comrade Zvereva, an irreproachable collaborator, had been turned over to a former syndicalist, Kirk. "A dirty business," said the big chief. "I ought to go there . . ."

The door opened quietly. Someone brought in a red envelope. The chief turned his limpid eyes on Maria Pavlovna and asked:

"Generally speaking, isn't your Commission too corrupt?"

The sudden start of the severe old woman, whom he had known for twenty years, having corresponded with her when she lived in Paris, on Rue de la Glacière, and he was residing in West Kanskoe, in the Altai Mountains, on the Chinese border, made him add quickly:

"Don't take offense, Maria Pavlovna. You know yourself how quickly people get demoralized, especially the young ones. Now: decide this matter yourself; I rely on you. I'll come later on. . . ."

This proof of confidence constituted perhaps the worst way of deciding; for at that time the suspicious shadow of the chief dominated the Special Commission.

Another complication: a scandal was brewing. The President, speaking before a big assembly of the Party, had permitted himself an allusion to the germs of corruption discovered in the redoubtable Special Commission itself. "We will purge the organs of the terror pitilessly," he had cried in an oratorical flourish. "The sword of the proletariat must be clean." The audience had applauded for a long time.

Arkadi belonged to the Kondrati group. The whole group felt threatened through him. They would turn the President's outburst of demagoguery against him, no one having the right to divulge a case which had not yet been judged by the Party or by the Special Commission—but the sacrifice of Arkadi seemed imperative so that the coterie would not be smeared on account of his mistake.

Finally, the case of Zolin, although completely different, was vexingly present in everyone's mind. This low-echelon agent of the Special Commission, who had made himself counterfeit seals in order to obtain foodstuffs for vouchers which he wrote out himself, had been shot with no discussion.

Article XV of the Internal Regulations was as precise as a guillotine blade. The debate was short, punctuated by long embarrassed pauses. Maria Pavlovna, the only member of the Central Committee present, said in a neutral voice:

"I propose the application of Article XV."

Osipov put it to a voice vote:

"Ivanov?"

"For."

"Feldman?"

"For."

"Ognev?"

"For."

Fleischman, the first of the Kondrati group, voted "for." When Terentiev's turn to vote came, he took the floor. For a few moments only his big red face, his curling lips, and his low forehead were in the light. His porcelain eyes, of indeterminate hue, were rolling in every direction; his big round hands, as red as his face, made a few broken gestures, as if stammering.

"There's nothing here but a whole lot of fuss over a woman. Arkadi's clean. We have few men of his caliber. He's worth more than I am, I tell you, a hundred times more! I tell you we can't shoot him. I'm an ignorant man, see. Look at my big paws, look how I sign my name. . . ."

He grabbed a pencil, made the motion of writing his name. He was looking around the room for some support, but the eleven faces were mute. Osipov, his cheek resting in his hand, was listening sadly. Terentiev, blushing, stammered.

"I believe in him. The Revolution can't simply take a person's word, I know. We have to offer our heads, it's true, because we are without mercy. But I can't! I tell you we can't . . ."

He fell silent.

"Have you finished?" Osipov asked softly. "You're voting against it?"

Kirk looked avidly at Terentiev. Six votes remained; this could be the decisive ballot. Terentiev's face was flushed, his head bowed. The veins stood out on his neck, his two ugly hands were lying flat on the green cloth. He was struggling with himself, his back against an invisible wall.

"No," he said, choked, "I vote 'for.'"

Kirk threw in "against" with a kind of fury. Too late; he was the only one. Osipov, the last, articulated distinctly:

"Me, 'for.' By eleven votes against one the application of Article XV passes."

Late that night Kirk went and knocked at the door of Room 130 in the House of Soviets. Osipov, dragged out of bed in his shirt, barefoot, with his old riding breeches hanging loose around his skinny hips, greeted him anxiously.

"Well?"

"Well, nothing. You know, brother, we're committing a crime."

"A crime?" Osipov tossed back at him. "Because one of us got hit this time around? Don't you understand that one must pay with one's blood for the right to be pitiless? Do you by any chance imagine that we won't all end up like that?

"I would have saved him if I could have. But you saw what happened, there was nothing left to do but share the responsibility. You're a Don Quixote, with your lone horseman's ways. Maybe that amuses you, but it serves no useful purpose.

"And then listen, this whole affair no longer has any importance. No more than your death or mine would have this week. You've come at a good time, for I'm completely exhausted. Go wake up Gricha in the guardroom, take my motorcycle, and have yourself driven over to Smolny. Six hundred men have arrived from Schlüsselburg. They have to be housed, fed, armed, and whipped into a fighting force. Work fast."

17

The offices are at work as usual. That is to say, they are going through the motions of working. There are people waiting on lines in the streets. Special assembly at the factory. Special meeting in the district. Telephones. The city awaits the event gathering somewhere above it, in unknown regions, ready to pounce on its huge prey. Woe unto the vanquished! A young pregnant woman—for maternity disarms suspicion—and an old white-haired woman are preparing false papers for the underground organization which will carry on the activity of the Party tomorrow, in the lost city; they don't know that they have already been sold out to the enemy; that their addresses are known; that the false foreign passports they are buying are doubly false. . . . Regiments are gloomily preparing for a supreme battle, pregnant with a horrible every-man-for-himself. The Special Party battalions, billeted around the Committees, are grumbling that nothing is being prepared for the evacuation; that the leaders will have trains and cars for their getaway while the poor slobs will play martyr. The workers, in the factories, are demanding flour and pilfering pieces of metal, tools, fence boards, sheet metal, ropes, cables. . . . Clouds heavy with rain bring rumors of betrayals, arson, defeats, executions. The Cossacks have pillaged the palace of Gatchina. The great writer, Kuprin, has gone over to the enemy. "They're hanging every last Jew, every last Communist!" At the end of school, in a schoolyard spotted with mud puddles, Rachel and Sarah, who look as if they had been born under a palm tree on the edge of a biblical desert, suddenly find themselves surrounded by kids.

"Yids! Yids! They're gonna disembowel you soon!"

"Children too?" inquires blond-haired Madeleine.

"All of them! All of them."

The little Jewish girls go off hand in hand, and already the future terror surrounds them with a strange void.

"What's 'disembowel'?" Rachel asks her big sister. But the big sister, who feels like crying, quickens her pace. "Shut up, you never understand anything."

What makes you think the city can hold out when the whole Republic is going to crumble? Experts have studied the problem of transportation, the problem of food supply, the problem of the war, the problem of epidemics. They conclude that it would take a miracle. That's their way of telling the Supreme Council for Defense: "You're bankrupt!" They withdraw, very dignified, veiling their prophets' arrogance. One knows that the wear on the railroad line will become fatal in less than three months. The other that the big cities will be condemned to die of hunger within the same lapse of time. It's mathematical. The third that the minimum program for munitions production is perfectly unrealizable. The fourth announces the spread of epidemics. Their files contain all the temperature charts of the Revolution. This fever curve is deadly. History can't be forced. Production cannot be organized by terror, don't you see, with one of the most backward populations on earth! They barely refrain from passing sentence out of deference for the men of energy who have embarked on this formidable adventure, who are lost, but whose least errors will be studied for a long time to come. How to explain these men? That's really the problem of problems. There is fear in that deference; irony, too; perhaps even regret.

The experts have left. Two men face each other in the middle of the Supreme Council, which in fact resembles, with its long faces and its papers covered with specious figures, the board of directors of a firm which is losing money at a terrific rate. Liabilities: the White Terror in Budapest, the defeat of Hamburg; the silence of Berlin, the silence of Paris, the hesitation of Jean Longuet, the loss of Orel, the threat to Tula. Liabilities: the fact that we were nothing yesterday, that we are coming out of poverty, out of the shadows, out of perpetual defeat. Assets: the dispatches from Italy, the strikes in Turin, the exploits of the partisans in the Siberian *taiga*, the rivalry between Washington and Tokyo, the articles of Serrati and of Pierre Brizon. Assets: the knowledge, the will, the blood of the workers. Another asset: the terrible liability of a civilization which carries the wound of war in its side. Through propaganda, the eleven thousand people murdered by the White Terror in Finland are converted to assets. . . .

At this moment, in the midst of the masses' labor and silence, the debate is summed up in the heads of two men. They are the two whose tiresome effigies are seen everywhere: in people's homes, in offices, in clubs, in the papers, in the display windows of flunky photographers contending for the honor of having shot the negative, at the doors of public buildings. On one occasion these two men, in a good mood after a great success in the nationalization of the coal mines exchanged the following ironical words about this iconography:

"I say, what a glut of portraits. Don't you think they've gone a bit far?"

"The bad side of popularity, my friend. Whipped up by opportunists and morons."

Both men were sarcastic, but in different ways: one was jovial, with a high, bare forehead, high cheekbones, a prominent nose, a wisp of russet beard, and a great air of health, simplicity, and sly intelligence. He laughed often, which made him squint, and then his half-closed eyes were full of green sparks. In those moments he displayed a huge wrinkled forehead, a big mouth, and a jovial expression which revealed to the observer the features of an Asiatic mingled with those of a European. The other man, a Jew, with prominent lips whose great fold at times revealed an eagle's powerful ugliness, had a glance of penetrating intelligence, the carriage of a leader of men, an inner certainty which nearsighted people might confuse with old-fashioned pride, and a rather deceptive Mephistophelean mask in his laughter—for this man retained the capacity for joy of an adolescent for whom all of life is waiting to be conquered. They laughed at their own portraits.

"So long as we live long enough to stop them from being printed," said the one.

"Let's hope we live long enough not to be beatified," said the other.

They knew that you can't turn the world around without leaning on the oldest rocks.

The fate of the city is being decided between them. —What is a city, even that one! The southern front is more important. Here's where we have to hold on: keep the Tula arsenal, the central capital, the keys to the Volga and the Urals, the heartland of the Revo-

lution. Gain more time, even by giving up territory. Concentrate
our forces. Nothing will be lost after this very hard blow. We can
evacuate the city, since the situation is becoming untenable. The
enemy won't be able to feed it. It will be a brand of discord between the Whites and their allies. . . . —Already one of these men,
the one characterized by the greatest prudence in the execution of a
design conceived with the greatest daring, is preparing to gather
new weapons out of an accepted defeat.

The other man leans toward solutions of energy. The best
defense is offense. Two hundred thousand proletarians, even exhausted ones, ought to be able to hold out against an army ten
times less numerous bringing them the yoke. Two hundred thousand proletarians can be an amorphous mass doomed to slavery or a
host on the march toward some great victory or a horrible defeat,
an invincible, inexorable force stronger than traditional armies, itself capable of giving birth to impassioned armies. An obscure consciousness transforms submissive mobs into rebellious mobs; a clear
consciousness awakens the mass to organization and later brings
forth armies. All that is needed is a human ferment.

The argument for resistance prevails. The chief of the army
shakes his black mane. A flash of mockery veils the look of preoccupation in his pince-nez eyeglasses. The fold of his mouth relaxes.

"I'll send in the Bashkirs!"

The laughter of the two men disconcerts the Council for a
moment. The idea of turning this cavalry of the steppes on Helsingfors in case Finland starts to move is a brainstorm! (Whether the
Bashkirs are worth anything under fire is another question. . . .) It
will make the ink flow by the gallon in the West. Not bad. Manipu-
lating the enemy's press is an advantage.

"By ensnaring it in its own stupidity, the effect is certain."

"I'll catch it through its own stupidity, exoticism, and funk."

❋

Gray battalions streamed out through the streets of the suburbs. Three thousand silent heads arrayed under the thick white
columns of the Tauride Palace listened to Trotsky intoning, like an
anathema, the threat of revolution. Tomorrow this threat would
reach the land of white lakes and pensive forests; by degrees it
would penetrate, an evil shadow, into the pretty cottages of a

blond, fair-skinned people, proud of its cleanliness, of its well-being, of its daughters (who practice rowing, and read Knut Hamsun), of being the best-policed people on the globe and of having drowned its Commune in blood.

"The road that leads from Helsingfors to this city also leads from this city to Helsingfors!"

Three thousand pairs of hands applaud, for this is reversing the odds, turning a peril into a strength. The man who raises his hand in order to strike a blow feels stronger than the one who raises his hand to ward one off.

"We were silent, bourgeoisie of Finland, when you sold your country to the foreigner. We were silent when your aviators bombed us. We were silent when you massacred our brothers. The cup is full!"

Yes, full. Everyone felt it in that dark furnace where hazy silhouettes were fired with new anger.

"Well, then, strike! Dare to! We promise you extermination. We are massing the 1st Bashkir Division at your gates. . . ."

Let a young people from the steppes avenge their dead from the Urals and the dead of every murdered commune on these clean-shaven merchants who have been trading on our death for months. The hounded Revolution turns around and shows you a new face, Europe.

"You rejected the proletarians who came proclaiming peace. You banned them from your civilization because, armed with your science, they undertook to rebuild the world they carry on their shoulders. So be it! We have yet another side. We also have—the poet spoke true—Scythian cavalry! We will hurl them at your clean, tidy cities with their bright façades, at your brick-steepled Lutheran churches, at your parliament, your comfortable chalets, your banks, your pious, right-thinking newspapers.

❈

Riding down the broad straight avenues appeared cavalrymen dressed in gray or black sheepskin caps mounted on little roan horses who couldn't prance. The squadrons were preceded by commissars wearing pince-nez glasses. Some of them had medallions of Karl Marx's portrait pinned to their tunics as insignia. Most of them were yellow-skinned nomads with wide, muscular, rather flat faces and little eyes.

They seemed to be happy to be riding through a town where the horses' shoes never struck the soil, where all the houses were made of stone, where automobiles often bounded out of nowhere—but which was unfortunately lacking in horse troughs. And life must be sad there since there are neither beehives, nor flocks, nor horizons of plains and mountains. . . . Their sabers were bedecked with red ribbons. They punctuated their guttural singing with whistle blasts which sent brief shivers down their horses' manes.

In the evening the commanders, the commissars, the members of committees, and the men belonging to the Party, who were authorized to go out, wandered among the streets of ill fame looking for prostitutes. It was soon repeated around that they were almost all diseased. They paid well, for many of them were rich in their country; they were gentle, curious, caressing, and brutal with the women of the street—too white, too restless, and too talkative for their taste, and who were intimidated by their apparent awkwardness. They knew Dunya-the-Snake, Katka-Little-Apple, and Pug-Nose-Marfa. One of them left a curved, bone-handled dagger in Katka-Little-Apple's pink belly—in their country, the women know slow dances and choruses that men can never forget. Over their long red dresses they wear necklaces hung with rows of coins which are passed down from generation to generation: big silver rubles of Peter and the two Catherines, blackened eagles of all the autocrats, coins of three centuries. The pattern of their dresses goes back even further. They love coral; and they croon at the doors of low wooden houses or tall round tents as they grind their grain in mills which are nothing but cut-off tree trunks. Their motions are the same as those of the women of the first Turkish tribes who came to the land of the Belaia, driven by drought and war, so many centuries ago that the historians lose their way. Perhaps the ancestors of these riders were fashioning their beehives in the same shape as today long before there were Sophists in Athens.

Back from the fleshpots, a few of them were squatting in a circle in their barrack room, stirring up old projects. These men felt themselves a resuscitated people to the bones. Bitterly they recalled the great Kurultai of 1917 which declared their national independence. Word by heavy word they poured out their resentment at fighting for others, their hopes for glory, the more tangible hope of getting their pay, and thoughts heavier still. The man who had just possessed Dunya-the-snake in feline silence, his loins empty now, his nails black, his skull covered with insect bites under his mop of hair, recited the lines of the Nogai poet in a nasal twang:

> *"Rosy dawn will wake the horses of the East.*
> *The white birches will greet*
> > *the horses of the East."*

Kirim, squatting opposite him, continued in a singsong voice:

> *"The arrows of the sun will guide*
> > *the horses of the East."*

Kirim always wore a green skullcap embroidered in gold with Arabic letters, even under his huge sheepskin hat. This man was learned in the Koran, Tibetan medicine, and the witchcraft of shamans who can conjure spirits, bring love or rain, turn loose epizootics. He also knew passages of the *Communist Manifesto* by heart.

For laughs, they wake up Kara Galiev, who can be heard whistling as he snores.

"What time is it, Kara Galiev?"

Kara Galiev kept flocks for fifteen years on the steppe of Orenburg. The dry winds have eaten away the skin of his face like acid. He is wrinkled at thirty, as wrinkled as an old man of sixty, which he thinks he is at times, not having an exact count of his years. On his chest, hanging right against his rarely washed flesh, he wears a gold watch, like a great amulet, on the inside cover of which is engraved:

> *To Private*
> *Ahmed Kara Galiev*
> *Of the Red Army of Workers and Peasants*
> *For His Bravery*

Since he knows the place of every word, Kara Galiev sometimes imagines he is able to read. His plainsman's sleep is light. The time?

He takes out his watch, which hasn't run since it was presented to him to the sound of the *Internationale* under the red flags— without his knowing exactly why; for, on the same day, he had stolen a horse, taken flight at a shadow, and found a machine gun abandoned by the enemy in the middle of combat. He lifts the watch to his ear and shakes it. Ticktock, ticktock. The little sounds of time become perceptible for an instant. Kara Galiev noiselessly crosses the room in his bare feet, which are cloven like a faun's, and goes out to sniff the air of a starless night. Kara Galiev is infallible. Above his curly head so many different nights have unfurled their carpets of stars, their domes of ice, their infinity, their nothingness, that a new sense of time has been born in him. The darkness will be the same in an hour, in two or three, but he says:

"The third hour after sunset."

And it is the third hour after sunset.

The Central Office for Political Education sent lecturers to explain socialism to these warriors. They left for the front along with columns of young khaki-clad *mujiks* from Riazan, battalions of fighters in caps clutching cartridge belts over their old overcoats, smart squads from the fleet, dressed all in black, astonishingly clean and well fed. On Pulkovo Heights, not far from the Observatory whose great telescope was pointed at the clusters of stars in the center of Ursa Major thousands of light-years away, this thirteenth-century cavalry was decimated by high-explosive shells manufactured at St. Denis. The shaking of the earth caused by the artillery fire spoiled the observations of Moses Salomovich Hirsch, the astronomer.

❖

Detskoe Park, covered with dead leaves, was falling into an irreversible state of neglect. Oblivion was covering the pavilions and statues placed at the ends of its straight paths for the delight of empresses. Some Bashkirs were admiring the little white mosque at the edge of the lake. The Chinese Theater, surrounded by the deep silence of the pines, was filled with the heavy snores of an exhausted horde. A denlike stench escaped through the open doors. Convoys of wounded moved through the far end of the park; the last images of life reflected in their fading eyes were the golden tip of a minaret on the edge of the water, the color of a dull sky reflected in the smooth white lake, the columns of a belvedere on a distant hill and, forming a sort of shining crown, the gilded belfries of the Catherine Palace. Trifon, the terrified old keeper, a former palace footman, stood guard at the gates armed with a hunting rifle. Beside him stood a pale woman in a red kerchief. Bearded to the eyes, Trifon kept fiercely silent. Whenever the crackle of rifles firing somewhere reverberated through the air, Trifon took a few steps along the sidewalk, inspected the street and the grill of the new garden, removed his hat and hastily crossed himself—five, six, seven times—in front of the little blue and white church. The useless carbine clashed with his pious demeanor. He believed that the end of the world was at hand, but he never doubted that it was his duty to preserve the palace he had guarded for thirty years from pillage— even from the wrath of God himself. The keeper was shivering with fever under an overcoat which was too big for his wasplike waist. The cuffs of his striped trousers were heavy with fringes of mud. The woman in the red bandana had crazy eyes and dry lips that were almost black. She glowed inwardly with joy at having escaped hanging two days before. She reassured herself by reassuring her companions. "Don't worry about anything. I've got my Party card." And a mixture of secret laughter and touches of hate glittered in Trifon's tiny pupils as he stared at her. In the sepulchral half-light behind the padlocked doors and closed shutters slept vast halls floored with rare woods: the amber room, the Hall of Portraits peopled with ghosts in court dress, the Hall of Silver, the tawny-colored Hall of Lions, the Hall of Mirrors . . .

The Bashkir Division tended its wounds—which wasn't easy since there were no bandages—and slaked their fatigue in deep black slumber. A commander in a gold-braided green skullcap came alone to visit the palace. "I am Kirim, commander of the 4th, member of the Party!" The keeper insisted on removing the padlock himself. He guided the stone-faced visitor through the imperial apartments himself. Kirim walked along in silence, surprised, after days of chaotic fighting in the rain, by this semidarkness warmed by flashes of gold. He would gladly have slept on those floors as under the skies of pasture lands. The crystal chandeliers sent out a twinkle of lost stars in their infinitesimal motion. He spoke only once, in front of the malachite vases: "That's ours." The keeper, fearing his guest intended to carry off the vases, murmured: ". . . registered in the inventory of nationalized wealth . . ." and added, "They're very heavy . . ." —"I mean," Kirim continued severely, "Ural stone. Our Ural."

A little later, in front of a white colonnade, Kirim noticed a tall sailor who had apparently seen some action, for the bottom of his coat was stained with dark red blood. He was holding an officer's horse by the bridle. Booty. Shreds of splendid finery snatched by the armload from the wardrobe of the last Empress were lashed in a shapeless bundle behind his saddle under rough straps. Kirim came up and advised him with simplicity:

"Comrade, you'd do better to leave the wealth of the Republic right there. We must keep our consciousness."

The sailor, testing the girth of the saddle with his hand, tossed his reply cheerfully over his shoulder:

"The Republic can shove it . . . get my meaning? Don't get mad, my sourpussed little brother, I didn't take everything. There's enough left for you."

Kara Galiev appeared at the edge of the ornamental lake. He was limping. Other gray forms were half visible among the weeping willows. "Hey!" shouted Kirim. He pounced like a cat, grabbed the sailor around the waist, and the two of them rolled between the horse's legs. The animal, startled for a moment, watched curiously the double human form rolling around in the mud. Then his attention was caught by a green skullcap embroidered with an Arabic inscription: "There will be no city, said Allah, that will escape our terrible punishment."

Thus Egor's destiny was cut short.

18

Prince Usatov, the former president of the Southeast Railway, put two motions to a voice vote. General Kasparov's motion demanded that the administration create a special section for hostages entirely separate from the quarters for common-law prisoners. Privy Councilor von Eck's was only asking permission for the hostages to close their rooms themselves during the day in order to prevent theft. The privy councilor's "opportunistic moderantism" annoyed the intransigents. A bald jurist had just maintained that the exceptional situation of the hostages allowed them to demand to be treated as prisoners of war. . . . Having reached this point, the speaker had interrupted himself and stammered that "none of this would make any difference anyway."

A murmur of disapproval arose.

"We got the mattresses, didn't we?" triumphantly shouted the financier, Bobrikin, known as the Fat One, although six months of detention had made him resemble a great bat bewildered by the daylight. Professor Lytaev voted for the moderate motion, which caused his neighbors to jeer at the incurable liberalism of the university.

Ever since the night when he was dragged out of his cell at midnight, doubtless to be executed, only to end up, by accident or indulgence, in the hostages' quarter, he had been feeling very good, all things considered. His wife's letters arrived every day, along with packs of cigarettes. Thanks to a former pickpocket who had stayed on in the prison as a watchman and who had a warm spot for intellectuals, the Professor had fixed up a corner for himself in Room 3, almost directly under the high, grilled window, which hadn't been washed since the abdication of the Czar. The top of a

packing case was his writing desk. Back against the wall, legs
stretched out on the straw mattress, writing desk on his knees, he
would stare up at the top of the window, at the rough diamond of a
broken pane through which the white sky was revealed, and forget
the room behind him with its petty passions and great fears. Since
no hostages had been executed for some time, a few optimists were
arguing that the terror had been ended following secret negotiations which, according to rumor, had been undertaken with the International Red Cross. The pessimists merely shrugged. One of
these nights, in their opinion, a nasty surprise could be expected.
"These bandits don't give a damn for the Red Cross; and they're
much too crazy to stop halfway. I wouldn't bet very much on our
heads," said General Kasparov, who had his own reasons to be
worried. He trembled whenever the newspapers admitted the disas-
trous situation at the front, for he knew (having himself ordered a
massacre of prisoners not too long ago, before embarking on the
special train reserved for the flight of the General Staff) that
defeated men are merciless. The principal preoccupation of the
room remained the division of sugar and herring. Prince Usatov, the
elected dean, presided over these quarrels with the fair-mindedness
of an old nobleman accustomed to deciding questions of honor.
Thanks to him, the shipowner Nesterov (of the firm of Nesterov
and Bosch, known in the harbors of the New World and the Old),
who refused to touch dried fish, received an extra lump of sugar
every other day plus three extra spoonfuls of sour cabbage soup
each day.

A crow flew slowly across the broad shred of white sky which
Lytaev was contemplating, tracing a curve which vanished as it was
made; but this line, non-existent yet real, was enough to start the
old man thinking. The bird's flight: that's the fact; the curve is only
its law as conceived by my mind. Lytaev reached under his pillow
and pulled out some odd-shaped scraps of paper which had been
carefully smoothed down and were spotted with grease. Having
sharpened his stub of a pencil with a razor blade, a precious object
loaned to him by Prince Usatov, he resumed his writing. He took
lots of disconnected notes: it was his way of unraveling his
thoughts. He sent them to Marie.

"Never, perhaps, have I lived in such total serenity. There is
great happiness in being detached from everything and understanding everything. The happiness I feel is immense, bitter, painful and
calm. Life appeared suddenly before me stripped of everything that

encumbered it: habits, conventions, duties, worries, superfluous relations. We end up abandoning our souls almost entirely to these things. Do you remember that story by Kipling we read together at Vevey: 'The Miracle of Purun Baghat'? It's the tale of an old Westernized Hindu who retires high up in the mountains in order to finish out his life there with the earth, plants, tame animals—eternal reality. I'm an occidental. I have no wish to remove myself from men or from action: these too belong to eternity. I wish only to overcome my own impotence and to finally understand the curve described in the sky by the hurricane which is carrying us all along with it.

"All man's miseries are reduced to naked simplicity here. We live the life of the poor. And I understand the poor, their direct vision of reality, their power to hate, their need to overturn the world. I have no hate, however, except, perhaps, in the end, for the things I love the most—I believe we are almost all of us without hate in this prison. I may be mistaken, for I don't observe the others enough. I don't have the time, would you believe it?

"They say the terror is going to end; I don't think so. It is still a necessity. The storm must uproot the old trees, stir the ocean to its depths, wash clean the old stones, replenish the impoverished fields. The world will be new afterward. If the old oak whose heavy sap is barely able to circulate could think, it would call out for the lightning bolt and crumble with joy. Peter I was a great woodcutter. How many old oaks he cut down! Now greater woodcutters have come, we are in a class marked for the ax.

"What a dead thing we have made of history in our libraries! We looked for the explanation of the present in the past. It's the present which explains the past. Real history will be written when men's eyes are open.

"Many of those who are making the Revolution are madmen. Yet they will all serve, down to the last. And if there are some who know what they are doing, we can take our leave without regrets with our books and our dust-covered sciences (which have not been useless). Another science will be created. Marie, I believe there are such men! There is too much order and method in this chaos. I think I can glimpse them. They exist or they are about to come into being, about to awaken to themselves. And I love them, even if they appear cruel, even if they are cruel, even if they kill me without seeing me.

"If only we are strong enough to prevail! You see that I have gone over to the side of those who tomorrow perhaps . . . The other side's terror would be worse. It would uproot all the young shoots from this poor land. One side is defending their lives and life itself. The other, old privileges. The ones think of man. The others think only of their goods: not even about themselves; in here we have a former landowner whose only reason for wanting the Whites to win is to be indemnified for the confiscation of his stud farm.

"My spot is one of the best in our room, not far from the window. Through a broken pane I can see the sky. Betelgeuse was shining in the other night when we heard the cannon firing. What a miserable noise it was under those flickering white dots which are universes! I contemplated them with limitless detachment. After us, the stars will shine for other eyes, which will be better able to see them. Men are on the march, Marie. Whether it is by an absurd chance or by necessity that they must pass over our bodies, they are on the march.

"It is always the barbarians who renew the world. There is so much rubbish and hidden barbarism, sickness and lies in our culture! The barbarians who have come are the product of that culture. That's why some of them are ugly and demented. They will be swept away like us, along with the old beliefs, the old images, the old poisons, money, and syphilis. . . ."

There was no light in the evening. Lytaev had to stop. We are never able to share everything, especially when we want to reveal the best in us. Lytaev silenced the insurmountable fear he felt for death; and the fact that his desire to live was as great as that of a child who has just discovered death.

*

Egor walked in circles around his cell, swaying from left to right, from right to left, half forgetting where he was. He was singing to himself. The Volga rolled her green waters through plains and forests, boats carrying hardy lads toward rich booty, Stenka's head rolling under the block, Stenka's head carried off on the waves . . .

The spy hole clanked open. A drooping mustache appeared:

"Silence. The rules forbid singing."

Egor felt his whole being rebound like a ball striking the ground and bouncing off in a new direction.

"Eat your own rules, stink-face, sewer rat, prison rat, mustache of my ass! I sing if I want to. You didn't make the Revolution!"

Behind the closed spy hole, Mustache-face stood for a while, nonplused. Seventeen years of loyal service in this jail through three revolutions, marked only by overcrowding, unheard-of relaxations in discipline, and a merry-go-round of people coming and going that could drive a man crazy, had adapted him to the silences of the galleries, and to the rules which, maintained by every successive administration, were as permanent and immutable as the succession of the seasons. Yet there were times in his life when he had trembled, heart in his throat, to see men returning to the prison as masters, whom he remembered well, having escorted them to the exercise yard behind the pimps. And so he hesitated a moment, torn between his sense of discipline and a vague apprehension. At that instant the new commissar of the House of Detention, Comrade Ryjik, emerged from the courtyard, followed by the quartermaster. (The previous commissar, caught selling food on the black market, now occupied a cell on the fifth floor; the guys on fatigue duty spat in the boiled water they gave him to drink.) Mustache-face greeted Ryjik in the regulation attitude of a guard before the warden. Ryjik, whose cheeks were covered with a dirty-looking stubble of beard, frowned. Where had they dug up this old animal, trained in the prison service to jump through hoops of paper like a circus dog? Although the days back in 1914 when Ryjik occupied cell 30 on the fourth floor were far away, he thought he remembered that ruddy face with its tarred mustache.

"One of our best men," whispered the quartermaster. "An old-timer: the only one who really knows his job. Never steals."

". . . Comrade Commissar, there's a sailor here who is creating a disturbance."

"What's he doing?"

"He's singing."

Ryjik shrugged his shoulders. "Well, then, let him sing." He stared at Mustache-face with a kind of hatred. "Hand out grenades to all the reliable men right away. (Not to this one, naturally.) Have them carry them on their belts. When I give the signal, 'clean out' the counterrevolutionaries' rooms and cells. Give each man his own assignment. Also 'clean out' the rooms of hostages in Category One."

"And the common criminals?" inquired the quartermaster.

Ryjik reflected; his instructions were silent on this point. After all, bandits only prey on property owners.

"Turn them loose, at the last moment."

At a corner in the corridor they ran into the person Ryjik wanted at all costs to avoid meeting. A gang of men in undershirts with trousers dragging over unlaced shoes were running toward the showers. One man loomed, dark, erect, terrifying. Close up he was no longer terrifying, just ordinary. Such is the power of concreteness that ten paces are enough to strip a man in appearance of the mystery surrounding him. How he had lost weight, aged in a few days: skin browned, mouth stretched at the corners, nose hooked, eyes like dark embers!

"Hello, Arkadi."

"Hello, Ryjik."

Handshakes.

"How's it going?"

"So-so. *Nothing*. Do you think we'll hold on?"

"It'll be hard. . . ."

Even in the days when Ryjik was pushing flatcars weighing several tons around railroad yards in Siberia, the load he felt in the small of his back at the end of the day was no heavier than at this moment. A weight of ice pressing down body and soul. Already there was nothing more to say to each other. Ryjik heard his own voice with a kind of astonishment, as if someone else, inside of him, had spoken in his place. This someone was now lying carelessly:

"Your case hasn't been decided yet. There are too many problems already, as you must know.

"Would you like to see that . . . your woman? I can arrange that for you. Good. In an hour, brother. Farewell."

In Russian, they say "sorry" for "farewell." There is deep wisdom in the word.

Arkadi lit a cigarette with trembling hands. He knew this slight but perceptible tremor in his hand well, having observed it on many occasions. He smiled, nonetheless, into the void. And so the little blond soldier accompanying him also smiled, his whole round face illuminated by two greenish drops of water.

❖

Ryjik locked the door of the director's office. Leather armchairs, dirty blotter. *The Constitution of the Soviet Republic, the*

Regulations of the House of Detention. Ryjik felt horribly alone, caught in a trap. No air. The dark panes of a glass cabinet returned his ugly image. Shame at having nerves like an intellectual made him feel even hotter. He pounced at the telephone. Replace me immediately! I'm not made for this kind of work. Send anybody, but relieve me, you understand, within the hour! —That's what he would shout at them. The sugary voice of a well-bred young lady informed him that Comrade Osipov had left for the front. No one was left at the Special Commission except Comrade Zvereva, on duty. . . . At the office of the President, a heavy masculine voice indicated that Comrade President was in conversation with the capital by direct wire and would not be free in the near future. Kirk was at the Special Defense Council meeting which was taking place on Trotsky's train. Ryjik finally got hold of Kondrati.

"What do you want from me, Ryjik? Be brief."

How to tell him that . . .

"Kondrati, I'm exhausted. I can't stand up any more. Send someone to replace me."

"Exhausted? Are you out of your mind? Don't you know what we're up against? Stay at your post and leave us the fuck alone." The wire went dead. Ryjik was suddenly aware of the cold, of the lurid lighting, of a touch of rheumatism.

He walked several turns around the office, just like so many of the men pacing circles in their cells at that moment. He felt more closed in than they.

He unlocked the door and rang. Mustache-face appeared.

"What's your name?"

"Vlasov."

"Do you have any spirits, Vlasov?"

"Who can live without liquor? Good grain spirits, sir, distilled on the sly by the peasants, not far from here in . . ."

"Fine. Bring it."

The first glass, a tall beer glass, sent its crude warmth coursing through Ryjik's stiff limbs. The way the fire gets into your pores when you warm yourself in front of a brazier burning out on the snow at night. Mustache-face stood with his arms at his sides, smiling obsequiously. "It's good for the soul," he said, licking lips that had not drunk. What a prick! thought Ryjik. But aloud he said:

"Sit down and drink."

Since there was only one glass, they took turns drinking.

○

Egor entered the visitors' room and found Shura.

A nondescript soldier with grenades around his belt watched his every move without seeming to see him: such was the look of boredom on his inexpressive face. "I've brought you a saw," whispered Shura. Her brilliant lips were so close to the man's lips that their breath mingled with these words. "Slide it into my sleeve." The supple resistance of the flexible blade felt like a stiff fern on the underside of Egor's arm. Timochka, the soldier, saw quite clearly the Chinese-looking woman with cat's eyes slipping something to her lover. And he spoke as if in a dream, softly, slowly:

"Take it, little brother, take it! For all the good it will do you. . . . But you, Princess, you're very kind."

Egor and Shura might have thought they were dreaming themselves to look at Timochka congealed in his boredom. His words passed through them, unreal.

"Bastard," said Egor, who believed only in the real.

"They know everything, Shura, those pigs. The bank job. The job at the Cooperative. Old Kalachnikov's business. The anarchist deal. There was no point in arguing; it didn't take ten minutes to settle my account. . . . Is it really you? It's me. Up against the wall, my boy. . . . That's as much conversation as was possible. If I don't find a way to skip, I'm done for. Once there was a man; now there isn't. Understand?"

The strange oval of her pale face looked up at him with intense pleading in the half-closed eyes.

"Don't be angry, Egor, I want to tell you something . . . something . . . Egor, don't be angry . . . I want them to put me against the wall with you, don't be angry . . ."

Egor put his arm around her and the tension of his muscles communicated his inner agitation to her whole being. She saw the blood rush to his face, a drunken joy twist his broad smile, sending lightning flashes zigzagging across his eyes. Did he cry out? Or did it only seem to her that he cried out?

"Shura, my little golden-eyed cat! Are you mad? Don't be stupid! Try to understand. They put a bullet through my head. Well, so what? Life goes on, eh? People go on, eh? You go on, eh? And the spring, do you think it will be any less beautiful? The thaw, the ice floes, the first green shoots, life—see?—and you, you!"

He shook his shaggy head; and dull fury boiled up in his skull, for he suffered rage at never being able to express himself (when lots of agitators with nothing to say are able to reel off phrases by the mile).

"Shura, my little golden-eyed cat, leave this place without looking back. Don't forget me"—he spat violently—"no, forget me; it's better that way, and I don't give a damn. Forget me. Live. Live, I tell you. Go to bed with the whole city. No, choose the strongest ones. No, let them choose you. Live. And don't be afraid of anything. Of anything, do you hear? Like me. There's nothing to be afraid of!"

Timochka waited for the last stroke of ten o'clock to sound before saying:

"Citizens, the visit is over."

19

What decides the way things turn out? A thousand events comprising in turn a million lesser events all add up without anyone knowing how; the wave attack advancing confidently is broken up by machine guns which it expected to knock out without any trouble as on the day before and the day before that; men who were fleeing turn around, stop fleeing, discover their own ferocity, spring back into action; those who were pursuing them stop, spent, discover their own exhaustion, turn around, flee.

The workers at the Great Works labored in gray darkness, without electricity, in order to mount artillery pieces on trolley-car chassis for street fighting. The workers at the Izhorsk and Schlüsselburg factories formed battalions of volunteers. They were consumptive, nearsighted, worn-out men of forty-five, wretched-looking soldiers in threadbare overcoats marching into the cold wind with backs bent and shoulders sloping under the weight of cartridge belts. Many of them fell in the muddy fields of Pulkovo and Ligovo; but the sight of officers dressed English-style going elegantly into battle with revolvers in their fists made them fight like mad dogs. The Bashkirs ran away in one place and fought furiously to hold another. The Siberian battalions fought in a spirit of bored solemnity as if they were working at some heavy, unpleasant job. A rough job—killing men while trying not to get killed yourself—let's face it; but the sooner it's done the sooner you get to go home, which is the real goal, for the earth is waiting. It doesn't always wait; it also receives a man without delay, as soon as he extends his watchful face six inches beyond the protective cover of a tree trunk at an unexpected angle.

There was also the heroism of the sailors, for newspaper head-

lines. They went into battle with such dash, as if going to a party!
All these dance-hall Casanovas with women's names, hearts, and
braids tattooed on their chests! Nonetheless, a hundred of them
reported sick before the battle; and half of them were thrown into
the brig—most of these happened to be actually sick as luck would
have it—on charges of malingering. Wounds in the hand and foot,
numerous during the first engagements, became rare after a few
summary executions to set an example. No matter. The sailors were
splendid; for they would have paid dearly in case of a defeat. The
blood of the admirals and captains "sent west" to satisfy the fleet's
sense of justice proved to be a valuable incentive. It came to pass
that the Commander-in-Chief of all the Republic's armies, a great
statesman but a rather poor horseman[1] leaped onto the nearest
horse in order personally to lead a bunch of disordered runaways
back into combat. They were astounded at the sight of the formidable, confident man, whose picture was posted everywhere, looming
among them, looking strangely like himself, extraordinarily natural
yet larger than life. They saw him, they heard him. With a bold energetic gesture he pointed to the little copse crackling with gunfire
from which everyone was fleeing; a little copse which was no more
terrible than any other, in reality. Why were they fleeing, in fact?
The runaways took off again in the opposite direction, shouting the
"hurrahs" of the charge. The Commander wiped the sweat off his
brow. Ouf! He had almost lost his pince-nez glasses. On the other
side of the noisy little copse, which was thus retaken by some
brawny lads from Kaluga, where they drawl their *a*'s, stood (in the
first version of the story) the crack troops of Prince Bernet outfitted
with German equipment, who were immediately routed; according
to the second version, there was nothing there, the enemy having
retreated from their side in time; according to the third version, the
copse was only a screen of trees; according to the fourth, invented
ten years later, the copse didn't exist and nothing of the kind ever
happened.

The city was bristling with barricades made up of heavy armor
plates, paving blocks, and stacks of cordwood, situated so as to rake
the main arteries with gunfire. Cannon planted perfidiously in deep
ditches pointed their muzzles along the level of the pavement.
Others were concealed behind the iron gates of gardens. An empty

[1] The man is none other than Trotsky.—Trans.

bazaar, its windows piled with sandbags, prepared to resist a long siege. Trenches dug by civilians, dragged from their homes for this nighttime duty, surrounded statues, cut across squares, and formed labyrinths in front of churches. Genuine bourgeois, albeit impoverished ones, accomplished their labors on the earthworks with simulated good will. The defeated party announced that it was mobilizing three dozen of its members for the defense of the Revolution, an elite corps commanded by Fanny herself; she got lost between the lines, lived off the peasants for two weeks, gloriously seized a cannon abandoned by the Germans during the 1918 offensive, and left behind her—in unknown hamlets where no other carriers of ideas had been seen since the Lutheran ministers came from Sweden in the seventeenth century—the seeds of a heretical socialism. A corps of anarchist partisans volunteered to defend the institutions of the dictatorship. Their services were accepted. Two days later it was decided to disarm them, the worst danger having passed. They refused to go along with the idea. The decision was reversed, the situation having worsened. . . . The simple face of victory was at last rising into the light. The anarchists wondered if they were not playing a fool's game. The Special Commission sent in bogus converts to study them. Stassik favored the idea of a fruitful "expropriation," Uvrarov, a clandestine departure for the Ukraine; Gorin, an alliance with the Party. The result was three splits. The ones who got the worst of it were the unity-men, whose sole desire was to oppose splintering, a tendency which obviously showed their most contemptible lack of principles.

Posted on every street corner, newspapers printed on dirty-green paper with muddy ink suddenly proclaimed such incredible news that people first thought it was false. *Detskoe Selo Taken.* ("—you see, they really were there!") *Krasnoe Taken* ("So it was true!"), the city has been saved. "Soldiers, sailors, workers, Communists, Commanders, Commissars! in spite of fatigue, in spite of everything, forward, forward! Decapitate the hydra! Victory! Victory! Victory!" Signed: The President of the Revolutionary Council for War. The Red Army of Siberia telegraphed the taking of Tobolsk. A telegram from the Revolutionary Soviet of the Southern Front announced the taking of Voronezh, which no one knew had been lost. Victory on every front. We will live. Future, you are ours until the end of the centuries—or until the spring; that's almost as beautiful and much more probable. In the windows of the Telegraph Agency

huge colored cartoons, drawings, and captions by the futurist Mayakovsky showed Lloyd George and Clemenceau crestfallen. The
squadrons of Shkuro and Mamontov, tainted with the odor of massacres, were in flight before the Red Cavalry. In the rear of the
White Army Nestor Makhno paraded his carts bristling with un-
seizable machine guns through the villages of the Ukraine, working
the fields in the intervals between combats. How many lost children
you have, Revolution, ready to shoot each other in your name!
Their hands reach out to each other from the Obi to the Dnieper:
Mongolian faces, singing Cossacks, rude countrymen, idealistic
ex-cons, bandits dreaming of cities of the future, proletarians giving
their last strength to repair the last locomotives, illiterate proletarians scrawling their crude signatures on orders written out by
deferential ex-generals who have learned to say "comrades," proletarians on horseback leading Kazakh nomads to the conquest of
Turkestan, proletarians bent over piles of statistics measuring hour
by hour the death of industry, engineers dreaming of the electrifica-
tion of a future "America" without gold seekers; for the real gold
has been found (it lies in the heart, the brain, and the muscles of
man). We will have more of it than all the vaults of the Federal
Reserve Bank. Think of all those cellars filled with yellow metal:
what a strange aberration! We will have a hundred million, two
hundred million free men; two hundred fifty million Europeans will
see themselves in us as they never have been. We will awaken
India: three hundred million oppressed people, the oldest wisdom
on earth, fallen low, extremely sick, but we will bring it health; we,
a West repudiating the cannon, we who through machines will liberate man from the machine! We will awaken China: four hundred
million men. . . . A billion Asiatics will hear our call. Shanghai and
Bombay will see strikes and insurrections holding aloft our em-
blems, applying our methods. Millions, hundreds of millions of men
on the march, this is what we are. Today, here, we have arrived.
What else matters?

*

Rain washes over newspapers freshly glued to the walls.
*COUNTERREVOLUTIONARIES, SPIES, AND CRIMINALS
SHOT.* This column, single-spaced in 8-point type, with the names
set off in bold, is the one people read the most attentively under the

dreary, piercing rain. "List of counterrevolutionaries, spies, criminals, blackmailers, bandits, and deserters executed by order of the Special Commission." Thirty-four numbered names. Artiushkin, Losov, Kaufman, Aga Oghol, Kasparov, former general, "1. Vadim Mikhailovich Lytaev, university professor, known counterrevolutionary, affiliated with the Right Center organization, convicted of having harbored a White agent. . . ." Paramonov, ex-officer. Ma Tsiu-dey, laundryman, convicted of several murders. "15. X, known as Nikita, counterrevolutionary. 16. Nicholas Orestovich Azin, alias Danil Petrovich Gof, 25 years old, member of the Right Center organization, courier for the Whites. 17. Olga Orestovna Azin, 28 years old, his accomplice. 18. Arkadi Arkadievich Ismailov, 34 years old, member of the Special Commission, guilty of corruption. 19. Kuk, Beliaev, Smolina . . . 27. Egor Ivanovich Matveev, known as Egor, 30 years old, ex-sailor, bandit . . ." Ivanov, Fokin, Sacher . . . Names take strange shapes on this list, coming to life, then bizarrely dying out before eyes which once saw flesh and blood beings moving through a universe in which nothing remains of them but these little characters traced in ash. People who don't know them move their lips spelling them out. Dead, dead, executed, heads gaping, buried no one knows where . . . "When, then?" "Read the date: on the night of . . ." "We slept peacefully that night, is it possible!" Nothing different on the street, the world is ordinary. Yet there comes a moment, long and brief like a swirling fall. Abyss. And the man reading these names thinks of himself: a double within him, who would never admit his own existence, substitutes his name for these names, his age for these ages, his life for these extinct lives.

Among the crowd assembled in front of the poster stands an old woman and a couple. The woman seems very old because of her old-fashioned dress and her gray lips; she must have aged all at once. She is reading; and suddenly the little aluminum pot hanging in her hand falls to the sidewalk. The old woman hears nothing. A little girl in a red beret picks up the little pot and hangs it back onto the inert hand, which seems paralyzed. "Auntie," says the little girl, "hold onto your pot or you'll drop it again." The old woman answers nothing. She straightens up a little, which makes her look funny, for her normal carriage has recently become stooped. The black-braided bonnet sitting on her gray hair has slipped down onto the back of her neck; she looks like a madwoman; you might think she is about to laugh, scream, break out sobbing, or fall. But she walks away mechanically through a desert of frozen lava. An unimaginable silence surrounds her. —A young blonde with deep eyes like sparkling blue water leaning on the arm of her lover, who wears the uniform of a vanished school, runs over the list distractedly. "Two women," she thinks, "28 years old, 31 years old . . . ah!" She herself is twenty. It's nothing but a ripple which quickly disappears over shallow water. They walk away with swinging strides. "Georg," she says, "I have become much more conscious . . ."

Johann Appolinarius Fuchs, painter, had been worried for some time that something bad had happened to the girl next door. Strangers armed with a Housing Order had moved into the absent girl's apartment without bothering to remove her personal effects. A newborn baby was now squalling in there, and a redheaded woman with a square chin was wearing Olga's dressing gowns. Whenever they met, Fuchs lowered his eyes so as not to look at her face, but then he discovered her hands, which were huge. He winced when he recognized her step in the hall and the brutal way she flushed the toilet. He was living miserably from the sale, for paltry sums, of the last of his racy eighteenth-century books. This very day a new drop in the value of the ruble had reduced his purchases to some poor-quality black bread and rotten fish. At random he walked into the General Information Bureau of the Commissariat of Public Education (LEARN! INFORM YOURSELF!) and found a little ageless woman explaining to two peasant women that the authority of the Bureau did not in any way cover arbitrary confiscations of furniture in the countryside. Fuchs was able to snatch the day's papers without any problem, which put him in a good mod. The sky had cleared, autumnal sunlight spread in tawny shimmering pools along the sidewalks of the central prospect. A rider was galloping toward the station down the middle of the street—which was deserted for two miles in a straight line—on a Siberian pony with long dirty hair the color of yellow bricks. The rare passers-by didn't even turn around at the sight of this Scythian tearing along at a full gallop between two rows of tall modern buildings, noble churches, severe ornamented palaces, theaters, and libraries.

Prostitutes were walking up and down in pairs in front of the monumental buildings of the former Eliseev fancy food store. Fuchs reflected that half of his food supply corresponded more or less to their current asking price. Lyda, grown thinner, a tall pale girl with a small face lighted by timid gray eyes, was there as usual, walking arm in arm with a girl friend. The year had gone by for her without any other events than bad colds, long waits in front of the pawnshop, the fear of diseases, and bad times with some rough customers. "Nothing will ever change for us," she would say, "it will always be the same or worse." It was in her room, sprawled across a narrow single bed with a bolster supporting two little white pillows, that Fuchs opened the newspapers. ". . . 17. Olga Orestovna Azin . . . 17. Olga Orestovna . . . 17, Olga, Olga, Olga . . ." The tiny dried-ash characters danced before his eyes; and he also glimpsed a blond head which seemed to have captured light, hands folded over a blue dressing gown; he heard a living voice: and all of this mixed up with terrifying shadows and the constant, obsessive, insurmountable, vertiginous sensation of that blond head suspended over the abyss, of her terrified expectation, of a horrible wound—of a horrible wound . . .

"What's the matter, Johann, do you feel ill?"

A pale, bony, brunette head with mascaraed eyes hovered over him in worried concern. This head too; why not? All heads are alike, there is only one kind of suffering, one death, one life, it's obvious.

"Johann, Johann!"

The sound of his name reached him through half-worlds after the passage of eternal seconds.

"It's nothing, honey. It'll pass. It's the t-t-t-times."

He was shaking from head to foot. "Do you know someone on this list, Johann?" Lyda didn't recognize anyone. "Lie down, Johann, my friend, don't think about it any more. Relax . . ." She rubbed his temples and forehead like a child's.

20

There were funerals and celebrations. They dug up the hardened earth of the Field of Mars in order to lower red coffins, covered with ribboned wreaths and borne on gun carriages, into wide common graves. From atop the granite ramparts, the President of the Executive affirmed the immortality of the working class. A scarlet banner suspended above the mounds crackled in the cold wind. "Eternal Communist Memory for Those Who Fell." Johann Appolinarius Fuchs found this Elzevirian inscription, on which he had worked for three days, rather beautiful. The oppressive cadences of the funeral marches marked the rhythm of the passing troops. The morning was damp; an invincible gloom came out of the earth. The victors marched past. They didn't appear to be passing into glory but rather to be returning, exhausted, from regions of misfortune. The men saw war naked, without parades and lies, as it appears to those who fight and want no more of it. Yet they would march with the same firm step to the end of the earth in order to put an end to it.

Four thousand men filled the white-and-gold hall of the Opera that evening.

A bitter smell of warm earth rose up from their gray ranks toward the white goddesses of the vaulted ceiling who held garlands out into the smoky blue. The hands of four thousand men were draped over the armrests of loges and balconies—hands of Riazan farmers, Bashkir shepherds, northern fishers, weavers who had become machine gunners. These clumsy hands knew nothing of eloquent, refined gestures; they were happy to be doing nothing and to possess things peacefully at last for one evening. The stage was brilliant, with a beautiful golden backdrop of painted cardboard.

Chaliapin appeared in tails and white gloves, just as he had before the Emperor not long ago, greeting this audience as he had the other (the audience which had passed before the firing squad) with a deep bow and the smile of a masterful charmer. Voices cracked through the hall: *The Knout! The Knout!* Love songs are beautiful, doubtless, but what this audience, this army crowded into a concert hall, likes is *The Song of the Knout.* They know the knout! Its taste on your back, its taste across your face; and also how to apply the knout, the capitalists know a few things about that! Sing us that one, comrade, and you'll hear bravos the like of which that other hall—the one that will never return, the one you miss perhaps deep down in your soul, the other hall with its low-cut dresses and its monocles—never gave you! Hands which have moved stones, earth, manure, metals, fire, and blood will applaud you! —And the perfect voice sang out *The Song of the Knout.* That's a song, brothers!

The singer was bowing his way out, wreathed in luxuriant smiles. *Encore! Encore!* He was about to return to the front of the stage and to give in again to the enthusiasm of the crowd when, from out of the wings, a simian hand grabbed his arm. "Wait, comrade. With a flick of the wrist, he repaired the crease in his cuff, crumpled by the ungainly grasp of this little, faceless, sunburned old soldier whose eyes were nothing more than dull brown spots. The surprised hall saw a little man dressed in the long coat of the Bashkir Division appear in the place of the great actor. Someone exclaimed: "Kara Galiev! The soldier advanced upstage with a heavy tread and stopped at the prompter's box. There, he raised his arm; at its end the hand was wound with white bandages. He was muddy to the waist. It never occurred to him to remove his cap, which was scrunched down as far as his eyebrows. He shouted:

"Comrades!"

What now? Another disaster?

". . . Gdov is ours!"

A new acclamation burst from the warm darkness of the hall. On the stage the handsome singer reappeared behind the messenger from the front. Bowing slightly, sparkling with whiteness, ebony blackness, grace and smiles, he too applauded this obscure victory snatched from the mud of the Esthonian border.

*

Snow covered the fresh graves which were already half forgotten. Life is for the living and they have trouble staying alive. Once again the long nights seemed reluctant to abandon the city. For a few hours each day a gray light of dawn or dusk filtered through the dirty white cloud ceiling and spread over things like the dim reflection of a distant glacier. Even the snow, which continued to fall, lacked brightness. This white, silent, weightless shroud stretched out to infinity in time and space. By three o'clock it was already necessary to light the lamps. Evening deepened the hues of ash, deep blue, and the stubborn gray of old stones on the snow. Night took over, inexorable and calm: unreal. In the darkness the delta resumed its geographical form. Dark cliffs of stone cut off in sharp right angles lined the frozen canals. A sort of somber phosphorescence emanated from the broad river of ice.

Sometimes the north winds blowing in from Spitsbergen and farther still—from Greenland perhaps, perhaps from the pole across the Arctic Ocean, Norway, and the White Sea—gusted across the bleak estuary of the Neva. All at once the cold bit into the granite; the heavy fogs which had come up from the south across the Baltic vanished and the denuded stones, earth, and trees were instantly covered with crystals of frost, each of which was a barely visible marvel composed of numbers, lines of force, and whiteness. The night changed its aspect, shedding its veils of unreality. The north star appeared, the constellations let in the immensity of the world. The next day the bronze horsemen in their stone pedestals, covered with silver powder, seemed to step out of a strange carnival; from the tall granite columns of St. Isaac's Cathedral to its pediment peopled with saints and even to its massive gilded cupola—all was covered with frost. The red granite façades and embankments took on a tint of pink and white ash under this magnificent cloak. The gardens, with their delicate filigree of branches, appeared enchanted. This phantasmagoria delighted the eyes of people emerging from their stuffy dwellings, just as millennia ago men dressed in pelts emerged fearfully in wintertime from their warm caves full of good animal stench.

Not a single light in whole quarters. Prehistoric gloom.

*

The red flags at the gates of old palaces were turning black. Ryjik no longer kept track of the time. His day had neither beginning nor end. He slept whenever he could, by day, by night, sometimes at the beginning of meetings, when the speaker was long-winded. —Toward midnight, just as he was getting worried, a hushed voice in the ear trumpet of the telephone communicated to him the results of the Aronsohn raid. "Hello, Ryjik? That you, Ryjik? Raid over; picked up three bundles of letters and documents; seized twelve pounds of butter, seventy pounds of flour, two dozen cakes of soap. . . . Wait a minute, what else, yes, photos, and cans, eighteen of them. . . . —No, no arrests. The bastards flew the coop. They fired a few shots . . . —Xenia? Xenia got two bullets in the belly. . . ." These last two words only took on their full meaning in his mind slowly. They exploded and faded. They lit up again in the depth of his consciousness like the little blue safety lamps in boiler rooms which sometimes indicate that the pressure has gotten too high: *d a n g e r*—then there was the carnal image of a wounded belly. Ryjik went down to the library. His jaw was rigid, his eyes vague.

Two soldiers were chatting by the light of a night lamp next to the big Dutch earthenware stove. Ryjik, his back against the stove to let the heat penetrate him, closed his eyes. The night reigned, magnificently silent, over the snow, the ice, the city.

"You look awful, Ryjik," said one of the men. "I'm beat myself. Flour was up to one hundred rubles today."

In the silence which followed, Ryjik heard bells ringing—bells, bells, bells—jangling, far off, grating, hectic, exasperating, comforting. . . . He ought to say that Xenia . . . but he didn't want to say it, and he lent his ear to the bells, the bells . . .

"We're in bad shape, with these prices," continued the heavy voice which had just spoken. "Listen to what this guy's telling, Ryjik."

They listened without seeing each other, for their eyes fixed involuntarily on the flame of the night lamp: a little wick floating in oil in a tin trefoil. . . . The other man, a foreigner, spoke the mutilated language of an ex-prisoner of war; and he was saying mutilated things, too, of another age, another world. Europe, comrades. . . . The silent dead factories of Vienna, the poor quarters swarming with rachitic children, the crippled decorated veterans selling matches outside night clubs on Kaerntnerstrasse. And the execution of the Hunchback, no, not in Vienna, in Budapest, between the Christmas and New Year's celebrations, a celebration just as brilliant for which they fought over invitations. . . . Ah, the Hunchback was magnificent! Even the newspapers said so. The others sang as they waited their turn, you could hear them easily, they didn't dare shut them up. The society people gave the executioner an ovation. Here.

The man got up and looked inside his tunic for a shapeless billfold from which he removed a piece of paper on which was written a single penciled line.

"Here's one of the last lines written by the Hunchback:

"*Ich gehe mit einer Alle umfassenden Liebe in das Nichts* [I enter with an immense love into the night]."

Ryjik said harshly:

"Too lyrical. Everything is much simpler. It's easier to die than . . ."

And he walked out. He was suffocating. The freezing night cooled his face. Crystallike bells continued to jingle in the distance, far off. Ryjik said aloud the three magic words: "It is necessary. It is necessary." The bells covered them. It is necessary. It is necessary . . . The world was empty like a great glass bell.

That night only twenty-one carloads of food supplies arrived in the city (three of them were pillaged). Just as long as we hold out until spring! The proletariat of Europe . . .

Martyshkino, Leningrad, Moscow
1930–31

Victor Serge

Victor Serge was born into the revolutionary movement as people were once said to be born "to the manner." His parents were part of the emigration of Russian *intelligenti* which streamed into western Europe during the dark decade of repression that followed the assassination of Czar Alexander II by the terrorist arm of the populist Narodnik party on March 1, 1881. He was born Victor Lvovich Kibalchich (Serge was a pseudonym) in Brussels on December 30, 1890, a child of want, exile, and revolt.

Serge's earliest memories were of adult conversations dealing with "trials, executions, escapes and Siberian highways, with great ideas incessantly argued over, and with the latest books about these ideas." Idealism and readiness for sacrifice were the values that reigned in his parents' milieux. "On the walls of our humble and makeshift lodgings," he recalled in his *Memoirs of a Revolutionary*, "there were always the portraits of men who had been hanged." Serge's father had barely escaped hanging for his part in the 1881 attack on the Czar, and one of Russia's most famous martyrs was Serge's relative on his father's side, Nikolai Kibalchich, the genial chemist who fashioned the bombs that were used against Alexander II.

Serge's birthright was a tradition of rebellion and sacrifice in the face of czarist autocracy and repression, a tradition begun by the Decembrists in 1825, passed on through Chernyshevsky, Herzen, Bakunin, and the generation of students who had gone "to the people" in the 1870s, to culminate in the terrorism of 1881, a tradition that combined the most intellectualized idealism with danger and desperate deeds.

Growing up in comfortable, complacent Brussels, but in a

household where extreme poverty caused the death of an older brother and where the atmosphere was charged with revolutionary fervor, Serge, even as a child, became obsessed with the idea that he was living in a "world without possible escape," and determined that the only acceptable career would be that of the professional revolutionary. Since his father, an impoverished scholar, despised public education—he called it "stupid bourgeois instruction for the poor"—Serge never went to school. He learned to read in his father's library of revolutionary books, and learned about life in the slum streets of Brussels. As an adolescent he worked as a photographer's apprentice. He was active in the socialist *Jeunes Gardes* but still found it "impossible to live" in a city where even the "revolutionaries" believed in gradual reform. In 1908, after a short stay in a Utopian colony in the Ardennes, he heeded the call of Paris, "the Paris of Salvat, of the Commune, of the CGT, of little journals printed with burning zeal; the Paris where Lenin edited *Iskra* from time to time and spoke at émigré meetings in little co-operative houses. . . ."

Disgusted with the watered-down Marxist and reformist-socialist doctrines of the day which promised "revolution for the year 2000" but neglected the impossible here and now, Serge and his young comrades in Paris were drawn to theories of Anarchist Individualism, the personal rebellion and "conscious egotism" of Nietzsche and Stirner: "Anarchism swept us away completely because it both demanded everything of us and offered everything to us." The revolution was to be personal, total, immediate. But in Paris, just as in Brussels, it was "impossible to live." There, poverty and hunger were the daily "impossibilities," and the young Individualists were soon converted to the theory (and practice) of "individual expropriation" based on Proudhon's idea that "legal" property is merely "theft." Driven by want, disease, and desperation, and inspired by half-digested revolutionary ideas, Serge's young comrades banded together and embarked on what was probably the most bloody and tragic series of bank robberies in modern times. Known as the "Bonnot Gang" and the "Tragic Bandits," they terrorized Paris for almost a year. All of them met violent ends—in gun battles, by suicide, and on the guillotine. Serge, then editor of *L'Anarchie*, was repelled by the slaughter and revolted by the excesses to which their idealistic theories had led. But he refused to break with his comrades and turn informer; after a sensational trial, the French state rewarded his silence with a five-year prison sentence as an "accomplice."

Of his term in prison (1912–17), Serge wrote: "It burdened me with an experience so heavy, so intolerable to endure, that long afterward, when I resumed writing, my first book [*Men in Prison,* a novel] amounted to an effort to free myself from this inward nightmare, as well as the performance of a duty toward all those who will never so free themselves."

Released from prison at the height of World War I and banned from France, Serge made his way to Barcelona, a city "at peace," busily turning out weapons for both sides in the great conflict. It was there that he abandoned Individualism and began to agitate in the ranks of the Syndicalists. In Barcelona he wrote his first article signed "Victor Serge," and Barcelona on the eve of insurrection (twenty years before the great Spanish Revolution and Civil War) is the setting for the first half of his novel, *Birth of Our Power.*

Though he was involved in Spain, the Russian Revolution, which had just erupted at the other end of Europe, beckoned to Serge. This was "his" Revolution, the end of that "world without possible escape." He left Barcelona and attempted to join the Russian army in France in order to be repatriated to the revolutionary homeland. But he succeeded only in getting himself thrown into a French concentration camp as a "Bolshevik suspect." After the armistice he was sent to Russia as a hostage in exchange for some French officers interned by the Soviets. He arrived in red Petrograd (the setting for the final chapters of *Birth of Our Power* and for *Conquered City*) in January 1919, at the height of the Civil War and famine. It was here that the evolution of Victor Kibalchich, homeless exile and Anarchist-Individualist, to Victor Serge, spokesman for Soviet power, was completed.

Serge's libertarian sympathies made him from the start wary of the authoritarian nature of Bolshevik rule. But, as a revolutionary, only one course was open to him: he threw himself, body and soul, into the work of defending and building the Soviet Republic. During the Civil War he served as a machine gunner in a special defense battalion, collaborated closely with Zinoviev in the founding congresses of the Communist International, became a commissar in charge of the czarist secret police archives (under Krassin), and eventually a member of the Russian Communist Party. At the same time, however, he openly criticized Bolshevik authori-

tarianism, frequented Anarchist, Left Menshevik, and Left Socialist
circles, and interceded in favor of many prisoners of the Cheka
(predecessor of the G.P.U. and the N.K.V.D.). At this time, too,
Serge was translating into French the works of Lenin, Trotsky, and
Zinoviev. Among poets and writers, he was friendly with Yessenin,
Mayakovsky, Pilniak, Pasternak, Panait Istrati, and Maxim Gorky
(a distant relative on his mother's side).

By 1923 he was a confirmed member of the Left (Trotskyist)
Opposition; at that date it was still possible to be simultaneously
"loyal" and an "oppositionist" in Soviet Russia. But his presence in
Russia was troublesome; he was made editor of the *International
Communist Bulletin* and sent off to Germany and the Balkans to ag-
itate, a task which he performed with perfect loyalty and discipline.

When Serge returned to Moscow in 1926 to take part in the
inner-Party struggle against Stalin, however, the political climate
was greatly changed. A little over a year later he was expelled from
the Party and held in prison for several weeks; his relatives, including many who had no political affiliations, were also made to suffer.
It was during this period (1928–33) that, relieved of all official functions and systematically deprived of any means of earning a living
because of the Stalinist "blacklist," Serge turned to serious writing.
Already known in France for his pamphlets and political articles, he
soon attracted a larger audience there as a historian (*The Year One
of the Russian Revolution*, 1930) and novelist (*Men in Prison*, 1930;
Birth of Our Power, 1931; *Conquered City*, 1932).

Surely no writer has ever produced under more difficult conditions, and the vivid tension and rapid episodic style of his works
may well have been dictated in part by his personal situation. "I
knew that I would never have time to polish my works properly.
Their value would not depend on that. Others, less involved in
struggle, would perfect a style; but what I had to tell, *they* could
not tell. To each his own task. I had to struggle bitterly for my family's daily bread in a society where all doors were closed to me, and
where people were often afraid to shake my hand in the street. I
asked myself every day, without any particular feeling, but en-
grossed by the problems of rent, my wife's health, my son's education, whether I would be arrested in the night. For my books I
adopted an appropriate form: I had to construct them in detached
fragments which could each be finished separately and sent abroad
posthaste; which could, if absolutely necessary, be published as they

were, incomplete; and it would be difficult for me to compose in any other form."

Serge was arrested again in 1933, and this time sent to Orenburg where he was joined by his young son, Vlady. He might well have perished there, like so many other Soviet writers, during the period of the great purges, had it not been for his reputation in the West. A group of young Parisian intellectuals campaigned for his freedom, and his plight was brought to the attention of pro-Soviet luminaries like Romain Rolland, André Gide, and André Malraux, who may have interceded in his favor with Stalin. In 1936 he was removed from Orenburg, but he was also deprived of Soviet citizenship, relieved of his manuscripts (both actions in violation of Soviet law), and expelled from the Soviet Union. His return to Europe was heralded by a vicious slander campaign in the Communist press.

Serge settled first in Brussels, then in Paris, where he continued to battle for the ideals of Soviet democracy and against the rising tides of Stalinism and fascism. His next novel, *S'il est minuit dans le siècle*, 1939, told the story of the heroic resistance of the Oppositionists and Old Bolsheviks in Stalin's concentration camps, and he analyzed the Stalinist counterrevolution in books like *From Lenin to Stalin*, 1937, and *Destiny of a Revolution*, 1937. Serge was one of the few to recognize the outrage of the Moscow frame-up trials (which deceived a whole generation of Leftist intellectuals and even the United States ambassador in Moscow) and to raise a voice against them.

Revolution had again broken out in Spain, and long before his contemporary and admirer, George Orwell (cf. *Homage to Catalonia*), Serge saw through Stalin's machinations there. While the workers and farmers were dying valiantly for the Spanish Republic, the Communists were quietly "eliminating" their political rivals in the rear. In spite of Serge's efforts, by the end of 1937 the Stalinists had murdered Serge's comrade Andrès Nin, the leader of the Spanish P.O.U.M. (independent Marxist party), and jailed and killed countless others. "We are building a common front against fascism. How can we block its path with so many concentration camps behind us?" he wrote to André Gide (with whom he later collaborated) on the eve of the latter's voyage to Russia.

World War II soon put an end to the limited possibilities for action that had remained open to Serge and his friends. As if reluctant to admit the catastrophe he had long predicted and fought against, Serge was one of the last to leave Paris before the advancing Nazis in 1940, although he was clearly marked for death by the Gestapo. Arriving penniless in Marseilles, with the Gestapo at his heels, he fought for months to get a visa while the great democracies closed their doors to him. At the last moment he found refuge for himself and his family in Mexico.

Isolated as he now was from the European socialist movement that had been his life, forced to be an impotent witness to the debacle of Europe under Hitler, menaced by N.K.V.D. assassins (who had recently murdered his friend Trotsky, also in Mexico), deprived of a journalistic platform by his Stalinist opponents, Serge might well have been thoroughly demoralized by his years in Mexico. But he continued to write, though without hope of publication, and produced some of his finest works (*The Case of Comrade Tulayev* and *Memoirs of a Revolutionary*) "for the desk drawer." At the end of the war, in spite of failing health and financial difficulties, he made plans to return to France. But his many projects for new books and new struggles were cut short by his death on November 17, 1947.

At the lowest ebb of his fortunes (in 1943), Serge summed up his life as follows: "I have undergone a little over ten years of various forms of captivity, agitated in seven countries, and written twenty books. I own nothing. On several occasions a press with a vast circulation has hurled filth at me because I spoke the truth. Behind us lies a victorious revolution gone astray, several abortive attempts at revolution, and massacres in so great number as to inspire a certain dizziness. And to think that it is not over yet. Let me be done with this digression; those were the only roads possible for us. I have more confidence in mankind and in the future than ever before."

THE WRITER AS WITNESS

Serge's dedication to absolute political honesty and clear-sightedness (*probité* and *lucidité*) as the only bases for building a genuine revolutionary movement had its corollary in his devotion to artistic truth.

The noun "witness" is a rough English equivalent of the Greek *martus,* from which our word "martyr" is also derived. The idea of being a witness to one's faith implies not only testifying to a creed but also participation and active suffering, freely accepted, in the name of something larger than one's personal ego. It also implies a privileged situation. Poets and other creative artists have long claimed this kind of status for themselves. Whether they chose to suffer in the name of the forward march of humanity (Hugo and the social romantics) or for the purity of art and the ideal (Baudelaire and the symbolists), they have regularly assumed that, the greater the risk and the deeper the plunge into the mysteries of existence, the richer will be the prize with which the artist returns and which he offers up to an often uncomprehending humanity.

Victor Serge was such a martyr-witness. He felt that "artistic detachment" was not a means of being objective about reality, but only a fashionable means of avoiding a confrontation with it. And he plunged headlong into a maelstrom of social destruction and revolutionary upheaval. His commitment to revolution was made long before Communist state power made it easy and at times profitable for writers to become *engagé,* and it continued long after many of them had returned to their ivory towers proclaiming that their newfound god had failed. At the time of his death, Serge was one of the rare survivors of three revolutionary generations. He had occupied a unique position, a position from which he, perhaps better than any other writer, was able to render both the heroism and the tragedy of a whole age of revolution.

For Serge, "He who speaks, he who writes is above all one who speaks on behalf of all those who have no voice"; he wrote out of a bond of solidarity with the men whose often tragic destinies fill the pages of his works—the heroes and the victims, the brave and the cowardly, the anarchists, Bolsheviks, bandits, madmen, poets, beggars, and the common workers. He defined the need to write as a need "first of all to capture, to fix, to understand, to interpret, to recreate life; to liberate, through exteriorization, the confused forces one feels fermenting within oneself and by means of which the individual plunges into the collective unconscious. In the work itself, this comes across as Testimony and Message. . . ." He goes on to say, "Writing becomes a search for poly-personality, a means of living several destinies, of penetration into others, of communicating with them. The writer becomes conscious of the world he brings to life, he is its consciousness and he thus escapes from the ordinary limits of the self, something which is at once intoxicating and enriching with lucidity" (*Carnets*, Paris, 1952).

This attitude made it possible for Serge fully to appreciate the experiences of his turbulent life and to distill them into the concrete characterizations in his fiction. His life as an activist was unique in that he managed to be in virtually every revolutionary storm center during the first part of this century. But his experiences were nonetheless typical for a man of his times; individually, they recapitulated the experiences of millions of men caught up in the struggles of European society.

In the solitude of his Mexican exile, after a chance meeting with Trotsky's widow, Natalia Sedova, Serge wrote sadly in his diary: "[We are] the sole survivors of the Russian Revolution here and perhaps anywhere in the world. . . . There is nobody left who knows what the Russian Revolution was really like, what the Bolsheviks were really like—and men judge without knowing, with bitterness and a basic rigidity." That ineffable quality, "what things were really like"—the aspect, tone of voice, emotional context of a human event, personal or historical—that is what the novelist's ear and eye can catch and what makes of his social and historical fiction a truer record of living reality than the historian's data or the theoretician's rational frames.

Richard Greeman

Bibliography

Works by Victor Serge Available in English

NOVELS:

Men in Prison, translated with an Introduction by Richard Greeman (New York, Doubleday, 1969; London, Gollancz, 1970; Penguin, 1972).

Birth of Our Power, translated by Richard Greeman, Introduction by Harvey Swados (New York, Doubleday, 1967; London, Gollancz, 1968; Penguin, 1970).

The Case of Comrade Tulayev, translated by Willard Trask (New York, Doubleday, 1950; London, Hamish Hamilton, 1951; Anchor, 1963; Penguin, 1968).

The Long Dusk (Les Derniers Temps), translated by Ralph Manheim (New York, Dial Press, 1946).

NON-FICTION:

Year One of the Russian Revolution, translated and edited by Peter Sedgwick (London, Allen Lane, The Penguin Press, 1972).

Memoirs of a Revolutionary, translated and edited by Peter Sedgwick (London, Oxford, 1963). Includes notes and a bibliography of Serge's works.

From Lenin to Stalin, translated by Ralph Manheim (New York, Pioneer Publishers, 1937; London, Secker & Warburg, 1937).

Destiny of a Revolution (American title: *Russia Twenty Years After*), translated by Max Schactman (London, Jarrolds, 1937; New York, Pioneer Publishers, 1937).

For a complete bibliography of Serge's writings, see the Appendix to either the French or English edition of the *Memoirs.*